'He's too old for you, you know,' Lucian said.

'Who?' Madeleine asked, hoping that she was wrong in what she thought he was going to say.

'Why, Philippe, of course. He's old enough to be your grandfather. He cannot afford you any real degree of pleasure.'

Madeleine felt her face grow hot.

'I know he provides well for you, *mademoiselle*, but I too could do that. I am even richer than he and have no wife or other commitments. If you should tire of him, I. . .'

Dear God! The man was making her a proposition. 'Please stay away from me, Monsieur le Comte. Believe me, you are the last man on earth I would choose for my protector!'

Truda Taylor grew up in Devon and now lives in Northamptonshire with her husband and children, and a selection of cats and hamsters. She teaches seven-year-olds, and enjoys encouraging them to use their imaginations. After visiting the Vendée, it was her fascination with the history of that area which eventually led to her writing historical fiction.

Recent titles by the same author:

HEARTS OF THE VENDEE
HAZARDOUS MARRIAGE

THE COMTE AND THE COURTESAN

Truda Taylor

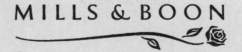

MILLS & BOON

MILLS & BOON, the Rose Device and
LEGACY OF LOVE are trademarks of the publisher.
Harlequin Mills & Boon Limited,
Eton House, 18–24 Paradise Road, Richmond, Surrey TW9 1SR

© Truda Taylor 1996

ISBN 0 263 79753 8

Set in 10 on 12 pt Linotron Times
04-9607-81475

Typeset in Great Britain by CentraCet, Cambridge
Printed in Great Britain by
BPC Paperbacks Ltd

PROLOGUE

Brittany 1779

SUNLIGHT filtered through the trees in golden bars, painting intricate patterns on the soft, green grass and turning the long hair of the peasant girl to yellow silk. She was a lovely child, lithe and graceful with skin turned a pale peach by the summer sun. The Marquis halted his thoroughbred horse to watch her as she twirled and skipped between the tree trunks, her childish voice lifted in a lilting song. She appeared so fresh, so free, and her obvious innocence tugged at his jaded heart.

Unable to help himself, he followed her until she came to a run-down cottage situated at the edge of the village, his village. A burly ill-kempt man was waiting for her and, after berating her soundly, gave her a backhander that sent her sprawling. The Marquis felt his temper rising. How dared the oaf treat the little girl so callously? As he rode forward, she looked up and her beauty quite took his breath away. He was a collector of beautiful things, yet amongst his accumulation of paintings and sculptures he had nothing to compare with that lovely child.

In a few years, he knew, poverty and ceaseless toil would erode her looks, would wipe the sparkle of vitality from her tawny eyes. He decided then that he could not let that happen. Such incomparable beauty

5

deserved a more fitting setting, deserved to be cherished and admired. Ultimately, he paid a large sum of money for the privilege of bringing up the child and the following day took her to the manor house. They remained there for a few days whilst dressmakers were summoned to clothe her respectably and then he swept her away with him to his home in Paris. She was an incomparable gem, and pure. No doltish peasant should take her maidenhead, only he, Philippe de Maupilier, but he was willing to wait. Only when she had matured would he make her his mistress.

CHAPTER ONE

June 1789

FIREWORKS blazed in the night sky above Paris, picking out the jumble of roof tops with their silvery light. It was a warm evening and one of the windows of the smart little apartment near the Palais Royal had been thrown open so that the occupants might view the celebratory display. From now on, nobles, clergy and the third estate would vote as one and it was seen as a great victory for the people. Outside in the street, everyone seemed to be rejoicing. Inside the house however, the atmosphere was more ambivalent.

'*Vive* the Third Estate! *Vive la nation!*' someone challenged, glancing up at the open window.

'*Vive le Roi!*' came the inopportune reply.

The old gentleman, standing beside the beautiful fair-haired girl, stiffened. His hand tightened warningly on her shoulder as he turned his attention to the crowd below. The celebrations had momentarily ceased and the tension was almost tangible.

'*Vive le Roi,*' he echoed the girl, then judiciously added, 'the father of the people.'

There was a slight hesitation then the cry was taken up by the unpredictable crowd. '*Vive le Roi*, the father of the people!'

The Marquis de Maupilier drew the girl back and with a rueful smile closed the window. 'You really must learn to be more circumspect, my dear. Things are so unsettled at the moment.'

'I'm sorry, Philippe.' Madeleine Vaubonne knew she had been foolish but she was finding it hard to adjust to the changes that were coming so swiftly upon them.

He shrugged and reached out a wrinkled hand to caress her smooth cheek. 'Let us forget it shall we, *chérie*, and endeavour to enjoy ourselves.'

'But of course.' The girl slipped her arm around his waist and gave him a hug. He was her protector and she loved him dearly, more than the uncaring father who had all but sold her to him not long after her mother's death. Since the moment he had taken responsibility for her nearly ten years ago, Philippe had lavished every luxury upon her—dresses, jewellery, *objets d'art*, and, when she was old enough, this apartment near the Palais Royal.

Madeleine was grateful for all the things he had done for her, but most of all she cherished the gift he had not intended to make: that of his love. He had made her into a lady, albeit one of the *demi-monde*, and in private he treated her as a father would a favourite daughter. Theirs was an unusual relationship with a public façade far different from the private reality, yet it was a relationship that had served them both well.

Taking her hand, he led her across the crowded salon to where a group of his friends were gathered, several of them with their own 'ladies'. They were all aristocrats of some degree or other and, a few months ago, would have worn swords to signify their rank. Now, only Lucian de Valori, Comte de Regnay, was rash enough to do so. Opinion was turning against the aristocrats and, since the recent riots, it was only a foolish or an

exceptionally courageous man who would dare to antag-
onise the mob.

Madeleine was not pleased to see de Regnay in that
company. He was younger than Philippe's other friends;
the way he looked at her made her feel uncomfortable.
His attitude also irritated her for he was an aristo of the
old school with a strong belief in his own superiority.
Unlike most of the other gentlemen, the Comte maintained no paramour. It was said that he didn't need to,
that more than one high-class lady was willing to share
his bed.

Try as she might, Madeleine could not understand
what they saw in him. She had heard him described as
handsome, yet personally thought his features too hard
for that. His cheek-bones were high and his mouth stern,
rarely showing a glimpse of a smile. As for his eyes, they
were almost almond shaped—not at all becoming in a
man—and as dark and hard as obsidian. She did not
know his age but judged it to be around thirty, making
him more than ten years older than herself.

Philippe gestured to the Comte's sword and frowned.
'You really should dispense with that, Luc. I know you
pride yourself on your skill but, faced with a mob, that
won't save you.'

The younger man merely shrugged, not looking at de
Maupilier but at the girl. 'I do not intend to forgo any of
my privileges before I have to.'

'That's foolish, my boy,' Philippe replied, taking a
liberty that few would dare. 'At this moment the people
are extremely volatile.'

'Volatile! That's an understatement if ever I heard
one!' The portly chevalier standing next to Philippe
slipped his arm around the lady at his side. 'I don't mind

admitting that the riots last month terrified me. As you know, my home is not far from the corner of the rue de Faubourg Saint Antoine where Reveillon lived. The night his house was sacked I thought we would all be murdered in our beds. Even now people speak openly in the Palais Royal of massacring us. And what protection is there? None! Not now the Garde Français are refusing to obey orders.'

'It's this government,' the Viscomte de Brunierre replied. 'Its weakness seems to allow anything. I might as well tell you all now, that my wife and I have decided to quit Paris. Only this morning we found our door marked with a black "P" for proscribed.'

'Leave Paris, *chérie*? I shall be devastated!' The tiny redhead clinging to his arm began to pout.

'You will be well compensated, Monique my sweet,' he replied drawing her close against him and briefly cupping her breast.

Philippe frowned. The ladies present were all courtesans but when he and Madeleine played hosts he insisted on a modicum of good manners. It was not the first occasion on which de Brunierre had come close to overstepping the bounds and he would not be invited again.

'You may moan, but something had to be done,' Philippe answered a little sharply. 'The king considered himself a law unto himself. Look what happened to the delegation from the States of Rennes when they came to protest about the new import tax, a tax that violated the rights guaranteed by the act of union. They were locked up! Aristocrats who were representing the rights of their own people.'

'I thought the king gave in over that,' another gentleman said.

'He did,' Philippe replied, 'but only after a fourth delegation of all three orders was sent to him. If he hadn't it could have meant the end of the union.'

The Comte de Regnay smiled sardonically. 'You Bretons are all the same at heart, independent and uncivilised the lot of you.'

For once the older man did not respond to this teasing. 'I am a Breton, Lucian, and proud of it!'

'Oh, come, sir,' the Comte protested. 'You sold your estate there and haven't been back to the area for years.'

'And you love Paris,' Madeleine put in.

Philippe laughed although there was a slight hollowness in it. 'That's right, I do. Now if only Paris was in Brittany then I would be a truly contented man!' Everyone laughed and he paused before adding, 'All these years I have retained a small manor there that came to me through my mother, isolated though it is. It has a special place in my heart.'

'Kercholin.' Madeleine gave him a smile that was full of affection.

'I never could part with it, my dear, not after I found you on one of the farms there.'

The Comte gave a sniff of disdain. 'Romantic rubbish, Philippe.'

Madeleine glanced at him and wondered if Philippe too saw the brief expression of distaste that crossed his face. Had it been anyone else then she would have thought she had imagined it.

Brunierre sighed. 'My wife is talking not only of leaving Paris but of leaving France. She has relatives in

England and, for the sake of our children, believes we should go on an indefinite visit there.'

'You would be foolish to leave so soon,' Philippe told him. 'Now we have a single assembly, things will probably settle down. What do you say, Luc?'

'I agree.'

'And if things get worse?' Brunierre asked.

'Whatever happens I shall not be driven from France.' The Comte managed to convey in his tone exactly what he thought of those who would.

He's so arrogant and full of his own self-esteem. I would love to see him humbled, Madeleine thought uncharitably, then flushed when she met his gaze and realised that he too had been able to read in her face exactly what she was thinking.

For the rest of the evening, she did her best to keep out of his way. Usually this posed no problem as he seemed to come to these gatherings mostly to talk to Philippe and the other men. She had engaged a string quartet for the evening and while they played, some of the couples began to dance. She was not at all pleased when the Comte, with Philippe's smiling approval, asked her to partner him. Good manners dictated that she accept him and she graciously murmured her thanks.

As he led her into the centre of the room and the musicians began to play another piece, she wondered yet again why Philippe should think so well of him. It could only be the attraction of opposites, she decided. Much as she cared for Philippe she was not blind to his faults. He was a man whose opinion was easily swayed, a man who only wanted to enjoy himself and would go to any length to avoid unpleasantness.

The Comte, on the other hand, appeared unbending

in his beliefs. His arrogance was matched only by his self-assurance and his ability to command without even lifting a finger. His life was devoted to pleasure, yet he managed to convey the impression that it was below his dignity to enjoy himself too much and that frivolous people and pastimes were to be disdained.

To Madeleine's surprise, he turned out to be an exceptionally good dancer, graceful yet entirely masculine, but he was certainly not entertaining. He made no attempt to talk to her and answered her own attempts at polite conversation rather brusquely.

'You did not have to dance with me,' she finally told him in exasperation.

'Did you not want to dance then?' His dark brows drew together in a frown. Together with his eyes they were a startling contrast to his heavily powdered wig.

'Not if you find it an effort.'

His well-shaped lips twitched just a little bit. 'It is no effort, *mademoiselle*, I assure you. However, if you are looking for pretty speeches, you will not get them from me.'

'I don't want pretty speeches,' she replied, then teasingly added, 'but a smile would not go amiss.'

When he did not respond to that, her patience ended and as soon as the dance was over, she stepped away from him. 'Thank you, sir, but I think I have had enough of dancing.'

For just a moment she thought he looked surprised. He glanced around to where Philippe was engaged in animated conversation with another gentleman, then said, 'In that case we will sit down. Perhaps I can fetch you some wine.'

With his usual high handedness, he guided her to a

chair in the furthermost corner of the spacious room. Mainly to be rid of him for a while, she allowed him to fetch her a glass of wine from the side table. When he returned, he took a seat next to her where he sipped silently from his own glass.

'He's too old for you, you know,' he finally said, surprising her and nearly causing her to choke on the wine.

'Who?' she asked, struggling to remain calm and hoping that she was wrong in what she thought he was going to say.

'Why, Philippe, of course. He's old enough to be your father, maybe even your grandfather. He cannot afford you any real degree of pleasure.'

Madeleine felt her face grow hot. In all the time she had been with Philippe, no one had ever said anything to her face although many of them must have wondered. Trust this man to trample her feelings so!

The sigh he gave when she did not answer annoyed her even more. 'I know he provides well for you, *mademoiselle*, but I too could do that. I am even richer than he and have no wife or other commitments. If you should tire of him, I. . .'

Dear God! The man was making her a proposition. 'I shall never tire of him,' she replied icily, 'and I shall thank you, sir, to go no further with your insulting offer!'

'Insulting?' He sounded genuinely perplexed and part of Madeleine could understand why. It was, after all, quite common for ladies to change protectors. 'It is something of an honour. I have never before considered it worth maintaining a mistress!'

Madeleine was astounded by his self-importance and

enraged by what she considered his duplicity. 'I thought
Philippe was your friend, yet you go behind his back,'
she told him tightly. 'Oh, I cannot find the words to tell
you just what I think of you!'

When she stood up she was really agitated and
surprisingly close to tears. 'Please stay away from me,
Monsieur le Comte. Believe me, you are the last man on
earth I would choose for my protector!'

He was pale beneath his powder and, if anything, his
black eyes had become even darker, yet she could see
no emotion in them. He stood and bowed stiffly.

'You have made yourself quite clear, *mademoiselle*,'
he told her in a voice that would have frozen a stone.
'I shall not force myself on you again.'

For the rest of the evening Madeleine tried to ignore
the Comte, yet on more than one occasion her eyes were
drawn back to his tall lithe figure.

Later, when the guests had gone and she and Philippe
were companionably drinking a last brandy before he
left for his own house in the Faubourg Saint Germain,
she told him about the Comte's offer.

Surprisingly he laughed.

'I knew he was going to make it,' he said after a while.

'Philippe!'

'Forgive an old man's vanity,' he pleaded with a rueful
smile. 'He was perfectly open about asking you and I
knew you'd refuse.'

For a moment Madeleine wondered whether to pretend she was considering the offer. It would certainly
teach him a lesson, but their relationship had always
been free from artifice.

'I'm sorry, my dear.' He squeezed her hand. 'I had no intention of hurting you.'

Madeleine sighed, and after a moment, returned his coaxing smile. 'You are forgiven Philippe... But I still do not see why you like him. He seems so...well, stiff somehow and cold, and so puffed up with his own importance.'

'That's true enough,' he replied. 'He is certainly aware of his own worth. I suppose it comes from having control of his estate since he was fifteen years old. Châteaurange is one of the oldest and richest estates in Normandy. Nevertheless, I like him, as I did his father before him, and he is handsome.'

He patted her hand affectionately. 'Lately, my dear, I have become aware of what you are missing. When I first took you into my care, I intended to make you my mistress in every sense of the word. Then I watched you grow and you became like a daughter to me.' He smiled wryly. 'Besides, a man's appetite wanes with the years although it suits me that my friends should not know it. Lucian is young and handsome, and very rich. You could do worse.'

'I doubt that,' she answered drily.

'Most women seem to find him attractive. In fact, he has quite a reputation with the ladies. Perhaps it is that very aloofness you so despise; they seem to find it a challenge. There was a young widow in England, as I recall, with whom he had a prolonged and, from all accounts, extremely passionate affair.'

The idea of the Comte being capable of any such emotion made Madeleine sniff in disbelief.

Philippe smiled. 'Do not think too badly of him,

Maddie. For all his other faults, he is an honest and a trustworthy friend.'

Although Madeleine nodded, she did not entirely agree with him. His words, however, were to come back and haunt her in the turbulent months that followed as the people of France embarked on a revolution that was to change the face of history.

CHAPTER TWO

April 1791

MADELEINE rested her forehead against the cold marble mantelpiece and stared down into the empty fireplace. Her heart was heavy and tears clogged her throat. Her protector was dying. Earlier that morning Dr Maupres had confirmed what she had already known in her heart. She had not wanted to admit it but, since Philippe had moved in to share her apartment, she had been unable to ignore the deterioration in his health. At first she had put it down to the shock of having his house attacked, of seeing the servants he had trusted desert him, but such had not been the case. Philippe was suffering from a disorder of the blood that was both advanced and incurable.

'Madeleine?'

She turned at the sound of that smooth, well-modulated voice and was not surprised to find that the Comte de Regnay had entered the room, unannounced.

Over the past two years his appearance had changed drastically. In spite of his earlier declaration, he had abandoned his sword. He still wore a wig, but his dress had become quite sober so that, had it not been for his arrogant bearing, he would have passed for a lawyer or a clerk.

Madeleine was surprised that he had remained so long in the capital when most of their other friends had

long ago departed for England, Strasbourg or the
provinces. She was even more surprised that he had
survived when his every gesture and word betrayed him
for what he was. Yet survive he had, virtually unmo-
lested by the aggressive citizens who had ruled the
streets. He had still maintained a carriage although the
coat of arms on its door had been painted out. Most
irritating of all, the majority of his servants had
remained loyal to him; one in particular, his personal
servant, Jean-Paul, still seemed able to procure for him
any luxury he desired. On more than one occasion,
Madeleine had wondered if his prolonged stay had
anything to do with Philippe's obvious need of him, yet
found it hard to attribute such an altruistic motive to the
so-arrogant Comte.

'I knocked but there was no answer,' he explained
with uncharacteristic hesitancy.

'Yvette left yesterday,' she told him, referring to her
only servant. 'Her father thought it unsafe for her to
stay with me any longer. I can't really blame him. She
has been harassed more than once on her way to the
shops.'

'I see.' He didn't sound surprised and made no
attempt to sympathise, sensing perhaps that it would be
quite unwelcome. 'In future, you really must make sure
that your door is locked.'

'Yes.' Lord! Upset as she was, the man still had the
facility to irritate her.

He moved closer and glanced towards the bedroom
door. For just a moment she saw a shadow of sorrow
cloud his eyes. 'How is Philippe today?'

'I had to fetch Dr Maupres for him early this morning.
He has been abominably sick and it has sapped what

little strength he had.' She took a deep breath to steady herself but her voice still cracked. 'He's dying. Dr Maupres says it could only be a matter of days.'

'Oh, my dear, I'm sorry! I had expected as much but hoped it was not true.'

She had turned away from him, so did not see the way he lifted his hand to comfort her then let it fall uselessly to his side.

'Is there anything I can do?'

She shook her head. 'There's nothing anyone can do. The doctor has suggested mulled wine if his stomach will take it. We don't have any so I shall have to go down to the shops. Madame Robard keeps a good quality burgundy.' She knew she was rambling but was unable to help herself. She stopped abruptly when she felt his hand on her shoulder.

'You must not leave the house today,' he told her with a frown. 'The mood on the streets is quite ugly. Word has spread that the King and Queen are about to depart for Saint-Cloud and the crowds do not like it. Make a list of what you need and I will see that Jean-Paul collects the items for you.'

He had done that for them before, obtaining things from parts of the city where Yvette or herself had not dared to go but where his own man seemed able to walk with impunity. Today, however, she felt sufficiently irritated with him not to want his help.

'Thank you, Comte, but I am quite capable of doing a little shopping,' she replied stiffly.

He sighed and for the first time she noticed how tired he looked. Perhaps he was not as immune to the pressure of life in the capital as she had supposed.

'Philippe will need you here,' he said flatly. 'Please, Madeleine, allow me to do what I can. He is my friend.'

His uncharacteristic humility pricked at her conscience and made her feel like a shrew. 'I'm sorry, Comte. Forgive me. . .I'm afraid I'm a little tired. I did not mean to be so ungracious. I'd be grateful for your help.'

'I wish you would use my given name,' he told her in a tone of weary exasperation. 'If you can't bring yourself to do that, then for God's sake address me as *monsieur*. We both know there are no longer any *comtes* in France!'

'Monsieur Valori it is, then.' Madeleine couldn't help thinking that the new form of address suited him a lot less than his title. It was almost amusing that he should have been placed in such a position. It was like referring to a pedigree spaniel as a hound.

He sighed and forced a smile that did not quite reach his eyes. 'Is Philippe up to seeing me, do you think? There were some things he asked me to do for him and I have come to report.'

'I expect so,' she said, moving across the room to the small vestibule that led to the bedrooms. She was a little irritated to find the Comte at her shoulder but said nothing to discourage him. When she opened the bedroom door and called out Philippe's name, he answered feebly.

'The Comte is here,' she told him.

'Lucian?' he rasped, struggling to sit up then deciding it was too much effort.

Without his wig he looked old and shrunken, his face already cadaverous. His smile was genuine, however, and Madeleine felt a little jealous of his obvious

pleasure. There was something in his relationship with
the Comte that she had never been able to understand
or emulate.

Leaving the two men alone, she returned to the
drawing-room where she sat down tiredly on the *chaise
longue*. She had not intended to fall asleep but the next
thing she knew, the Comte was bending over her. His
face was very close to her own and there was an
expression in his eyes that she could not define.

'Madeleine,' he said a trifle huskily. 'I'm sorry to wake
you but I have to leave now and I want you to come and
lock the door behind me.'

'Oh, yes,' she replied, still a little dazed. 'How rude of
me. I did not mean to fall asleep.'

'Philippe has asked me to bring Monsieur Leclerc
around this afternoon. Apparently there are matters of
business he wants settled.'

Madeleine paled. 'Surely you didn't tell him. . .?'

'That he is dying?' The Comte looked sombre. 'I
didn't have to, Madeleine. He knows. He was most
insistent that I bring Leclerc here today.'

Once again Madeleine felt close to tears. A lump
lodged in her throat and she found herself unable to say
anything.

'Oh, Madeleine,' he sighed and briefly brushed his
finger across her cheek. 'You will be well taken care of,
I assure you.'

Stiffening, she brushed his hand away. 'I was not
thinking of myself, *monsieur*,' she replied quite truth-
fully, 'and I certainly shan't need you to take care of me.'

His eyes flashed briefly but he made no reply. Instead,
he turned and moved silently to the door, not looking to
see if she followed.

'Jean-Paul will get you the wine,' he told her stiffly before taking his leave, 'and I shall return with Monsieur Leclerc at about five o'clock.'

He was, as usual, true to his word. Not just one bottle but a case of burgundy arrived just after noon, delivered by a rough-looking but polite citizen wearing the striped trousers and tricolour cockade of the revolutionaries. At five o'clock on the dot, the Comte and Monsieur Leclerc the lawyer arrived. They spent nearly an hour with Philippe, leaving him exhausted and even more pale. Madeleine silently cursed their thoughtlessness as she helped him to some wine and water and then settled down in a chair beside his bed, waiting for him to fall asleep.

'I'm glad that's all settled, Madeleine,' he said, sighing contentedly as he reached for her hand. 'I wanted to make some arrangements for you.'

'Philippe, what are you talking about?' she asked.

'You'll see. . .in the future.' His smile was almost mischievous. 'I want you to be happy. . .Lucian. . .trust him and do as he says. He has promised to see. . .you. . . home.'

Madeleine was not sure what he meant by 'home'. She wanted to tell him that she had no desire to leave Paris and that she certainly had no intention of going anywhere with the Comte de Regnay but she did not have the chance. He was already asleep and his face looked more relaxed than it had for days. Towards midnight, she left him and retired to her own bed where she fell into a deep sleep of exhaustion.

* * *

Philippe died sometime in the early hours of the morning. Quite peacefully, Dr Maupres said. Madeleine found it difficult to believe that he had slipped away without her even being aware of it. There had been such closeness between them that she felt she should have known.

Two days later, on the first day of May, he was interred quietly without the pomp and prestige that should have been his due. The Comte made all the arrangements; both he and Monsieur Leclerc were adamant that there should be no show. Thus he was laid to rest in the crypt of a small church on the outskirts of the city with only the three of them in attendance. The quiet occasion contrasted sharply with the public distress and bizarre pomp associated with the funeral of the politician Mirabeau who had passed away a few weeks before and was revered in death as a hero of the revolution.

As soon as the short service was over, the Comte and Monsieur Leclerc accompanied Madeleine to her apartment where Philippe's will was read. She cried a lot and, on one occasion, the Comte went so far as to squeeze her hand. In fact, she paid little attention to what was being said, so distressed was she. She knew Philippe had a nephew living in Caen and assumed that the bulk of the estate, now converted into gold and bonds, would go to him. Such proved to be the case and, if her own bequest was smaller than anticipated, she did not mind. She was not family, she reminded herself; besides, she already possessed a small fortune in jewels.

'When you return to Brittany, my dear, I can arrange for the documents pertaining to your bequests to be transferred to a colleague there,' Leclerc said, gathering his papers together. 'Your aunt's farm is near Vannes, I believe.'

'But I have no intention of leaving Paris,' Madeleine protested.

Leclerc frowned. 'I think you should be aware that the renting agreement expires on this property at the end of the year. It may not be possible for you to renew it. I can look into the matter for you, if you wish it. When the Marquis gave me no instruction to do so before, I assumed you would both be leaving Paris. Of course, I had no idea how ill he was.'

'Philippe intended for you to return to Brittany,' the Comte told her with a frown. 'In fact, he extracted a promise from me to escort you there. He was sure your aunt would be happy to take you in. I understand that their farm is unusually prosperous.'

Madeleine thought of her aunt who had been taught by the local priest to write and did so as regularly as circumstances would allow. She was her mother's older sister and had not approved of Madeleine being put into 'service' with the Marquis.

'I would be welcome but I do not want to go. Paris has been my home for too long now,' Madeleine told him, a trifle crossly. 'Do not complain, Comte; you will, after all, be spared the tedious duty of escorting me.'

The two men exchanged glances. 'I'll look into the renting agreement, then,' Monsieur Leclerc conceded.

'Please do,' Madeleine told him, 'for I shall not change my mind.'

The Comte sighed tiredly. He looked so genuinely concerned that Madeleine regretted her earlier curtness.

'Whatever you decide, I will do what I can to help

you,' he said. 'However, I most strongly urge you to change your mind. I don't think we have seen the worst of this so-called revolution.'

For the next few days, Madeleine existed in a kind of vacuum. The apartment seemed excruciatingly empty and yet, in some ways, it was full of Philippe. She almost expected to see him sitting in his favourite chair; on one occasion, she could have sworn she heard him call to her from the bedroom.

The Comte continued to call daily, usually in his carriage. He did not stay long, often for less than an hour. There was always a certain amount of constraint between them, which was was natural enough, Madeleine supposed, for it was Philippe who had been his friend. She felt that he saw her as something of an obligation and because of this, perhaps, failed to welcome him as she ought. He did not press her again about leaving Paris and seemed to give up the idea of doing so himself.

The weeks passed and still he continued to come and see her, making things easier for her whenever he could, but even with his visits, Madeleine was dreadfully lonely. Philippe had been her entire life and she had no real friends of her own. She took to shopping for herself, much against the Comte's advice, but at least she didn't feel so isolated.

Towards the end of June, the royal family, who since their attempt to visit Saint-Cloud had been kept as virtual prisoners in the Tuileries, made a desperate attempt to leave Paris. They had hoped to cross the frontier into the Austrian Netherlands, where German and Swiss regiments would help the King raise his banner, but their escape was badly bungled and the King's position became even more precarious.

The Comte, who brought Madeleine the news, appeared more dejected than she had ever seen him. He knew the King well enough to feel a certain amount of personal sadness for his plight. Furthermore, he believed it to be the end of any hope of a constitutional monarchy.

Over the next few days there were riots on the streets. Enraged crowds went about defacing or smashing shop and inn signs bearing the King's name and notaries, whose profession was designated by boards bearing the fleur-de-lys, hastily removed them. According to the Comte, someone had even placed a placard on the gates of the Tuileries proclaiming 'House to Let'.

When the King was returned to Paris, the citizens were forbidden by the Assembly to show him any respect. 'Anyone who applauds the King will be beaten,' said the signs. 'Anyone who insults him will be hanged.'

Feelings were running high. When a demonstration on the Champs de Mars got out of hand, the National Guard opened fire, killing a number of people—thirteen, the authorities said, although the word on the street was that it was nearer fifty. To prevent absolute anarchy, martial law was declared. On the Comte's advice, Madeleine stayed at home. She did not want for anything as the Comte or Jean-Paul called daily but she felt dreadfully confined.

* * *

It was more than two weeks after the massacre before
Madeleine judged it safe to venture out. Even then, she
knew the Comte would not approve, but she wanted to
buy some new black ribbon for her hat. The weather
was fine and she felt almost too hot in her pelisse as she
walked along the pavement in the direction of the Palais
Royal. Purchasing the ribbons caused no problem,
although if she had wanted a hat, madame Tarmonde
told her, then it would have been different: the hatters
were on strike.

After buying the ribbons, Madeleine was tempted to
stroll in the Palais Royal. It would have been nice to
have had an escort and to be able to wander without
constraint. Unfortunately that was not the case and she
did not have the temerity to venture there alone.
Somewhat reluctantly, she turned her steps homeward
and, about a block from her apartment, entered a
chandlers to purchase some candles.

The proprietor, Monsieur Bouchard, greeted her
pleasantly enough, but there was a distinct air of
hostility about the woman who was already waiting in
the shop. Before Madeleine could even place her order,
she announced that she did not like sharing the shop
with an aristo's whore. Madeleine tensed with apprehension but scrupulously kept her back turned, ordering
her candles and waiting tensely while a harassed
Monsieur Bouchard tied them together with a piece of
twine.

'So your protector is dead, eh?' the woman continued.
'Good riddance, I say, the lecherous old beast!'

Madeleine hated to hear Philippe referred to like that
but she judiciously refrained from answering. Neverthe-

less, her hand was shaking as she took some coins from her purse and reached for the candles.

'Did you hear me, bitch?' the woman persisted, catching hold of Madeleine's shoulder and swinging her around so roughly that her hat went flying across the floor.

The woman was pretty in a voluptuous, rather coarse way, with thick untidy hair that cascaded down her back and across her ample bosom. Her dark eyes, however, blazed with a degree of hate that was ugly to behold.

'For years you have lived in luxury whilst me and mine starved,' the woman continued. 'I'm glad the old bastard is dead. Without him, you won't have the means to be so high and mighty!'

The next instant the woman's free hand snaked out and her fingers clawed at Madeleine's cheek, leaving long, angry weals. 'Not so pretty now!' she hissed.

Madeleine felt fear but she also felt anger intensified by the stinging pain. The bunch of candles was in her hand and, without even thinking about it, she smashed them into the woman's face. The citizeness lurched backwards, coming sharply up against the wall. Rather dazedly she put her hand up to her nose which was already beginning to bleed.

Madeleine did not stop to see how badly she had been hurt but rushed from the shop, leaving her hat still lying on the floor. She was relieved when the woman did not follow her and kept glancing nervously over her shoulder all the way to her own door.

Her heart was pounding and her legs were shaking as she climbed the stairs to her apartment. She was afraid she had not seen the end of the woman; she felt sick with apprehension and fear. When she reached her landing and found the Comte de Regnay leaning negligently against her door, she had never been more pleased to see anyone. Arrogant and overbearing he might be, but he was civilised and the closest she had to a friend. She did not want him to know of her adventure and yet she desperately needed his support.

'Where the devil have you been?' he demanded in his usual high-handed manner. '*Dieu*, Madeleine. It's not safe for you to go out unattended.'

'I've been shopping.' Madeleine swallowed and struggled to control herself. Nevertheless, her hand still shook as she turned the key in the door. 'I didn't see your carriage,' she said, attempting to sound normal.

'It was a nice day so I decided to walk.'

'Yes, that's what I thought, too.' She kept her back turned to him so he should not see the damage to her cheek.

He sighed irritably. 'If I had known you wanted to walk, then I would willingly have escorted you. Why can't you understand. . .?'

'I really don't think I want one of your lectures just now,' she told him and was appalled to hear a tremor in her voice. Quickly, she walked away from him into the drawing room, not caring whether he followed her or not.

'Madeleine?'

She could hear the concern in his voice as she removed her pelisse and placed it across the chair.

Bowing to the inevitable, she finally turned to face him and was surprised to see him pale.

'*Dieu*!' he said; shaken. 'Who did that to your face?'

'There was this woman. . .' she began, still battling tears. 'She said such dreadful things. . .' In spite of his presence, she had never felt so isolated and alone. The woman's hatred had been a vile and tangible thing that had shaken her to the core. She had instinctively recoiled from it, but even now felt a little bruised of spirit and unsure.

The Comte stepped towards her and very gently tilted her chin so that he could view the damage more closely. A muscle tensed in his jaw.

'You had better wash it,' he told her in a calm voice. 'I don't suppose the woman's hands were all that clean.'

Madeleine nodded, suppressing a foolish urge to press her face against his palm. She badly wanted comfort and reassurance as to her own worth, even from him.

'Do you have some brandy?' he asked. 'You're as white as a sheet.'

She gestured towards the side-table then sat down shakily on the *chaise longue* whilst he went to pour her a glass. That done, he withdrew a clean handkerchief from his pocket and tipped some brandy onto one corner of it. Returning to Madeleine, he pressed the glass into her hand then, kneeling in front of her, once more lifted her chin.

'This will sting,' he told her in a surprisingly gentle voice as he dabbed at the livid marks with the handkerchief.

Madeleine winced but she did not draw away from him. Her cheek felt like it was on fire and she bit her lip to hold back tears.

Although she did not know it, her distress cut into the Comte like a knife. In his entire life he had never felt such a strong desire to comfort, to cherish and to console. He wanted to rush out and find that vicious citizeness and grind her underfoot. Instead, he drew

back and rather brusquely ordered Madeleine to drink
the brandy. This she did although she didn't like the
taste of it. It was much easier than arguing with him.
Moreover, she had somewhat belatedly come to realise
that he only had her best interests at heart.

When he sat down beside her, she heard him sigh. 'I
went to see the King earlier today,' he said. 'It wasn't
easy to get an audience and we were allowed little
privacy, but I felt I had to assure him of my support. He
asked after my Breton friend. Of course, he meant
Philippe and he was genuinely saddened to hear of his
death. I have promised to return to the Tuileries before
I leave Paris.'

'Oh, so you do intend to go.' Madeleine was surprised
at how desolate that made her feel and for the first time,
admitted to herself how much she relied on his help and
companionship. 'I shall miss you.'

'You can't stay in Paris, Madeleine,' he told her
determinedly. 'If you don't want to go to Brittany, then
let me take you to Châteaurange. You would be an
honoured guest, nothing more. Philippe would hate to
think of you living alone here. Things are going to get
much worse, my dear—I'm sure of it. The King is now
seen as a traitor by the majority of citizens and the same
will apply to any who appear to have supported him. I
dare not remain here much longer myself.'

'Do you think you are in danger then?' Madeleine
asked sharply.

He shrugged. 'No more than anyone else in my
position, but my instincts tell me it is time to leave.
Besides, I have neglected my estate long enough. Come
with me, Madeleine. I urge it most strongly.'

She could see how much more difficult life in the

capital was going to be without him. In fact, the prospect
was quite frightening. 'When did you intend to leave?'
she finally asked.

He could have answered, weeks ago, that he had only
remained there because of her. Aware that she was on
the point of accepting his escort, he wisely refrained.

'In two weeks, one month at the most,' he told her. 'I
would really like to be away from here before the onset
of autumn.'

Madeleine forced a smile and with as much dignity as
she could manage told him that she would be grateful
for his escort to his château, and then on into Brittany if
he could spare the time.

'Of course I can spare the time,' he replied and with
such a sense of relief that she realised he had been
waiting for her to make that decision for several weeks.

Philippe had been right about him, she thought. He
had proved a true and loyal friend. It was just that he
was so arrogant, so aloof and restrained. Nevertheless,
Madeleine resolved to make the effort to be nicer to him
in the future.

'I can be ready by the end of August,' she told him.

'That will suit me well enough,' he replied. 'It would
be foolish to leave my house empty at such a time so I
need to find someone to rent it from me. Fortunately, I
have already had enquires about it.'

'A good patriot, I trust,' Madeleine commented with
heavy sarcasm. 'That way you can be sure the house will
remain intact.'

'But of course.' He smiled at that, a natural unrestrained smile that relaxed the stern lines of his face and
made his dark eyes twinkle.

He really should do it more often, Madeleine thought,

then perversely hoped he would not, for it made him appear disconcertingly attractive and she really did not want to think of him in that way at all.

Over the next few weeks she managed to keep herself busy, packing clothes and deciding what items she would take with her to Brittany. Monsieur Leclerc called at the Comte's bidding and offered to arrange the selling of her furniture after she had gone. It would pose no problem, he told her; the proceeds would make a nice addition to her legacy which he would make possible for her to draw on in Vannes. In fact, the whole process of packing and arranging matters progressed more effortlessly than she had thought, and she found herself ready a day or two in front of the Comte's suggested departure date.

On the first day of September, Madeleine and the Comte began their journey. The Comte's retinue pulled up outside Madeleine's apartment just after the sun had risen, when the streets seemed awash with gold. It consisted of two vehicles, the Comte's carriage and a heavier, old-fashioned coach piled high with the possessions he had not wished to leave behind.

De Regnay himself was mounted on a superb grey horse that looked entirely too spirited. The beast pranced and sidled as Madeleine's trunks, two of clothes and two containing other items, were loaded onto the carriage by the postillion and Jean-Paul. The latter, a slight young man with roguish dark eyes, handed Madeleine up into the carriage and graciously wished her goodbye. She was surprised that he was not going to accompany them and determined to ask the Comte about it at the first opportunity.

The streets of the city were quiet at that time of the morning and they progressed without incident. However, when they reached the city wall, they found soldiers on duty beside the old gate. They stopped the carriages and looked pointedly at the amount of luggage.

'Damned aristos,' Madeleine heard one of them mutter, 'running like rats from a sinking ship and taking their wealth with them.'

'I am not leaving the country,' the Comte told them coldly without bothering to dismount. 'I am merely returning to my home in Normandy. If you doubt my word, I have a letter from Monsieur de Lessay verifying that.' The name he mentioned was that of a prominent politician. 'He will not be pleased if you delay us. He is hoping to rent my house and that will not be possible if you turn me back.'

The officer frowned doubtfully. 'May I see this letter, *monsieur*?'

Making no effort to conceal his irritation, the Comte passed the document across. 'I am not obliged to show it to you. There is as yet no law to prevent us leaving Paris.'

Whether the letter was genuine or not Madeleine did not know but the soldier seemed satisfied that it was. The Comte was a man of many parts, she decided, and much more resourceful than she would have thought.

In no time, they were through the gate and the sprawling houses that had grown up just outside the city walls, and travelling through the open countryside. Madeleine gave a sigh and settled back against the seat.

When she glanced through the carriage window, she saw the Comte kick the grey horse into a gallop and surge ahead. For a man who had spent a great deal of his life in the drawing rooms of Paris, he looked surprisingly natural on a horse.

and she allowed him to help her down. His grip was warm and sure, and oddly unsettling. Madeleine drew away from him as soon as was seemingly possible.

This is lovely,

They had pulled up at a grassy clearing

CHAPTER THREE

As THE sun climbed higher in the sky, the early morning haze disappeared, heralding a fine day. Madeleine lowered the window on her side of the coach and breathed in the sunwashed smell of the countryside. She had almost forgotten the scent of hedge parsley and the fresh, sweet smell of drying leaves and grass, and with the awakening memories came a new sense of optimism. Her time with Philippe had been good and in its way fulfilling, but it was over. She was entering a new phase in her life, and for the first time in weeks, felt able to look ahead with a measure of pleasure and confidence.

She had already written to her aunt and, although she did not know if the letter would arrive before her, she was nevertheless sure of her welcome. The farm was large and prosperous. It was set between woodland and river, and on a fine summer's day there was no better place to be.

Towards noon Madeleine began to doze. She was jolted awake when the coach left the roadway to pull up on a wide grassy verge.

'Why are we stopping?' she asked when the Comte himself opened the door for her.

He smiled that rare but genuine smile that inevitably softened her feelings towards him. 'I thought you might be hungry.'

'Yes, I am,' she admitted.

'Then we will stop for a picnic.' He held out his hand

37

and she allowed him to help her down. His grip was warm and sure and oddly unsettling. Madeleine drew away from him as soon as was seemingly possible.

'This is lovely,' she told him, looking around.

They had pulled up at the edge of a grassy clearing that was surrounded on three sides by trees. Already one of the coachmen had scampered down and was spreading a blanket out beneath a nearby willow tree. Madeleine was delighted when, on reaching the tree, she found that it bordered a small clean stream. With a contented sigh, she settled herself down on the blanket and the Comte came to join her there.

Today she found herself very aware of him, yet she chose to ignore him and instead watched as the coach was manoeuvred into the shelter of the trees. In a matter of seconds the man who had spread out the blankets returned, carrying a large hamper.

'You may leave us,' the count told him curtly. 'We shall serve ourselves.'

The man bowed in acknowledgement then went to join the other coachmen who were preparing to eat their own lunch. They had settled themselves down at a discreet distance. Madeleine thought it typical of the Comte to have his servants so well trained.

'I expect you will miss Jean-Paul,' she commented.

The Comte looked up from the picnic basket. 'Yes, I suppose I shall, his dry humour in particular.' He sounded faintly surprised by his own admission. 'But he was Parisian born and bred. I had not really expected him to accompany me.'

That explained quite a lot, Madeleine thought, certainly the ease with which the man had roamed the city streets.

'Has he left your service for good, then?'

The Comte nodded and, lifting out a bottle of wine, stepped down to the stream where he set it in the shallows. 'These days he can do much better for himself. He has the makings of a politician.'

Madeleine was surprised by his easy acceptance of that. 'Doesn't that upset you?'

He looked up sharply. 'That a servant can better himself? A few months ago it might have, but not any more.' He shrugged and gave a wry smile. 'Over the past few months I have grown to appreciate his talents. Now people like de Lessay, I have less respect for.'

Madeleine immediately recognised the name. 'De Lessay. Isn't that the Republican who is renting your house?'

'Pierre Dominique de Lessay, previously the Marquis de Beauforte. We are friends of a sort. Pierre is one who has moved with the revolution. Oh, he's not a true "patriot", but he has embraced the call for liberty and equality sufficiently to retain his influence and his power. All he has lost is his title and apparently he set little store in that.' He shrugged again. 'Pierre was ever a pragmatist and I suppose his attitude is better than running in fear to England or Austria but I still see him as a traitor to his class.'

Sitting down on the blanket, he opened the hamper and offered Madeleine a delicious-looking pastry filled with salmon.

Graciously she accepted one. 'I don't blame you for feeling like that. . .when I think what happened to Philippe. . .'

'Philippe was unlucky,' the Comte said gently. 'In spite of the disorder on the streets, the number of attacks on our houses has really been quite small. However, things are going to get worse. No one knows when more violence will erupt and the law has become a joke. Like today, for instance. The soldiers had no authority to turn us back. There is at present no law against emigration, but a word to the crowd. . .I can't say I'm not relieved to be out of the city.'

'I am too,' she admitted. 'I feel somehow more free.'

The Comte's eyes seemed to soften as he looked at her. 'I know what you mean. We should both have left sooner.'

'Why didn't you?' Madeleine asked, biting into the pastry.

He could have admitted that he had promised Philippe not to leave without her but it was not only that promise which had kept him there. Because he did not understand his own motives, he ignored her question, turning his attention back to the basket as he extracted an array of silver dishes covered with crisp white cloths.

'I hope you don't mind making do,' he said, handing her a china plate and cutlery wrapped in a spotless napkin.

Madeleine looked at the array of food and decided that his idea of 'making do' was certainly not the same as hers.

'There's more here than we will be able to eat,' she protested.

He looked a little surprised by her remark. 'I had no idea what you liked. Besides, my cook had nothing better to do. De Lessay is retaining his services but does not move in until the end of the month.'

There was going to be such waste. Madeleine found that she felt guilty about that. Had not the riots in Paris been caused by starvation? She had been nine years old when Philippe had taken charge of her, old enough to know and remember what hunger had felt like. She was quiet whilst they ate even when he retrieved the chilled wine and deftly poured her a glass.

'I wonder what I have done to upset you this time,' he finally commented in a tone of mild exasperation. 'Is the food not to your liking?'

Madeleine knew she was going to have to explain her feelings to him even if he laughed at her. 'It's delicious,' she admitted. 'It's just that there is going to be so much waste and. . .' She hesitated, then forced the words out, 'and other people are starving!'

'Madeleine, you are not becoming a Jacobin, are you?'

She thought he was teasing her but she could not be sure. There was only the faintest light in his eyes and not the slightest curve to his well-shaped lips.

'Of course not,' she replied testily.

'If it will make you feel any better, I will leave the remains and the basket with the first hungry-looking peasant we meet.'

He was teasing her and she was in no mood to accept it. 'Now you are making fun of me! It's attitudes like yours that are responsible for the present troubles.'

His mouth tightened in annoyance; it was as if a shutter had come down behind his dark eyes. She knew she had been rude and an apology hovered on her tongue until she realised that it would only make matters worse. Furthermore, she did not really want to take back her words.

He looked so arrogant, so untouched by events, sitting there in his perfectly tailored riding coat and breeches and with his wig immaculately curled and queued. The new revolutionary style of natural untidy locks was nicer, she thought sourly, and a lot more practical. No doubt the Comte looked ridiculous without his artificial coiffure.

Shortly after that the picnic was packed away and they commenced their journey. As before, the Comte chose to ride, thus relieving Madeleine of his company. In the late afternoon, they reached the outskirts of Dreux and there the Comte elected to stop, deciding that they had all had enough for one day.

The hostelry he had chosen was on the edge of the town. That it was one he had used before became immediately apparent. The coat of arms might have been removed from the carriage doors and the coachmen no longer in livery, but the patron seemed to know exactly who he was dealing with. In spite of the law abolishing titles, the fellow still referred to Lucian as 'Comte' and treated him with exceptional diffidence. Madeleine reflected that, in that particular inn, it was as if the revolution had never happened. Mirabeau and others like him would be turning in their graves.

The Comte introduced Madeleine as Philippe's widow which gained her sympathy rather than censure. In a way she resented the need for the deception, but realised that the Comte was right when he said that it would make matters easier all round.

They dined together in a private parlour and the food was excellent. Afterwards the Comte stretched out in a chair beside the empty fireplace, wincing slightly as he did so.

'Lord, I'm stiff!' he exclaimed. 'I haven't spent that long in the saddle for years.'

It afforded Madeleine a certain amount of satisfaction to know that even he could feel fatigue. That satisfaction was quickly quelled by the fact that he looked so unexpectedly masculine and appealing sprawled there. His almond eyes looked warm and slumberous and his usually immaculate cravat had been loosened. In spite of his aloof arrogance he really was a most attractive man, she acknowledged with a certain amount of surprise, and she wondered how she could have thought otherwise.

The following day they did not set out until mid-morning after partaking of a late but hearty breakfast. Once more the Comte elected to ride and Madeleine tried to convince herself that she was not disappointed. It was a little boring riding alone in the coach and, after a while, she acknowledged that she would have liked his company.

Once the journey had begun, they progressed rapidly, the Comte being anxious to make up for lost time. It was another warm day and, because the roadway was now completely dry, dust became a problem, making it impossible for Madeleine to leave her window open.

Around noon, the coach seemed to swerve. Madeleine heard the scraping of the brake, and then the vehicle came to an abrupt halt with a jolt that was sufficient to send her sliding from her seat and onto the floor. As soon as she had regained her equilibrium, she opened the coach door and climbed out on to the dusty roadway. The coachman was swearing roundly but Madeleine ignored him, her attention riveted on the small girl who sat crying at the side of the road. She couldn't have been more than about four, but her limbs

were without the chubbiness associated with a child of
that age. She was dressed in a short ragged dress and her
tiny feet were bare. The boy who was trying to comfort
her was scarcely older and certainly no more robust. He
glanced at Madeleine apprehensively.

'Did you hit her?' she demanded of the irate coachman and he shook his head.

'They ran straight across in front of me. It's a miracle
I didn't.' He gestured towards a small rundown dwelling
set back from the road and to their right. 'The brats
came charging out of there without so much as a glance
in our direction.'

On instinct Madeleine moved towards the children
but the Comte was before her. He curtly silenced the
coachman who was continuing his tirade on the stupidity
of the children; slipping lithely from the saddle, he
crouched down beside them.

'Is she hurt?' he demanded of the boy.

The lad just stared at him, too frightened or too much
in awe to answer. After only a momentary hesitation, he
took matters into his own hands and lifted the little girl
to her feet. He wasn't particularly soothing or gentle, in
fact his manner bespoke irritation, yet she seemed to
sense that he would not hurt her. She stood quite
steadily, sniffed, then lifted a badly grazed elbow for
him to inspect.

Somewhat awkwardly, he removed a clean handkerchief from his pocket and tied it around the injured limb.
Madeleine was impressed by his gentleness. It seemed
out of character, yet because of that was all the more
endearing. When the child lifted her ragged skirt to
reveal a graze on one bare buttock, he cleared his throat
and hurriedly stepped back.

Madeleine could not contain her laughter. 'I think she wants you to bandage that too!'

With his expression inscrutable, he moved towards his horse. 'She's well enough. The coach didn't hit her.'

'Shouldn't we. . .?' Madeleine was going to suggest that they find the child's mother but paused when she saw a young woman leave the cottage and come hurrying towards them.

'Foolish children!' the woman exclaimed. 'How many times have I told you to be careful of the road?'

Turning to the Comte she began a fearful, almost groveling apology. He rather curtly brushed it aside, but at least did not berate her as more than one noble seigneur would have done.

Madeleine moved to his side and together they watched as the woman hurried the children back towards the cottage. She, too, looked half-starved and Madeleine thought guiltily of the food they had wasted the day before.

When she glanced up at the Comte she found him watching her, a strange expression on his face. With a resigned sigh he followed the woman, catching up with her before she could enter her door. Madeleine saw him pull a purse from his pocket and push it into the woman's hand.

'For the children,' she heard him say.

He returned quickly and glared at her, defying her to make any comment. It made her want to laugh, the more so when he searched in vain for his handkerchief. Still biting her lip, she offered him hers. He wiped his hands on the tiny square then, after a momentary hesitation, pushed it into his pocket.

'God knows what I could catch,' he muttered, beckoning to one of the coachmen who had scrambled down to hold his horse. 'Get in the coach, Madeleine. We've wasted long enough as it is!'

'Yes, Lucian,' she replied meekly, using his Christian name easily for the first time.

Once settled in the coach, she gave in to the laughter she had been trying to control. The Comte was not as aloof or as self-contained as he liked to appear. He was a little spoiled perhaps, and sometimes thoughtless, but there was an innate kindness in him and something that was almost akin to chivalry. The way he had been with Philippe and the patience he had shown towards her should have told her that. Foolishly, she had let his arrogance blind her to his other qualities; his arrogance and an impertinent proposal she really should have forgiven him for.

She was surprised to find that such a proposal would not be nearly as repugnant to her now. Philippe had been right. Lucian would make a good protector. Unfortunately, she had decided that she no longer wanted that life. The kind of relationship she'd had with Philippe was hardly likely to be repeated and she had a feeling of repugnance about sleeping with a man just so that he would keep her. It was as well the Comte was too proud to repeat his offer for she would only have had to refuse him again.

They spent that night at an inn where the servants weren't nearly as obliging as they had been the night before. The Comte's authority procured him the service he required, but not without a certain amount of surly resentment. The degree to which people embraced the revolution seemed to vary from one town to the next, from one hostelry to another. There seemed no more reason for the varying attitudes than there was for the mobs in Paris. Even those who supported the revolution seemed to expect different things from it and underlying everything was a disquieting sense of fear—fear of reprisals, of anarchy, of a return to the old regime and, not least, of an invasion by a foreign power. Everyone seemed to know of the Austrian and Prussian troops gathered on the French border and that reprisals against the King and Queen could easily cause war.

They did not linger the following morning but left not long after the sun had come up. The Comte resented having to exert himself for service he was paying well for and couldn't wait to shake the dust of the place from his feet. Such an early start meant they had to spare the horses, thus progress was slow.

The sky had turned to pink and the sun was sinking below the tree-covered horizon by the time the coach entered the tiny village of Rangeville which was situated a mere two miles from the Comte's château. Madeleine had lowered her window; for the past few miles the Comte had been riding beside the coach, pointing out landmarks and making himself generally agreeable.

'Only another half an hour or so and we will be there,' he told her. 'The horses have had enough and I'm ready for a bath. Muscles ache that I didn't even know I had!'

'I'm sure you'll survive,' Madeleine told him drily.

He certainly looked healthy enough, and disconcertingly handsome. Over the past couple of days his face had tanned and his eyes glowed with health and something she could only interpret as happiness.

'As a matter of fact, you're looking rather well.'

Aware that she had said too much, she turned away from him.

The Comte smiled at her lack of sophistication and his eyes softened as he looked at her. He did not think she knew just how beautiful she was. Because she had been under Philippe's protection, other men had not pursued her and there was a freshness to her that he found surprisingly appealing. Even in Paris she had not powdered her hair, which was fair and fine: the colour of pale butter or the petals of a yellow rose before they fall. Her profile was delicate and yet her complexion spoke of health and her eyes of vitality. Cat's eyes, he thought, and most apt, for in spite of her gentleness he knew she would protect those she loved as fiercely as any tigress.

For the first time, he admitted to himself that he desired her more than any woman he had met before. It was ironic that she didn't even seem to like him for he'd never had trouble attracting the opposite sex. Generally, they fell over themselves to be agreeable and that had become a bore. It would be far more interesting trying to change Madeleine's opinion of him. No, not just interesting; it mattered to him. His smile faded at this disquieting realisation. Surprisingly, it mattered quite a lot.

He was thoughtful as he turned his attention back to the town; for the first time, it occurred to him that things were not quite as they should be. Previously, whenever he had returned, the villagers had waved and doffed their hats to him in greeting. Now they were quite deliberately turning away. His last sojourn in Paris might have lasted nearly four years, but surely he had not changed that much! Even without the coat of arms emblazoned on the coach doors, they should have recognised him. He felt more than a little peeved.

'What's the matter?' Madeleine asked, seeing the consternation on his face.

'Nothing important,' he replied, and yet he continued to feel uneasy.

When two women, who were gossiping outside a cottage door, flashed him a look of absolute horror before retreating inside, his feeling of disquiet increased. Was his reputation that bad, he wondered, or was it more to do with the spread of new ideas? Certainly he had not expected to find a hotbed of revolution on his own doorstep. He had always treated his peasants fairly and, by the lights of other landlords, rather well. Had his manager Jean de Siva done something to turn the people against him? If so, then it was contrary to the instructions he had been given and extremely foolish.

With a muttered oath, he kicked his horse into a canter, thinking that the sooner they reached the house, the sooner he would be able to get to the bottom of things. Madeleine watched him go, completely at a loss to understand his change of mood.

After a minute or two, the coach turned up a narrow lane to the right, travelling between yellowing trees that curved overhead like a tunnel. They passed through a wide gateway and, after crossing a narrow bridge, followed the drive as it curved around a copse of trees. It was only then that the château itself came into view.

Madeleine glanced out of the window in horror and confusion. She had expected splendour and there was evidence of that, but there was also evidence of destruction and fire. Although the façade of the great house remained intact, there was hardly a window that was not broken. In places soot had blackened the pale stone-work and the cherubs that supported the lintel above the front doorway looked like little chimneysweeps. In most places the roof seemed to have collapsed, the exception being the rounded tower that was connected to the château's western aspect. The corresponding tower on the eastern side had been completely gutted, and charred wood and other debris had collapsed into the river that served as a kind of moat.

The Comte dismounted and stood like a statue, viewing the destruction, quite oblivious to his horse which further trampled the partially flattened flower-beds. Without waiting for help, Madeleine got out of the coach and quietly went to stand beside him. She could sense his shock, his angry confusion, and her heart went out to him. Gently she slipped her arm through his. He hardly seemed to notice.

'I'm seeing it but I can't really believe it,' he said in a tight strained voice. 'How could such a thing have happened?'

Pulling gently away from her, he walked up the soot-stained steps and in through the front entrance. What had once been a sturdy door was now nothing more than a pile of ashes. Concerned, Madeleine followed him. The spacious hallway was like a blackened cavern criss-crossed with fallen beams and soot stained masonry. The Comte picked his way cautiously forward but the vibrations still sent a loose piece of ceiling crashing down, missing him but covering the shoulder of his coat with ash and plaster.

With an oath he withdrew, catching hold of Madeleine's arm and taking her with him. He was very pale and the expression in his eyes was bleak. Words of condolence hovered on the edge of Madeleine's tongue but they would only have been platitudes and she knew he would not welcome them. He moved towards the side of the château but before he could explore further, a dark coated-horseman came galloping up the drive.

A man of about the Comte's own age pulled the horse to an abrupt halt and hurriedly dismounted in front of him.

'Lucian,' he said, looking as if he might embrace the Comte. 'I would not have had you find out like this for all the world! Obviously you did not get my letter; it cannot even have reached Paris yet.'

'I received no letter,' the Comte answered flatly. 'What the devil happened, Maurice? And why was it you who wrote and not Jean?'

'Jean has gone,' the other man replied, his face full of sympathy and concern. 'I know not where. I doubt he had the courage to face you. As for what happened. . . it's a long story. Come back to the house with me. It will be better if we discuss it there.'

'I'm surprised you're not afraid to offer me hospitality,' the Comte replied with a sneer. 'The peasants seem to have turned so thoroughly against me. There was not one who dared to greet me as we passed through the village.'

'No doubt they felt too guilty to look you in the eye.' Maurice reached into his coat and, after removing a silver flask, took a hasty swig. Wordlessly he offered it to the Comte, who only shook his head. 'There was less malice in this than you might think. It was more a question of hysteria and ignorance. They were like children, Lucian, rebellious, thoughtless children who could not see where their actions would lead.'

'Was anyone hurt?' the Comte asked, not sounding as if he really cared.

Maurice shook his head. 'The servants were allowed to leave, even Jean. . . Come back to the house with me, man. It's been a shock for you and, quite frankly, you look like death.'

The Comte glanced at Madeleine. 'I've been remiss,' he said. 'I should have introduced the two of you.'

He was falling back on etiquette, she realised, using it to support him in a situation that had really knocked the ground out from under his feet. She couldn't help but admire his self-control, yet she could sense the anger and devastation lurking just below the surface of his composure. With unwarranted formality he introduced her to Maurice Champion, his man of business and his friend.

'Up until now, Maurice has helped to manage my affairs,' he continued with a bitter smile. 'It remains to be seen whether I have enough of a fortune left to require his services in the future.'

The young lawyer continued to look concerned. 'Come back to the house, Lucian,' he suggested for a third time.

After a moment's hesitation, the Comte nodded almost imperceptibly. 'Very well,' was all he said before turning towards his horse.

Madeleine was desperately worried as the coach headed back towards the village. She felt sympathy and concern for the Comte, but she was also a little afraid. His emotion had been damped down but she knew it would take very little to provoke an explosion. In fact, that explosion was not long in coming and when it did it was almost a relief.

They entered the village and, bearing left, passed a small green. There in the centre, as in a thousand such villages all over France, a liberty tree had been erected to commemorate the revolution. It was not a proper tree but a striped pole resembling a maypole that was decked with tricolour flags and ribbons. It was a symbol of the village's allegiance to the revolution, but to the Comte it was like a red rag to a bull.

As they approached the green, he called the coach to a halt, then sat for what seemed an age, staring at the tree. Finally, he turned and, riding up to the coach driver, collected a length of stout rope that was left over from that used to fasten the luggage down. Rather curtly, he ordered the coachman to swing the vehicle around; having dismounted, he fastened one end of the rope to the rear of the coach and the other around the liberty tree. By this time the doors of the houses facing the green had opened and people were beginning to filter out, their fear of the Comte overcome by their curiosity.

Leaning from the coach window, Madeleine watched in horror as the Comte ordered the coach forward. She felt a sharp jerk and looked back to see the beribboned pole lying on the ground. A picture of arrogance and anger, the Comte rode into the centre of the green.

'That is what I think of your liberty!' he snarled, standing in his stirrups and staring around him. 'If it is liberty that caused the wanton destruction of my home, then it is the liberty of fools! This is my land and I will not have a symbol of such anarchy and mindless violence erected on it. Is it liberty that keeps the King a virtual prisoner in Paris? Is it liberty that dispossesses the church and forces priests to swear allegiance to a civil power? You people do not know the meaning of the word!'

After the things she had seen and experienced in Paris Madeleine tensed, waiting for the villagers' response. At the very least she expected a verbal assault, but the Comte's charisma and justifiable anger carried the day. The people stood silently, more respectful than sullen. They were country people, his people, and more than one of them felt guilty about what had been done.

the rents were to be eased, they were readily believed.
It was seen as part of a plot to reduce the tenants'
profits and make it impossible for them to buy their own
land. The fact that, even with a cut in rent few would be
able to do so, was simply not registered with
them.

CHAPTER FOUR

THE Comte paced restlessly back and forth across the
worn carpet in Maurice Champion's study. He was pale
and tense, as yet unable to completely accept his loss.

'Are you telling me I should do nothing?' he
demanded of his friend in angry frustration. 'Am I to
forgive and forget just like that?'

'I can understand how you feel,' Champion replied
quietly. 'I'm just trying to explain something of what
happened although, in truth, I do not fully understand it
myself. I was surprised that our people were so easily
led. It was the men from Alençon who began it. They
were on their way to Paris, to the Jacobin club they said,
and they obviously wanted to practice their oratory.
Even so, I don't think matters would have come to such
a pass if your manager had not just increased Pierre
Boulin's rent.'

The Comte stopped his pacing. 'But you've already
told me that the fellow was lazy, that he let his own barn
burn! He should have had to pay for the replacement.
Jean was acting just as I would!'

'I doubt that,' Champion told him. 'You are not
stupid and feeling was obviously running high. There
was something personal in it, too. In spite of being a
good manager, Jean was never able to talk to the
tenants. He was brusque and arrogant in manner and
Boulin was downright rude to him in front of others.
When the men from Alençon began the story that all

the rents were to be raised, they were readily believed. It was seen as part of a plot to reduce the peasants' profits and make it impossible for them to buy their own land. The fact that even with a cut in rent few would be able to do so, doesn't seem to have registered with them.'

The Comte sighed and walked to stare out of the window. As his mind digested the facts, he became increasingly angry, not so much at the peasants but at the stupidity and waste.

'You had been in Paris too long, Lucian,' Maurice continued. 'The peasants liked and respected you but, recently, they had begun to think of Jean as their landlord. I suspect he had even begun to believe it himself. What began as a march to the château, to protest Pierre's rent rise, rapidly got out of hand. Jean came out of his cottage to threaten the peasants with a musket and in panic shot Raymond Lablanc's youngest son.'

The Comte swore softly and turned back to face the room.

'The boy will live but has lost the use of an arm,' Champion told him. 'Jean was dragged from the manager's cottage and soundly beaten. It's a miracle he was not killed and says something for the forbearance of the people. Then, after allowing the servants to leave, they torched the château. It was wanton destruction.'

He paused, then admitted, 'I was there, Lucian. . . I tried to reason with them, but it was hopeless. Short of trying to fight them all, there was nothing I could do.' He sighed unsteadily. 'All that art, the ancient tapestries and silver. It was such a waste. Perhaps I should have tried harder.'

The Comte slumped down in a chair; for a moment his eyes closed in anguish. 'It would not have been worth your life, Maurice.'

Champion walked across and briefly squeezed his shoulder. For a moment they were both silent, too full of emotion to speak.

'What about rebuilding?' the Comte asked after a while. 'You know more about my finances then I do myself.'

'You have lost a lot, Lucian,' the lawyer replied quietly. He shrugged. 'Possibly, in time... Fortunately the very people who burned you out will continue to pay their rent. You could even increase it a little in retaliation. However, the farms must remain viable, otherwise...'

The Comte smiled bitterly. 'If I take too much, then in the long run I'll get less. Is that what you're trying to tell me?'

Champion nodded. 'You are far from destitute but it will take a colossal amount to rebuild. Since the abolition of manorial dues, your income is a great deal less. Of course you could sell off some land, but I wouldn't advise it.'

'Because the land is my income,' the Comte supplied. 'I could end up with a fine house and no land to support it.'

'Exactly! As I've already said, it's unlikely that more than one or two of your tenants will be able to take advantage of the new law and buy their land—perhaps the Beliers, for their farm is by far the most profitable, but that is all. You are not ruined, Luc, far from it, but to recreate Châteaurange would be well beyond your

means and may not even be advisable in the present
political climate.'

'Well, that's clear enough.'

'I'm talking about now,' Champion insisted. 'Who
knows about the future? If we invest wisely, in your
children's time. . .' he shrugged.

'Children?' The Comte smiled wryly. 'I've never
thought that far ahead. I've never even considered
marriage. I like my freedom and my pleasures too
much.'

'I think you have become a little too used to both, my
friend,' Champion teased, trying to lift his friend's
spirits. 'What woman would have you?'

'Are you hinting that I am spoiled?' the Comte asked,
with the hint of a smile.

'Abominably!'

The reply was in jest yet slowly the smile faded from
the Comte's eyes. 'Perhaps you are right. I have been
too long in Paris. *Dieu*, Maurice! The château wasn't
really a home, but such senseless destruction. I feel that
I could kill someone over this!'

Madeleine was reading in the drawing-room. She had
washed and changed and was feeling refreshed, if a little
ill at ease. Madame Champion, a pretty dark-haired
young woman, had been welcoming enough but had
lacked the social grace to set Madeleine at her ease. To
make matters worse, she obviously stood in considerable awe of the Comte and had become positively
tongue-tied in front of him. Madeleine could sympathise
to a certain extent, for at his most imperious he was
certainly daunting, but he had gone out of his way to be
pleasant to his hostess.

When he entered the room with Maurice Champion, Madeleine thought he looked as vulnerable and human as anyone else. He, too, had washed and changed, but the signs of strain remained on his face. She was surprised by how much she ached for him, by how strong her desire to comfort him was. In spite of his arrogance, he was a good man and he certainly didn't deserve what had happened to him.

When he sat down in the chair beside her, she surprised herself by reaching across to touch his hand.

'Are you all right?' she asked quietly.

'Of course,' he replied with that closed expression she had come to dislike. Then, with a tight smile he added, 'You don't need to be concerned about me, Madeleine.'

But I am, she thought. I can't help myself. She knew he was not made of stone; he had shown her that in a dozen different ways and she was annoyed that he still felt he had to pretend with her. It came as something of a shock to realise that she was actually beginning to feel protective towards him.

The meal that followed was not a great success. The food was plentiful and well prepared, for the Champions were wealthy enough to retain an accomplished cook, but Madame Champion appeared agitated and ill at ease. She did not once look the Comte in the eye and spoke only to her husband and Madeleine. She was, in fact, rather rude, something her husband awkwardly apologised for the moment she left the room to check on the preparation of dessert.

'She does not mean to be discourteous,' he explained. 'It is just that she is feeling guilty. Her father and brother were there when the château was burnt and lifted not a finger to help me prevent it. If it is any consolation to you, she has not spoken a word to them since.'

The meal was concluded mostly in silence. As the only other woman present, Madeleine did her best to draw her hostess out but with little success, and the Comte, after an initial effort, seemed disinclined to try. It was a pattern that continued on into the evening and Madeleine was relieved when it became late enough for her to escape to bed.

The room the Champions had given her was large and well furnished, one of four on the second floor. Their house was the only one of any size in the village and opulently furnished. Apparently Maurice travelled twice weekly into Mamers to deal with business there, but Madeleine suspected that the bulk of his income came from managing the Comte's affairs. Given those facts, she could understand although not completely sympathise with the other woman's anxiety.

She was not in the least tired and, once she was ready for bed, settled down in one of the two chairs set before the fireplace to finish the book Madame Champion had loaned her. Although it was only early autumn, a small fire smouldered in the hearth and she felt quite cosy. Time passed without her being aware of it and she had actually reached the last chapter before she was disturbed by a knock on her door.

'Madeleine, I saw your light.' It was the Comte's voice. 'I would like to speak with you if I may.'

'Just a moment.' Madeleine checked that her robe was properly closed and tightened the sash. It was a pale gold in colour, only slightly darker than her hair.

When she opened her door, she found the Comte leaning lazily against the door jamb. He had shed his jacket and his cravat was decidedly askew. His eyes looked sleepy, appealingly so.

'Can I come in?' he asked. 'I only want to discuss the arrangements for the rest of our journey.'

His voice was a little slurred and she frowned.

He smiled wryly. 'Yes, I have had a drink or two but I'm far from drunk. It's quite safe, Madeleine, I assure you.'

Feeling foolish, she stepped aside for him to enter.

'I thought we might leave tomorrow,' he said.

Madeleine was surprised. 'So soon? Are there not things to be settled?'

'Maurice wants me to speak to the peasants but to be honest I don't trust my temper.' He shrugged. 'Maybe in a few weeks. . . In the meantime, I certainly don't want to stay here. Maurice's little mouse of a wife nearly jumps out of her skin every time I speak to her. Besides, we've already sorted out what's important. Maurice can manage what's left of my income.'

It was on the tip of her tongue to remind him of just what had happened when he had left others to handle things. Without being asked, he settled down in one of the chairs in front of the fire and stretched out his long legs.

'Aren't you going to offer me a drink?' he asked, glancing pointedly at a bottle of brandy and some glasses that had been placed on a side-table.

'I thought perhaps you'd had enough,' she replied drily. 'In any case, I was going to bed.'

'You're no fun, Maddie,' he teased with a mixture of irritation and amusement, then rose to help himself.

She scowled at the shortening of her name. He was using it with increased regularity and she was not at all sure she liked it. She wanted to be annoyed with him and yet the shadows lingering behind his smile prevented her. After what had happened he had every reason to get drunk.

He must have read her thoughts. With another wry smile, he lifted his glass and added, 'Don't worry, I've never thought this the answer to anything.'

'I'm pleased to hear it.' Her tone implied she could not have cared less. Rather ill at ease, she sat down in the chair across from him. 'What time did you want to leave?'

'Before noon, if possible. In fact, I've already told Maurice we'll be going. He's a good friend and offered hospitality indefinitely, not that I could stand it. I'm leaving the second coach here and Maurice is going to store some of my trunks. This house isn't large, but it does have extensive stables which is fortunate as he is already housing the horses that were rescued from the fire.'

He sighed deeply. 'I've given him permission to sell all but five of them. Tomorrow we'll continue as planned. Pierre, the fellow who handled the second coach, will drive as the other two coachmen wish to remain here with their families. That was to have been the arrangement in any case. What I really wanted to know was whether you would like me to find a maid to keep you company on the remainder of the journey. I know we left Paris without one, but that situation does not have to continue.'

Once again Madeleine was surprised by his thoughtfulness, the more so because he seemed to have so many problems of his own. However, she couldn't envisage turning up at her aunt's farm with a servant in tow. She would feel awkward enough having the Comte for an escort. She rather hoped he was not expecting hospitality—not that her aunt wouldn't offer it, but Kermosten was a working farm.

'I think I would rather manage without a maid,' she told him. 'Will you be hiring yourself a new gentleman?'

'Not yet, anyway. I had thought to train one of the château's servants.' He smiled lazily. 'Perhaps I'll grow a beard.'

Madeleine looked at the shadow already darkening his jaw-line and found herself intrigued by that idea. It would be dark, she realised, like his eyes.

'Lucian,' she said seriously, 'you've been very good to me, but you've such problems of your own. If you wanted to forget about escorting me, I would understand. You must feel so awful about what has happened.'

'More awful than I have a right to. My visits to the place were few and far between. To tell you the truth, I found it rather lonely even when my father was alive. If it hadn't been for Maurice it would have been deadly. Children need the company of other children, you know, and I was never allowed near the peasants.'

Company her own age was something she, too, had been denied once Philippe had taken charge of her. Her patron had always been there for her, however, and she thought how much worse it must have been for the young Comte. Yet another stone in the wall she had built between them crumbled away.

'I want to leave here, Maddie,' the Comte continued. 'In any case, I have to go to Brittany now. A friend has asked me to deliver a letter for him... Actually, I'm glad of something else to occupy my mind. I don't know

what I'm going to do yet, where I'll go. I only know I
want to stay in France. To tell the truth, I feel direction-
less, like a ship that's lost its rudder.'

Smiling ruefully at his own unaccustomed eloquence,
he stood to place his glass upon the mantelpiece. 'You
don't mind leaving so soon, then?'

Madeleine shook her head and rose to see him out.
The movement brought them closer together.

The expression on the Comte's face softened and,
with a sigh, he reached out to touch her hair that lay soft
and shining across her shoulders.

'Today it looked like sunshine,' he said solemnly, 'yet
in the candlelight it shines like molten gold.'

Madeleine had not thought him capable of such
poetry; when his hand strayed from her hair to her
cheek she did not push him away. Suddenly he seemed
so warm, so human and exciting. A slight fluttering
began in her stomach which she was at a loss to
understand.

For just a moment he hesitated, then bent to kiss her
cheek. Of course she permitted it. They were friends,
after all, and it was nice to feel so close to someone both
physically and emotionally. When his lips moved to her
mouth, her eyes flew open in surprise. It was the briefest
of contacts and before she could protest, he had drawn
away.

'Goodnight, Madeleine,' he whispered a trifle huskily.
'Sweet dreams.'

He had gone before she was even aware of it; for
several seconds she stood staring at the door. Her heart-
beat had increased and she could still taste the sweetness
of the wine on his lips. Unable to help herself, she
sighed. No one, not even Philippe, had kissed her on the

lips before and she was surprised to find that she had liked it. . .she had liked it so much that she had wanted it to continue. She was twenty years old, yet it was the first time in her life that she had felt the awakening of desire. It was not a comfortable feeling and for a long time that night she lay sleepless and confused.

The following day, late in the morning, they set off once more. The Comte, because he was feeling the effects of his indulgence the night before, chose to ride in the coach with Madeleine. His horse, which she had only recently discovered was named Charlemagne, was tied behind. There had been times on the journey from Paris when she would have welcomed his company; now, she found it oddly unsettling. He was not a demanding companion and seemed quite happy with the silence that all too often stretched between them, but Madeleine found herself unable to relax. At one point she caught him watching her from beneath half-closed eyelids; she felt like a fly beneath a magnifying glass.

Eventually he fell asleep and then Madeleine was able to study him. She liked his face, she decided, with all its contradictions. His lean jaw and high cheekbones spoke of arrogance and determination but his mouth, with its slightly fuller bottom lip, hinted at the softer side of his nature, a side she had only recently become aware of. It was there in his face and yet she doubted many people would notice it because he deliberately presented such a controlled façade. With his eyes closed and his face relaxed, he looked much younger than she had first thought and not in the least intimidating.

They spent the night at an isolated country inn where

Madeleine retired to bed as soon as it was polite for her to do so.

When they continued their journey the following morning and he announced his decision to ride, she was relieved. Solitude was preferable to the emotions that seemed to surface whenever he was in her proximity. They travelled on in easy stages, breaking their journey in Mayenne and again in Vitré where they stayed at a tiny inn standing below the fortress walls.

They were on a deserted bit of road, heading towards the Breton capital of Rennes, when the incident occurred. One minute the coach was travelling quite steadily and the next there was a terrific lurch and the vehicle had crashed over on to its side. Madeleine was thrown sideways. She heard the scraping of metal and wood across the stones of the road, the screaming of a horse in agony. Then her head connected sharply with the side of the door and for a moment she literally saw stars. When her vision cleared, she found herself lying on her back, staring up at the side of the coach that now loomed over her head. The door lifted and she saw the Comte's anxious face peering down.

'Madeleine,' he called in a voice that sounded tight and strained, 'are you all right?'

'Yes, I think so,' she replied, yet when she tried to sit up her surroundings tilted alarmingly.

He swore softly and, pushing the door right back, lowered himself down beside her. 'Perhaps you should lie still for a moment,' he said with gentle concern. 'You're as white as a sheet.'

'Really, Lucian, I'm fine,' she protested. 'Just help me to climb out of here.'

She saw that he too was very pale and concluded that he had been as shocked by the incident as she.

'What happened?' she asked, attempting to keep her voice steady.

'We lost a wheel, God knows how, and because the road had subsided a little on that side, the whole coach went over. The two offside horses went down and I had to shoot one of them. Then I had to unhitch the other beasts before I came to look at you or the coach would have been kicked to pieces.'

'What about the driver?' she asked.

'A broken leg, I think. To be honest, you were my priority. Do you think you can stand now?'

She again insisted that she was all right and, with his help, managed to scramble up on to the side of the coach. When she glanced back down at him, she was surprised to see him grinning.

'Pink lace, Madeleine,' he quipped as he swung himself up to join her. 'How frivolous.'

He led her down the crumbling bank and into a meadow where the coachman lay white-faced and in obvious pain. With a concerned frown, the Comte removed his jacket and slipped it gently beneath the fellow's head.

'There's a blanket in the coach,' Madeleine told him, and he obligingly went to fetch it.

'I'm going to have to ride for help,' he informed her when he returned. 'Nothing has passed us in the last hour and Pierre can't lie here too long. I hate to ask it of you, but would you mind very much staying with him? Of course, I could take you with me, but I'll make better time alone and. . .'

'Of course I don't mind staying,' she replied.

'I'll be as quick as I can,' he assured her, looking concerned.

He was gone little more than an hour but for Madeleine the time dragged. There was nothing she could do to help Pierre and as the sun sank lower in the sky she became quite chilled. The Comte returned just as it was getting dark, with a party of peasants and a wagon. Pierre was carefully lifted into it and Madeleine climbed in beside him. They were taken to an inn some five leagues in the direction they had been travelling. It was not a very prosperous concern and was obviously not used to dealing with visitors of quality, but they were made welcome enough and Pierre was efficiently taken care of.

The meal that evening was unsophisticated but wholesome. The Comte surprised Madeleine by being more tolerant than she would have expected. When a nervous serving girl spilled the vegetables onto the table cloth he made no comment and quite cheerfully accepted the lack of any decent wine. On more than one occasion, he glanced worriedly at Madeleine and asked her if she was all right. When she mentioned feeling cold, he fetched her shawl from her room and insisted that she drink a glass of what he told her was decidedly inferior brandy. His consideration and concern was rather endearing, the more so in view of the fact that he was obviously tired himself.

Before he retired to bed, he went to see how his coachman was faring, then called in at Madeleine's room to pass on the news. Once again, she entertained him while dressed only in her nightgown and robe and was surprised how natural it felt. As soon as he had gone, she climbed into bed and fell instantly asleep.

How long she slept she did not know, but she was awakened by a loud crash followed by a succession of more muted thuds and bangs. She was lying there, wondering just what was making the noise when the unmistakable sound of a pistol discharging sounded close at hand. Her stomach turned over when she finally realised that the sounds were coming from the Comte's room, which was next door.

She did not stop to consider the consequences as she leapt from her bed and, shrugging on her robe, hurried out into the hallway. Other doors were also opening and there was a great deal of shouting. Then she caught sight of the Comte, standing alone in the doorway of his room. One of the onlookers was holding a branch of candles, and in the flickering light the Comte's complexion was the hue of waxed linen. He was breathing heavily and perspiration glistened on his forehead. Nodding to the portly landlord who had just hurried upstairs, he gestured behind him. As he turned, Madeleine saw that a bruise was beginning to appear on one of his cheeks.

'There is an intruder,' he said tightly. 'I think I have killed him.'

The landlord went into the room, emerging a few minutes later. 'He's dead all right,' he told the Comte. 'The pistol, *monsieur*, where did it come from?'

'It's his,' the Comte replied. 'Once he realised that he'd disturbed me, he intended to shoot. We struggled for the weapon and it accidentally went off. I assume he intended to rob me, for he was busy searching my trunk when I awoke.'

'Good riddance from all accounts,' muttered one of

the on-lookers. 'You have had a lucky escape, *monsieur.*'

The landlord nodded his agreement. 'I am so sorry, *monsieur*, that such a thing should happen here. I cannot tell you how sorry I am.' He then proceeded to try and do just that.

The Comte was rapidly losing his patience. He was tired, cold and bruised in a dozen places. Moreover, he was struggling to maintain his façade of cool indifference. He had never killed a man before, not even in a duel, and he was feeling rather sick.

'I do not hold it against you,' he cut in brusquely, 'but I'd be grateful if you would dispose of the corpse as soon as possible.'

'Of course! Of course!' the man replied. 'In the meantime, if there is anything you desire. . .?'

'My main desire is to get back to my bed,' the Comte told him sharply, and only Madeleine guessed that he was not as composed as he appeared. When his gaze met hers, his expression softened. 'Go back to bed, Maddie,' he said gently. 'The excitement is over.'

She did as he suggested but found it impossible to go back to sleep. When she closed her eyes she could hear the shot and she shivered to think how easily the Comte could have been killed. It occurred to her then that their journey had been exceptionally eventful. Life, it seemed, was just as dangerous outside Paris.

When she joined the Comte for breakfast the following morning, she realised that he had slept no better than she. There were shadows beneath his eyes and he appeared unusually quiet and preoccupied. As soon as he had eaten, he left for the stables to check on the condition of his horses and to get news of the damaged coach. He returned, looking even grimmer than before.

'The coach will take weeks to repair,' he told her. 'The joints have sprung in a dozen places.'

She groaned, full of sympathy for him. 'Oh, dear. . .I suppose it will cost a great deal.'

He shrugged. 'I'm more concerned with the inconvenience. There isn't another coach for sale or hire within miles of here, but I've managed to purchase a farm wagon. It's either that or leave our luggage here. I'll use my two leaders to pull it and Pierre can take the third horse back to Rangeville with him once he has recovered.'

'The wagon sounds like a godsend,' she assured him. 'But it is an extra expense and you must let me reimburse you.'

'I am not destitute, Madeleine,' he replied with just a hint of a smile. 'I have no intention of accepting your money.'

She knew it was no use pursuing the matter, but she felt badly about it. She was certain that he had lost the bulk of his wealth and that he was too proud to admit it. As for travelling in a wagon, she was quite pleased about that. She would have felt awkward arriving at her aunt's farm in the Comte's coach and, in that respect at least, matters had turned out rather well.

As for the Comte, the idea of travelling in a farm wagon appealed to him for an entirely different reason; it offered a greater degree of anonymity. Although he had said nothing to Madeleine, he was convinced that the man he had killed the night before had been more than a common thief. The fellow had sworn at him whilst they had been fighting and his accent had come from the gutters of Paris. Furthermore, he was not at all sure that the wheel coming off the coach had been truly an accident but rather a tactic to slow him down. The vehicle was fairly new and his people had been trained to keep it in good repair.

He had already told Madeleine about the letter he had promised to deliver for a friend. What he had not divulged was the name of that person—Louis Capet, the imprisoned and discredited king. When he had agreed to act as courier, he had not considered the danger involved. If he had, then he would still have aided the king. He would not, however, have combined the errand with escorting Madeleine to her new home.

CHAPTER FIVE

THEY decided to put off their departure for another day and Madeleine was not sorry for it. She was stiff and sore and was glad to be able to sit in the parlour and relax. The Comte, however, was restless, and seemed torn between an obligation to keep Madeleine company and a desire to prowl around. One of his remaining horses had been slightly injured in the accident and he spent considerable time in the stables, overseeing its well-being. This in spite of the fact that he had already pronounced the groom there more than competent. Madeleine had never noticed this restlessness in him before and wondered how he had dealt with this surplus energy whilst living in Paris.

When she tackled him on the subject he shrugged. 'I fenced,' he said, as if he had not considered the matter before, 'for at least two hours each day and I suppose that was quite demanding.'

Madeleine was surprised. The information was so at odds with the image he had presented there.

The following morning she dressed as simply as her wardrobe would allow, not wanting to look conspicuous in the rough vehicle. When she emerged from the inn, the Comte was already on the wagon seat and their trunks were stacked behind him. Charlemagne was tied to the tailgate and both he and the horses between the shafts appeared rather frisky. Somewhat impatiently the Comte told her to hurry.

She climbed up on to the hard seat, then stared at him in surprise. Not only was he dressed more casually than she had ever seen him, in buckskin breeches and an open-necked shirt, but he had dispensed with his wig. Philippe's hair had been poor and thin beneath his and for some absurd reason she had expected the Comte's to be the same. She could not have been more wrong. It was thick, dark and glossy although ruthlessly shorn to within an inch of his head. Madeleine felt a strong desire to reach out and touch it, to see if it was as soft as it appeared.

The Comte saw where she was looking and frowned irritably. 'The wig was not at all suitable,' he explained with just a hint of embarrassment. 'Besides, it seems to be the fashion to go without.

'I like it,' she replied without thinking and was surprised to see colour tinge his cheeks. She gave a delighted laugh and was roughly thrown back into her seat as he abruptly urged the horses forward. She couldn't resist teasing him. 'It reminds me of a hedgehog!'

She had obviously offended him for it was some time before he spoke again and then it was only to tell her that there were blankets beneath the seat should she feel cold. Fortunately, it was a lovely morning, for the wagon provided no shelter, and although there was an autumnal chill in the air, that soon disappeared. The countryside they were now travelling through was wilder and more hilly than that of the Comte's native Normandy and more thickly wooded. Oak, ash, beech and elm trees covered the hills with a rippling green canopy interspersed with taller, more rangy pine.

They reached Rennes in the late evening and put up at a modest inn on the outskirts of the town. To Madeleine's surprise, the Comte adopted the name Vaubonne and informed the landlord that they were brother and sister. The place was not up to his usual high standard and he again surprised her by declaring his intention of spending an extra day there. Naturally, she was disappointed. She did not want to waste the time but the Comte had been so good to her that she didn't like to dispute the matter. When he told her that he was tired and that he wanted the extra day's rest, she said nothing although she privately thought he looked rested enough. The following morning, however, when he joined her for breakfast, she changed her mind. He really did look exhausted, as if he had not slept at all. When she voiced her concern, he smiled guiltily.

'As a matter of fact, I didn't get much sleep,' he told her. 'I had some business to attend to.'

'At night?' she asked and then coloured as it occurred to her just what that business could have been. She felt intensely disappointed in him and, to her surprise, more than a little jealous.

The Comte knew exactly what she was assuming: she couldn't have been more wrong. He had spent the night on horseback, not in some woman's bed. The vital letter had been delivered. Unfortunately, it had not marked the end of his responsibilities in that regard. He wanted to tell Madeleine exactly where he had been. Only common sense made him hold his tongue although he found it much harder than he would have thought. For a man who normally did what he pleased, it had become disconcertingly important that she think well of him.

The following day they set off once more, the Comte driving and Madeleine perched up beside him. They approached the small market town of Ploërmel in the middle of the afternoon, following the narrow roadway that wound down into a picturesque valley. The Comte would have been quite happy to break their journey there but Madeleine wanted to press on. She was sure she remembered a pretty inn just to the south of the town where she had once stayed with Philippe. If they spent the night there, then it was only half a day's ride to the farm. With obvious reluctance, the Comte gave in. They stopped only long enough to refresh themselves and then set off again, travelling slowly to spare the horses.

By the time the sun was beginning to set, it had become obvious that Madeleine's memory was at fault. They had not come across the inn or any other sizeable dwelling. Madeleine became increasingly tired and worried. The Comte refrained from saying 'I told you so', yet she knew he was thinking it which did not improve her temper one iota.

'We're going to have to stop soon,' he told her in a tone of weary exasperation. 'The horses have had enough and, quite frankly, so have I. Already the light is beginning to fade.'

Madeleine did not relish spending the night in the open yet knew she had no grounds for complaint, the fault being entirely her own. She gave a sigh of relief when, after rounding a tree-covered bend, they saw a small group of buildings in the distance. As they neared the buildings, however, her feelings again hit rock bottom. What had once been a busy hostelry was now nothing more than a burned-out ruin.

'Well, that's it!' the Comte exclaimed tiredly. 'Inn or no inn, this is as far as we go.'

'Who would. . .?' Madeleine began, thinking that the fire must have been set deliberately.

'No one!' The Comte's voice sounded clipped and she knew he was remembering his own home. 'Most likely it was a kitchen fire.'

With a sigh, he passed the reins to Madeleine, then jumped down to investigate. She watched as he stepped through the blackened doorway then came out again to explore the outbuildings to the rear. The one furthest away seemed not to have been touched by the fire but from her seat in the wagon she had no way of knowing what it was like inside. The door was obviously stuck and she saw the Comte put his shoulder to it. If she hadn't been so anxious then she would have enjoyed watching him, she decided, for somewhere along the road from Paris, his courtier's walk and manner had been replaced by a more natural, athletic grace.

When he came out of the building, his face didn't look quite so grim. His hands were obviously dirty, for he rubbed them together then, with a shrug, finished them off on his breeches. Madeleine hid a smile, thinking that, just over a week ago, he wouldn't have dreamt of doing that.

'We can shelter in the end building,' he told her as he approached the wagon. 'It was obviously a storage shed of some kind. It's a bit dirty but quite dry and infinitely better than sleeping in the open.'

He climbed up into the wagon and, reclaiming the

reins, drove the vehicle through what had once been the stable yard and on to a patch of grass beyond. There, he unhitched the horses and tethered them to the low branches of an overhanging tree. Whilst he was doing this, Madeleine went to explore the outbuilding for herself. It was dark and dusty and smelt of earth and rotting wood, but the majority of it was dry. There appeared to be just one hole in the roof and that at one corner. There was an upturned barrel in the shed and a few logs. Apart from that, the place seemed empty, but the light from the doorway did not penetrate the corners and she dreaded to think what might be lurking there. She would sweep it out, she decided, and, returning outside, asked the Comte to cut her a branch from the tree to do it with.

'Cut it with what?' he demanded a trifle irritably. 'The only sharp thing I have with me is the sword hidden in my trunk and I have no intention of ruining that.'

Before she could make a sharp reply he reached up and, snapping a branch, twisted and turned it until it came free. Without saying another word he passed it to her, then leant against the doorway, arms folded, watching as she struggled to brush any loose dirt and debris outside. The whole exercise wasn't particularly effective but Madeleine felt it was better than nothing. When the ensuing dust made her sneeze, the Comte's amused smile broke into an open laugh.

'Oh, Madeleine, my dear,' he teased, 'I had never suspected this streak of domesticity.'

'I wasn't being domestic,' she snapped irritably. 'I just don't fancy sleeping with spiders.'

It wasn't until she said the word sleep that she realised that was what they would be doing and within feet of

each other. The thought was more than a little disconcerting. Did he snore? Philippe certainly had; she had
often heard him through their connecting door.

'Come with me to fetch the blankets,' the Comte told
her. 'Then you can show me what you would like me to
unload for tonight.'

Glad that he was unable to read her mind, Madeleine
readily obeyed. Together, they unloaded two small
trunks from the wagon, one containing her valuables
which she did not want to leave unattended, and the
other such essential items as a brush and comb.

By the time this had been done, the shadows were
lengthening and the temperature was already beginning
to drop. Glancing up at the broken roof, he suggested
that they try a fire. The hole, he thought, would act as a
kind of flue. This necessitated another trip outside for
twigs and dry leaves. These were collected easily
enough, although setting them alight proved an exercise
in patience. The Comte had only the spark from his
pistol and although there had been no rain, the twigs
were a little damp. Eventually, he managed to get it
going although it was a while before they dared add
even a small log. As darkness closed around them,
Madeleine was grateful for the fire's comforting glow.
The heat it gave out was negligible, however, and they
had to put up with a great deal of smoke.

Madeleine sat on one of the blankets with a second
draped around her shoulders, feeling cold and miserable. Her eyes stung and she was hungry. She knew their
position was mainly her fault but that did not stop her
feeling irritable, something that was irrationally
increased by the Comte's apparent lack of discomfort.

'Is there anything left to eat?' she asked hopefully.

'I'm afraid not.' He settled back indifferently against one of the walls. 'I take it you're hungry.'

'I'm starving!'

He shrugged.

'I don't suppose you could hunt for something.' As soon as she had said it, she knew how ridiculous the suggestion was.

'Hunt for something!' He stared at her incredulously, irritation edging his voice. 'Hunt with what, exactly?'

It was pure contrariness that made her continue with what she knew to be a ridiculous suggestion. 'Well, you have a pistol.'

It was one of the few times she had seen him really annoyed and had to admit that up until then, he had been quite patient with her. 'One does not hunt with a pistol; besides, it's pitch black outside! I'm not some blasted peasant to go prowling around in the dark. Show some sense, will you?'

She was obviously in a worse case than she had thought, for his sharply spoken rebuke made her want to cry. Not that she would dream of doing such a thing. For a moment they lapsed into silence, both of them regretting the angry words.

'If you're hungry, try to go to sleep,' he suggested after a while.

She sniffed in exasperation. 'I'm too cold to sleep.'

'If I put more wood on the fire, we'll suffocate.'

'I know...I'm sorry, Lucian. I really didn't mean to take my bad temper out on you. I realise now that we should have stayed in...'

'It's no use crying over spilt milk, you know.' He grinned then, and she felt herself smiling in response. 'Are you really cold?'

'Yes, and uncomfortable!'

Without saying another word, he tossed his blanket aside and went out into the darkness, returning a few minutes later with one of his jackets and what looked like an expensive bottle of brandy.

'There, that should fit over your own jacket,' he said, handing her the coat.

She muttered her thanks and, slipping it around her shoulders, watched as he opened the bottle and sniffed appreciatively at its contents.

'Cognac,' he told her. 'I was saving it for an emergency. I almost brought it out at that last inn. Now I'm glad that I didn't. This will warm us up.'

Ever mindful of his manners, he offered the bottle to Madeleine. She had rarely drunk spirits before and, in spite of its quality, it burnt her throat and made her eyes water.

'You had better go slowly if you're not used to it,' he cautioned.

The dim glow from the fire illuminated his amused smile and glowed in his dark eyes. Madeleine's heart gave a strange little lurch.

'You've changed, you know,' she said seriously after taking a few more sips, then surprised herself by adding, 'You're much nicer now.'

He laughed. 'That's a backhanded compliment if ever I heard one.' He was silent for a moment then added, 'If nothing else, the past year has taught me how to make the best of a bad job.'

'Like escorting me?'

'No, Maddie,' he replied with what was almost a tender smile, 'that has been no hardship, I assure you.'

'So gallant, Luc.' She was surprised when a giggle escaped her. 'I've never noticed that in you before.'

They continued to share the bottle in companionable silence until Madeleine began to feel quite light-headed. On more than one occasion the Comte cautioned her to go easy and eventually, when the bottle was half empty, judiciously placed it to one side.

'Are you warmer now?' he asked.

'A little,' she replied, surprised that she had to think about it. Her head felt fuzzy and suddenly she felt pleasantly tired.

'Come here,' he said, holding out his hand to her. 'We'll be warmer if we sit together.'

Without really thinking about it, she accepted his offer and, taking her blankets with her, went to join him. She draped one across her shoulders and spread the other over her legs.

'That's not fair,' he told her in a teasing voice. 'As you're sitting on my blanket, you have to share one of yours.'

Without asking permission, he pulled at the blanket across her legs until it covered them both. Madeleine still had the extra one draped across her shoulders but he gallantly made no comment about that.

How she ended up in his arms, she was never quite sure, but somehow she found herself snuggled into the hollow of his shoulder whilst he rested back against the wall. He smelt of the outdoors, of night-time laced with summer grasses and the faint tang of woodsmoke. It was a pleasant combination and Madeleine sighed contentedly.

'Are you comfortable?' he asked in an amused and slightly husky voice.

'Mmm. . .and warm.'

'Madeleine,' he said softly, 'do you realise that you're tipsy? I don't think you know just what you're doing to me.' His hand brushed across her hair, then gently tilted her chin so that he could kiss her.

His lips were gentle, coaxing a response from her, beguiling her with their sweetness, their promise of comfort and caring. Madeleine had never felt so cherished, so boneless and relaxed. In that moment, to respond seemed the most natural thing in the world. A slow warmth began in her stomach that was nothing to do with the brandy and she groaned softly, letting her arms creep up and around his neck. She felt the hard beating of his heart, the frantic drumming of her own and she marvelled at the sensations he was arousing in her.

For a moment the Comte drew back and, looking down at her, felt a stab of desire stronger than anything he had experienced before.

'God, Maddie,' he groaned, 'I've been aching to do that for days.

In the firelight her hair looked more bronze than gold, her eyes were closed and her lips were swollen from his kisses. More disturbing still was the button that had sprung open on her blouse revealing an enticing glimpse of one full breast framed by the lacy edge of her chemise. She looked vulnerable and sleepy. He knew she was feeling the effects of the brandy, but it would have taken more willpower than he possessed to pull away from her. For months he had been watching over her, wanting her, becoming close to her and, in truth, he saw no reason to hold back. She had been Philippe's, why should she not be his? She would do well as his mistress, far better than she would on an isolated Breton farm. They could set up an establishment together in Rennes for they had both liked the old town.

It was easy enough to reason away what remained of his conscience and he took her lips again with a soft groan. Again she kissed him back, almost purring with pleasure as her arms tightened around him. She was so responsive, almost innocently so, as if she did not know where their embrace would lead.

A warning bell went off somewhere in the back of his mind but he was too absorbed to heed it. He had drunk freely enough himself and the light from the fire cast shadows that seemed to fill the small room with mystery and magic. Outside, some animal cried out on the darkness for its mate and the noise struck a chord deep in his soul.

Madeleine made a sound more of contentment than passion, as primeval as the sound of the sea. He wanted to protect her, to be there for her and cherish her in his own fashion, but he needed her, too, and he would take what he needed. It had always been that way for him, an attitude bred into him since birth, and yet it did not negate his tenderness. He ran slow, gentle kisses over her, brushing her mouth, her cheek and lingering in the hollow of her neck. Gently, his hand touched her breast, skilfully caressing it.

Madeleine felt herself drifting in a soft sea of sensation, her whole existence bound up in Luc's arms. His lips found her neck, brushing it with fire before returning once more to her mouth. She was intoxicated by him, by the intriguing mixture of warmth and strength, softness and latent power, and she did not protest when he rolled her over, pressing her more closely against him. It was as if she was in a dream and yet she had never been so aware of him, of his smell and touch, so practised yet so gentle.

A sigh escaped her lips as he kissed her again, this time with increased passion. Almost of their own accord, her hands glided over the lean hard muscles in his shoulders. She could feel the tension in him and she vaguely wondered at it. She was too inexperienced to appreciate that his tenderness had turned into a burning desire rapidly racing out of control.

With a groan he skimmed his hand expertly down her side, lifting her skirt and sliding it seductively up over the silk of her thigh. Only then did her mind call out a warning, only then did it occur to her where his delightful caresses were going to lead. He was on the verge of making love to her, only she had been too befuddled by the brandy, too absorbed in the novel sensations he was arousing in her, to recognise it before.

Even as she slipped her hands between them and began to push him away, she regretted the need for it. She still ached for his kisses, his fiery touch, and in some far corner of her mind regretted that something so exciting should be so wrong for her.

'No, Luc,' she cried, pushing against his chest. 'Please, you must stop. I don't want this!'

'Of course you do,' he rasped, catching hold of her hands and lifting them above her head, his mouth burning kisses across her cheek.

'No, I don't!' It was a lie, although she would dearly have liked for it to be true. 'I will not become your mistress. . . No, Luc! I said no!' Then in desperation she added, 'I've never done this before!'

It was the panic in her voice that finally reached him,

penetrating the haze of brandy and passion. For a moment he lay absolutely still and Madeleine could hear his ragged breathing.

'What?' he demanded, as if he did not believe what he had heard.

'Philippe and I never. . . It was all a pretence. He was like a father to me!'

The word he muttered as he rolled away from her was shockingly crude, but he had stopped; she realised, even in her inexperience, that many men would not have. For a moment, he sat with his back to her, shoulders tensed and head bowed. Madeleine ached to reach out and comfort him.

'You and Philippe never. . .? By the saints, that's hard to believe!' But believe it he did. Her panic had been all too genuine.

'Luc, I. . .' Tentatively she reached a hand towards him then let it fall to her side.

'Don't say anything,' he rasped, struggling to control himself when desire was almost a physical pain.

'I'm sorry. . .' Tears clogged Madeleine's voice. In truth, she felt as empty and deprived as he.

'*Dieu*! I told you to be quiet. I've never taken an unwilling woman, but if you continue apologising I might very well start now!'

Rising stiffly to his feet, he headed towards the door, straightening his clothing as he went. He wrenched it open, then swung it sharply behind him. If it had not been for the ridge of earth that prevented it closing entirely, it would have slammed.

Madeleine settled back under the blankets, feeling too tense and miserable to cry. She felt like the lowest form of animal and yet she knew that stopping him had been for the best. Gradually, however, anger began to replace the emptiness she was feeling. She had grown to like him so much and now he had spoilt everything. How could they be friends now?

Moreover, she believed that he had taken advantage of her. From the beginning he must have known where his kisses would lead. She dreaded facing him in the morning, yet knew there was no alternative. When she reminded herself that they were nearly at the farm and that he would soon be leaving her, she was surprised to find it no consolation at all.

It was light when Madeleine awoke and a pale ribbon of sunshine was flowing through the half-open door. She felt stiff and sore but she was also warm. All the blankets now covered her, carefully tucked in, but there was no sign of the Comte.

As soon as she realised where she was, the events of the previous night came rushing back in a torrent, so confused they seemed like a dream. Stiffly she rose and, opening the door of the shed, looked around outside. There was no sign of the Comte and for one dreadful moment she wondered if he had deserted her; then she saw his horse grazing peacefully beside the carriage horses. Assured that he would put in an appearance sooner or later, she followed the short path down to the river bank. There, she splashed her face then dried it on her handkerchief. When she turned away from the water, she found the Comte standing behind her. His face looked pale above the beginnings of his beard and his eyes were shadowed.

'Do you want me to apologise?' he asked tightly.

Wordlessly, she shook her head. 'We were both a little drunk, I think.'

'It was more than that,' he replied evenly, 'and you know it.' Tiredly he rubbed at his eyes. 'You and Philippe...we all thought... You led us to think...' He swore. 'You could at least have been open with me!' His voice sounded harsh, accusing.

'It was none of your business,' she answered tightly, 'and Philippe had his pride. I was always more like a daughter to him.'

He was feeling guilty as it was and that statement only made him feel worse. Philippe had asked him to care for her. If it hadn't been so sickening, then it would almost have been funny. He had actually thought the older man had intended for him to take over as her lover. She was pure and he did not know whether to be pleased or disappointed. It was strangely satisfying to know no other man had touched her, yet that very purity made her less likely to accept the proposition he intended to make.

'You may be inexperienced, Madeleine, but you responded to me. You seemed happy enough in your relationship with Philippe. Why not enter into a similar one with me? I'm sure it would suit you far better than wasting away on some farm.'

The disappointment Madeleine felt was sharp enough to be a physical pain. 'And would you treat me as a daughter, too?' she asked, deliberately pretending to misunderstand him. 'You are older than me, Lucian, but not that old.'

'You know that is not what I meant,' he answered impatiently. 'Ours would be a much more conventional arrangement.'

'Yes, I'm sure it would.' Madeleine was furious with him for making the suggestion, for ruining the friendship they had so tentatively forged. Hadn't she refused him once before?

'Months ago I told you that I have no wish to become your mistress and I have not changed my mind.' She drew an angry breath and lied through her teeth. 'I responded to you because I was drunk, not because my feelings have changed towards you! You took advantage of me!'

'That's not true!' he replied, stung. 'I had no idea that you were so inexperienced. You certainly gave no indication of it. If you must know, you seemed as hot for it as I. That, combined with the sickening way you used to drape yourself all over Philippe. . .' He shrugged. 'If you don't want men to treat you like a whore, then you shouldn't act like one!'

It was the reference to Philippe that upset her more than the insult. Without thinking about it, she brought up her hand to soundly slap his face. Then, with her palm still stinging, she ran from him. Tears threatened and she was determined that he should not see them, should not know that he had the power to hurt her so.

Half running, half walking, she hurried along the river bank, not knowing where she was going, only that it was as far as possible away from him. In the back of her mind she knew that she would have to face him sooner or later but not until she had herself firmly under control.

The Comte didn't think that he had ever felt so disgusted with himself. Her accusation had justifiably angered him but his response had definitely not been that of a gentleman.

It was self-disgust that made him hurry after her, that and a desire to apologise and try to explain something he didn't fully understand himself. Above all else, he wanted to erase the pain and contempt he had seen in her eyes. For a man who had always gone his own way, who had never felt the slightest need to justify himself or seek approval it was a particularly unsettling experience and further added to the irritation and anger that seethed inside him.

'Madeleine!'

She heard his angry exasperated cry and, looking back over her shoulder, saw that he was following her. Running from him was childish, she realised, and without being aware of it she slowed her steps.

He caught up with her where the riverside path widened and divided, one track heading into the trees on the left. Grasping her shoulder he roughly spun her to face him.

'*Dieu*, Madeleine! There is no need for you to run.' As he spoke he shook her gently in exasperation. 'I only wish to. . .'

She never knew what he was going to say for at that moment he was wrenched away from her. She saw the blur of a meaty fist and heard the sickening thud as it connected with the side of the Comte's face. The blow almost lifted him off his feet and sent him crashing against the side of a small boulder. The other side of his head connected sharply with the cold, hard stone and he sprawled limply on the grass.

Madeleine screamed in surprise and fear.

'It's all right,' the newcomer assured her. 'I mean you no harm. In fact, I seem to have come up with you at exactly the right time.'

For a moment Madeleine could only stare at the stranger. He was very tall, she realised, and broad as well, a veritable giant. His hair was blonde and shaggy and the lower half of his face was covered in thick, red-gold beard.

'It's as well my mother asked me to look out for you,' he continued, 'although in truth, if it had not been for that and the portrait you sent us two years ago, then I wouldn't have known you.'

It was only then that she recognised him. He was her aunt's first-born son, her cousin Leon. His colouring had not changed but in other respects he bore scant resemblance to the lanky teenager she remembered.

'Well?' he prompted, his eyes narrowing with disappointment and anger, 'are you not glad to see me, and so opportunely too?'

Madeleine did not reply. She had already moved to kneel beside the Comte. '*Dieu*!' she exclaimed, a catch in her voice. 'I'm afraid you have killed him.'

The Comte was lying on his back, his face as white as chalk. Blood was oozing from a wound on his temple and trickling back into his hair. His eyes were closed and he made not the slightest sign of movement.

With an expression of annoyance, Leon knelt to feel for a pulse in the Comte's neck. 'He is stunned. That is all. . . I'm surprised you care.'

When she glanced questioningly at him, he added, 'The fellow was attacking you.'

'No! You misunderstood,' she hastened to assure him. 'It was a silly quarrel. He's been a good friend to me, truly he has! We must take him to the farm.'

Leon would rather have left the Comte at the nearest hostelry but Madeleine was insistent and eventually she got her way. The young Breton lifted the unconscious man with surprising ease and carried him back to the wagon. The trunks were collected and, with the Comte's horse and Leon's sturdy pony tied behind the vehicle, they set off.

It was only then, as she sat on the wagon floor attempting to protect the Comte from the worst of the jolting, that Madeleine had time to analyse her feelings. She did not know when or how exactly it had happened, but at some point the Comte had become very dear to her. It was a disquieting thought. She had been angry with him and disappointed but she would never have wished him harm. Gently, she smoothed his cheek, feeling the roughness of his beard. At that moment the only thing she wanted was for him to be all right.

CHAPTER SIX

RAFTERS, that was what they were! The Comte had been staring up at them for some time before the realisation came to him. He was naked and lying in a bed in someone's loft and his head was aching abominably. Summoning his strength, he tried to sit up, then regretted it immediately as the pain that sliced through his skull was almost enough to send him spinning back into unconsciousness.

'So you're awake at last,' said a female voice, pleasant in spite of its heavy Breton accent. 'How are you feeling?'

He was too busy fighting the nausea that threatened to overcome him to make any reply. He had never felt so ill. The woman's footsteps sounded unnaturally loud as she covered the short distance from the single wooden chair to the bed. Somewhere in the back of his mind he noted that she was wearing sabots. A cool hand touched his brow, stirring memories of some distant childhood illness.

'Try to stay awake,' she commanded gently. 'Come on, look at me.'

Reluctantly he obeyed and found himself staring into a pair of concerned tawny eyes that reminded him of Madeleine.

'Where?' he managed to ask and was surprised how weak his voice sounded.

'Kermosten Farm.'

93

She had a nice smile, he thought, and was still attractive in spite of her age, which must have been more than forty. She was dressed in a black peasant's dress trimmed with spotless white and the hair that peeped out from her cap was a pale blonde.

'Who. . .?' he began.

'Shh. . .' she chided. 'So many questions. Do you think you could take a drink if I helped you to sit up?'

Before he could protest, she slipped a hand beneath his head and, lifting it, pressed a cup to his lips. He drank simply because it was less trouble than protesting.

'I asked you who you were,' he said a trifle peevishly when she allowed him to lie back down.

Gently, she smoothed his short hair. 'I'm Madeleine's aunt. . . She's been most concerned about you.'

The Comte frowned. He still couldn't understand what was wrong with him. He could remember quarrelling with Madeleine on the river bank and then nothing.

'Was I taken ill?' he finally asked.

'You were knocked unconscious,' she replied quietly. Then, after a momentary hesitation, added, 'My son Leon hit you. He thought you were going to hurt Madeleine.'

'Oh.' The Comte seemed to think about this for a moment then, closing his eyes, complained weakly, 'That's ridiculous, you know.'

Madame Lemieu smiled. 'Of course it is,' she said soothingly. 'You've taken the greatest care of her.'

He shifted slightly and had to stifle a groan. His head felt fuzzy and he was finding it difficult to think but there was something else he wanted to know. 'Where is she?'

'At the moment she is unpacking,' Madame Lemieu

answered quietly. 'Go back to sleep now. You'll feel
better directly.'

As he settled back against the pillows, he was con-
scious of a feeling of disappointment. Madeleine's aunt
had been very kind but he would like to have seen
Madeleine; would like to have known that she cared
enough to come and see how he was. Obviously she was
still angry with him and he was surprised how much that
hurt.

Madame Lemieu frowned thoughtfully. The Comte
was not at all what she had expected. Madeleine had
been right, she decided, and Leon, as usual, had been
too eager to pass judgement. The man lying before her
was no villain. Moreover, she found it difficult to equate
him with the arrogant aristocrat Madeleine had
described. He simply struck her as a very sick and rather
endearing young man who was doing his best to conceal
how disorientated and ill he was actually feeling. With a
sigh she lit the candle that had been placed on the
bedside table, then bent to retrieve the cushion she used
for her lace-making.

The next time the Comte opened his eyes it was daylight
and the sun was streaming through the small, high
window, illuminating dust motes in its golden bars. His
head was still aching, but the pain was bearable and he
felt much stronger. Cautiously he sat up and looked
around the spartan chamber in which he found himself.
The only furniture apart from the bed consisted of a
small bedside table and the wooden chair in which
Madame Lemieu had been sitting.

Catching sight of his clothes folded across the arm of
the chair, he decided to get up. This required consider-

ably more effort than he had anticipated. His legs felt like rubber and the pounding in his head increased alarmingly the moment he was vertical, but he persevered. Donning his shirt was easy enough but he found that he had to sit down again in order to manage his breeches and his boots proved quite beyond him.

With his legs still feeling weak, he padded barefoot across the wooden floor and somewhat shakily descended the stairs. At the bottom of them, he paused, bracing an arm against the wall to steady himself. He found himself in a narrow hallway with four doors, two on either side, leading off it. Ahead of him another narrow window illuminated a stairwell and he made his way towards it. Stone stairs this time led down in a spiral, the steepness of which almost put him off. Bracing his hand against the stone wall, he carefully made his way downwards, narrowly missing knocking a crucifix off the wall with his shoulder. An enticing smell of freshly baked bread assailed him and he realised, with some surprise, that he was hungry.

The stairs led down into the farmhouse kitchen where Madeleine and her aunt were busy at the stove. It was a large room, the hub of the household, with low beams and a rough flagged floor. A large rectangular table flanked by benches took up part of the room. Two rocking chairs and a high-backed bench were set in front of the hearth and there was another roughly finished work table close to the wood stove. Pans and ladles of all shapes and sizes hung from the walls and onions were slung from the beams.

The Comte found the domesticity of the scene oddly comforting. As a child he had sometimes ventured into the château kitchen and he could remember the cook there giving him treats. How odd, he thought. That was something he hadn't thought about in years.

As he reached the bottom step, Madeleine's aunt turned. 'Good heavens!' she exclaimed, placing the loaf she had just taken from the oven down upon the table. 'You really shouldn't be out of bed.'

Clucking like a mother hen, she helped him across to one of the chairs, scolding him for his impatience whilst Madeleine looked on.

He protested that he was quite all right when in reality he was glad to sit down. In all his life he couldn't remember feeling as weak.

'Would you like something to drink?' Madeleine asked a little shyly. 'Milk, perhaps?'

Her face was flushed from the heat of the oven and there was a smudge of flour on her nose. The Comte decided that she looked even more attractive than usual, attractive and irritatingly wholesome. She was wearing a dark dress and a full-length apron, the bib of which only seemed to emphasise the curve of her breasts.

'There's cider if you prefer it,' she added.

'Milk would be best,' Madame Lemieu advised.

'Milk then,' the Comte agreed with a wry smile, thinking it had been years since he had drunk the stuff.

Madeleine ladled some milk out of a crock standing on a stone counter in the corner, and brought it to him. Her smile was a little wary as she put the cup in his hand.

'Is your head still aching?' she asked.

'A little.' That was an understatement if ever he had uttered one but he was not going to admit to too much weakness. With a reassuring smile, he accepted the milk.

'This must be quite a large farm,' he commented.

Madame Lemieu smiled proudly. 'The largest and

most well run in the area. At the moment we are renting it but we will soon have enough money to buy. It will be nice to have land to pass on to our sons.'

The Comte grunted his understanding. He really didn't feel like making conversation but good manners dictated that he try. 'How many sons do you have, *madame*?'

'Two now, Leon and Guy.' A momentary shadow crossed her face. 'Our youngest died in infancy, but Madeleine's brothers are also like sons to me. No daughter, though. The Lord did not see fit to bless us in that way, which is why I am so glad to have Madeleine here.'

She frowned as she tipped the dough onto the table and began to knead it enthusiastically. 'I might as well tell you now, Comte, that I did not approve of the way my brother-in-law packed Madeleine off to Paris. He was a weak and selfish man and my sister would have turned in her grave. I know things were hard for him after Monique died, but he must have known we would have taken Madeleine in. It was a blessing that the Marquis turned out to be such an honourable man. I thank God for it every day.'

So she knew the details of Madeleine's relationship with Philippe and was obviously protective of her. Suddenly the Comte was swamped by a feeling of unreality. Here he was in some godforsaken farmhouse actually feeling anxious in case he should offend the farmer's wife.

'Are you sure you are all right?' Madeleine's question cut into his dreaming. She actually looked concerned.

'Yes,' he replied after a moment and forced himself to drink some of the milk.

'I really don't think you should have got up.'

'I was bored with lying in bed, Maddie, and curious to see where I was.'

Madame Lemieu smiled approvingly and began to chat about the farm and the nearby villages. 'Of course, Vannes is our nearest centre,' she continued, 'but it's a two- to three-hour drive depending on the weather. Madeleine's younger brother has a fishing boat there. He has done very well for himself. We see quite a lot of him. It's not the same with Reynard, my elder nephew. We never know when he's going to appear.' Her frown was a little disapproving. 'I do wish he'd settle down like his brother Thierry, but I'm afraid there's a deal too much of his father in that one!'

The woman could certainly talk, the Comte thought a trifle unkindly as he rested his head back against the chair. It was warm in the kitchen and already he was beginning to feel drowsy. After a while he gave up trying to keep his eyes open and allowed himself to relax. He felt curiously detached from what was going on around him, peaceful almost. Distantly, he heard the clatter of pots and pans, the sizzling of fat, hushed voices and muted footsteps. Madame Lemieu said something and there was laughter in Madeleine's voice as she replied. With a sigh, the Comte drifted off to sleep. He did not see Madeleine hurry to take his empty cup before it plummeted to the floor or her concerned frown.

'Are you sure he'll be all right?' she asked her aunt.

Madame Lemieu smiled. 'He obviously has more strength than we gave him credit for. He'll live, my dear. There is no need for worry.' She glanced thoughtfully at Madeleine, then in her direct way asked, 'Is there more than friendship between the two of you?'

'No.' Madeleine wasn't sure why she felt so guilty. It was not a lie.

The older woman nodded her approval. 'That's good. There is no way a man like him would ever be able to marry you.'

The Comte slept for nearly two hours. Then it was the arrival of Monsieur Lemieu and his sons that disturbed him. He awoke to find the kitchen full of large men talking gruffly in a language he did not understand, Breton, he supposed. Dishes clattered in the background as the meal was set upon the table.

'So you're awake at last,' commented Madeleine's uncle in heavily accented French.

'*Monsieur.*' He made an attempt to rise but the older man gestured for him to remain seated.

'We don't stand on ceremony here, lad,' Lemieu said, frowning at the open wound on the Comte's temple. 'Anyone can see you're still not yourself.'

At first glance the Comte found that he liked the older man. There was both kindness and intelligence in the grey eyes which dominated an otherwise unremarkable, weathered face.

Lemieu accepted a mug of cider from his wife then turned back to the Comte. 'I believe I must thank you for seeing Madeleine safely home.'

'It was a pleasure.'

The farmer smiled and gestured towards the other men whose conversation had abruptly ceased. 'These are my sons, Guy and Leon. They are not always mindful of their manners, but they are good boys.'

Guy Lemieu inclined his head and smiled. He had a pleasant open face and his father's chestnut-coloured hair. Alongside his brother, he looked almost willowy.

Ignoring the pain in his head, the Comte stood up to acknowledge the young man's greeting. When he turned towards the blonde giant, he was both surprised and annoyed by the hostility he saw in his eyes. Surely he was the one who should feel aggrieved? He thought the peasant owed him at least an apology.

'*Monsieur.*' He acknowledged Leon politely enough but his spine had automatically stiffened. For a moment they faced each other, sizing each other up and it was Leon who finally looked away.

'I think perhaps we should eat,' Madame Lemieu put in nervously.

Her husband agreed and swiftly introduced another man who had been waiting in the background. He was Raoul Duprey who worked on the farm and occasionally joined them for meals. Duprey was shorter and stockier than the Lemieu boys, quieter too. It didn't take the Comte long to realise that the young peasant was very much Leon's consort and admirer.

The seven of them sat down to dine at the rough wooden refectory table. As head of the household, Monsieur Lemieu sat at the head of the table directly across from his wife. The Comte found himself seated on a bench with Guy on one side of him and Madeleine on the other. The meal consisted of some kind of rabbit stew, well seasoned and cleverly flavoured with herbs, served with new bread and creamy butter. When he complimented Madame Lemieu on her cooking she smiled warmly.

'It's simple fare,' she told him, 'but warm and nourishing. . .and there's always plenty, thank God.'

That was certainly true enough and the Comte found himself amazed by the amount the other young men ate.

Conversation was carried on in a mixture of Breton and French, the latter, Luc realised, in deference to his presence. The Lemieus' command of French was quite good as, he was surprised to note, was Madeleine's Breton.

Luc managed to clear the food on his plate, but when Madame Lemieu offered to refill it, he shook his head and excused himself from the table. His headache had intensified and he knew that he had to lie down. Swinging his legs over the form, he stood up and was surprised to feel so wobbly. Looking concerned, Madeleine rose with him.

'I'm fine, really I am,' he told her.

A little unsteadily he made his way to the stairs. Spots were dancing in front of his eyes by the time he reached the loft and he was grateful to stretch out across his bed. The sky was turning pink beyond the high window. The brightness hurt his head and he rested his arm across his face to cover his eyes.

He sighed and tried to identify the feeling that was eating away at him. It was a moment before he realised that it was loneliness. Seeing Madeleine so settled and happy in the bosom of her family had made him realise just what he lacked. She no longer needed him. He should have felt relieved by that, but instead he felt empty and a little hurt. After a moment he got up and went to the trunk that someone had kindly placed at the bottom of his bed, rummaging through it until he came to a carefully folded piece of vellum. He had carried more than one letter for his king.

Before he had left Paris, he had been assured that no one knew of the letters except the king and the servant who had smuggled them out of the Tuileries. That might

have been true at the time, but at some point the
authorities had found out about them. The accident to
the coach and the man he had discovered in his room
attested to that. How much they knew about the actual
contents, however, he could not guess.

In any case, the first letter had already been delivered
during their stop in Rennes, to Armand Tuffin, Marquis
de la Rouerie. De la Rouerie was a veteran of the
American War of Independence who, although he
wanted more power for the Breton parliament, was also
a Royalist. The Comte did not know exactly what was in
that letter, but de la Rouerie had obviously been pleased
with it and, after reading it, had asked if he could rely on
the Comte's support. That assurance had been readily
given.

This second letter was addressed to the Comte himself. The royal seal on it was broken for he had read it
once before. As he scanned the page again, he found
himself assailed by the same feeling of disquiet that had
affected him the first time.

The letter declared that the Comte de Regnay was
Louis's man and requested that others should help him
in any venture he should undertake in the King's name.
The Comte had not asked for the letter and had found it
something of a shock. He had been moved by the King's
plight, but had not previously considered that he personally might be able to influence affairs. It was a novel idea
and not a particularly welcome one.

Tiredly, he massaged his throbbing temple. Obviously
the King felt that there was help to be had in the west
and was hoping the Comte would play a part in rallying
that help for him. Such an undertaking could take
months, even years. The Comte had nothing more

pressing to do with his time and there was no one to really care what happened to him, so he supposed he was in a better position than most men to hazard his life. It was with that rather melancholy thought that he closed his eyes and drifted off to sleep, the missive still clasped in his hand.

By the following morning, the pain in his head had receded to a dull ache and he felt altogether stronger. After going down to collect some hot water, he washed and shaved. He availed himself of a clean shirt and hose and, feeling better than he had for hours, made his way to the kitchen. Madame Lemieu chatted away as she served him a simple breakfast. She used his title whenever she addressed him and he found himself becoming quite irritated by it. It sounded so unnatural in the rustic kitchen.

'There are no longer any comtes in France,' he finally told her.

She shrugged. 'We still use the term here in Brittany and shall continue to do so regardless of what they say in Paris.'

That made him smile. 'My given name is Lucian, but my friends call me Luc. It would please me if you and your family would feel able to do that.'

She seemed a little surprised by his request but none the less pleased. In some inexplicable way, he felt he had taken a definite step forward. Of Madeleine, there remained no sign and he began to wonder if she was deliberately avoiding him. He remembered saying some harsh things to her during their quarrel and suspected that she had not completely forgiven him for it.

Feeling more than a little peeved, he made his way outside. It was a lovely morning and the sun felt warm on the back of his neck as he made his way across the farmyard. In the middle of the yard he paused to look around and was surprised how large and prosperous the farm appeared. There were numerous stone outbuildings, including a large cellar that was attached to the house itself and a long, narrow stable.

Lucian made his way to the latter, anxious to check on his horses. Once inside the building, it took a moment for his eyes to become accustomed to the darkness. It was cool in comparison to the outside and smelt of earth, hay and old leather. The two carriage horses were together in a large stall that he suspected was used primarily for cattle, but he could not see his grey stallion. Going back outside, he rounded the stable and found his horse in a fenced pasture behind, together with a graceful brown mare and two sturdy carthorses. When the stallion came over to the fence to greet him, the Comte could see that he had been properly groomed.

'Someone's been looking after you, haven't they, boy,' he said as he leant over the rough fencing to rub the stallion's nose.

'That was me,' said a pleased voice.

The Comte turned to find Guy Lemieu at his elbow. The young farmer looked hot and sweaty, but his smile was open and unrestrained. The Comte saw that he was younger than he had first thought, probably not yet twenty.

'I came to pet the horses,' Guy said, holding up an earth-encrusted hand in which he carried a bunch of carrots. 'My mare loves these.' He whistled through his teeth and the other horses came racing over.

The Comte watched in some amusement as his horse, too, turned up for his share.

'You're good with horses,' he commented, watching as the young farmer caressed the animals' necks.

'Aye. I've always had a way with them, although it's a skill that's not much called for on a farm like ours.' He grinned. 'Sasha is mine. I've had her since she was a foal and I persuaded Father to buy her for me. She's a fine animal and someday soon I hope to breed her. It's just a question of finding the right sire.'

The Comte asked the mare's age and, as they stood talking there in the sunshine, decided that he liked the younger man very much more than he did his elder brother. Finally, he asked after Madeleine and was told that she had gone down to the river to gather some watercress.

'She'll take her time about it if she's any sense,' the young man added. 'It's cool down by the water and very pretty.'

He directed the Comte along a track that ran down the side of the pasture then turned left into the trees. Walking in their shade, the Comte could hear the distant gurgle and hiss of the river, then a couple of minutes later found himself on its bank. Sunlight filtered through the overhanging trees, splattering the water with gold and tawny brown. Already stray leaves had fallen from the oak trees and were being carried along on the current like miniature coracles.

Madeleine was crouched over the bank where the water had cut out a small inlet. Shading his eyes against the reflected brightness, the Comte made his way towards her. She was too engrossed in collecting the dark green weed to notice him. Her sleeves were rolled up over her softly rounded arms and he thought again how lovely she was. She was infinitely desirable and yet there was an innocence to her that pulled at his heart. It had always been there, he thought, that elusive purity, only he had failed to recognise it for what it was.

The physical need he felt for her was stronger than ever. It had been bad enough before he had touched her; before he had learned how sweet her mouth tasted, how silky her hair and skin felt. Now it would be worse, for his dreams would have sensation and his fantasies would be coloured by reality.

When she looked up and saw him, her eyes widened and her smile was so obviously apprehensive that for a moment he wondered if she had been able to read his mind.

'Don't worry, Madeleine,' he said wryly. 'I have no intention of molesting you.'

'I didn't think that,' she replied.

'Didn't you?' With a sigh he sat down several feet from her. 'In fact, I came to apologise... Not for what happened between us, but for what I said. It was unjust and uncalled-for.'

She looked away from him to place a last piece of weed in the basket, then dried her hands on her apron. 'Perhaps we should just forget it.'

'If that's what you want.' Even as he said the words, he knew the impossibility of it.

Obviously relieved, she picked up her basket and moved closer to him. 'You're looking better,' she said after studying him for a moment. 'I can't tell you how pleased I am.'

He found her concern gratifying. He was even more

pleased when, after a momentary hesitation, she seated herself down on the grass quite close to him.

'I'm afraid Leon was always one to act first and think later.' When he made no comment, she asked, 'Can you forgive him for it?'

'There is nothing to forgive,' he replied shortly. 'He thought he was protecting you.'

'I over-reacted,' she said. 'I should never have run from you. You've been so kind, so generous.' She paused then asked, 'Now, about those expenses —'

'No!' he interrupted her. 'I refuse to discuss that.'

The determined set of his jaw told her it was no use persisting. A frown line had formed between his eyebrows and she found herself wanting to smooth it away.

She was silent for a moment, then said, 'I suppose you'll be leaving soon.'

He smiled crookedly. 'So anxious to get rid of me?'

'No, of course not.' She looked genuinely distressed. 'You've been a good friend and. . .I enjoy your company. . . But that's all I want from you, friendship.' She coloured charmingly. 'What happened between us the other night. . .I don't want it to spoil our friendship.'

'You have my friendship, Madeleine,' he assured her with an empty smile. 'So, you are determined to stay here. It seems such a waste. You'll be bored out of your mind in a matter of weeks.'

'If you think that, then you have no idea of what life is like on a farm,' she told him. 'Besides, I shall soon make new friends, perhaps even marry.'

He made a sound of disgust. 'Some stolid farmer, I suppose, whose house you will fill with boring, unimaginative children!'

He had not meant to quarrel with her, in fact he had

intended to cement their friendship, but the image his own words conjured up made him angry.

'I won't let you interfere in my life, Luc,' she replied tightly. 'I know what I want.'

'Do you?' he demanded. 'I wonder?' Climbing stiffly to his feet, he held out his hand. 'Come on. I'll walk you back to the house.'

With only the slightest hesitation, she accepted it. He pulled more strongly than she had anticipated and once more she was in his arms. For a moment he considered kissing her to try and force her to acknowledge the attraction between them, but there remained that element of doubt. In all his life he couldn't remember feeling so unsure of himself.

He didn't want to leave the farm, he realised, not yet, not without her, and he didn't have to. When he had first read the King's letter he had anticipated using it, if he used it at all, to rally men from around his home. Now it came to him that such work might be better done in Brittany and that the farm would make a convenient base. Perhaps in a month or so when she was becoming bored, Madeleine would be more interested in his offer.

'Gentlemen don't kiss their friends, do they, Maddie?' he said a little huskily, then gallantly stepped away from her.

That evening after supper, he broached the subject of a prolonged stay with his host, unashamedly playing upon his lack of a permanent home.

'In spite of what happened to my château, I am not completely without means,' he continued. 'I would pay generously for my keep.'

The farmer frowned and puffed thoughtfully at his

pipe. For one of the few times in his life the Comte felt at a disadvantage.

'I won't take your money, boy,' the older man finally told him. 'You can stay, but this is a working farm and everyone on it must do their share. We have already begun the harvest and after that there'll be the cider to make. You are welcome to stay but you must work.'

'Father, we don't need. . .' Leon began, but Monsieur Lemieu held up his hand. 'Do you agree to those terms?'

The Comte smiled. 'I have never had to work for my living, *monsieur*, but I expect I can do so as well as the next man.'

The farmer nodded. 'Fetch the cider,' he told his wife, 'and we will drink to our new, working guest.'

It was only as he was climbing the stairs to the loft that evening that the Comte allowed himself to reflect on Madeleine's displeasure. Although she had said nothing, he could see that she did not want him at the farm and he was surprised how much that hurt. She was afraid of him, he told himself, afraid of what he made her feel, but he was far from sure of it.

After removing his boots, he settled back upon the bed. Slipping his hands beneath his head, he stared up at the beamed ceiling illuminated in the flickering candle-light. It was not the standard of accommodation he was used to but, surprisingly, that did not seem important. Over the past few weeks his life had changed drastically and, although he did not realise it, he was changing along with it. The rather self-centred and bored gentle-man of fashion had gone forever. Almost out of nowhere he had found himself with a cause and a duty he intended to fulfil to the best of his ability.

CHAPTER SEVEN

'THE men are finished,' Madame Lemieu informed Madeleine, glancing through the open kitchen door. 'As soon as they have washed they will be ready for some refreshment.' Reaching a stone jar down from the shelf, she began filling tankards with cider. 'Take them some towels, Maddie, there's a good girl, and explain that we'll be waiting dinner for Leon.'

Madeleine's elder cousin had gone into Vannes that morning to purchase some seed and sell off some of their better cider. In fact, his father had not wanted him to take the time off but Leon had insisted that with Luc there he would not be missed, and Monsieur Lemieu had reluctantly agreed.

With a couple of cloths in her hand Madeleine stood back whilst her uncle, Luc, and Guy drew buckets of water from the well and used them to sluice off their hands and faces. It was only April and there was not a lot of heat in the sun, yet they all looked hot and tired. Planting was one of the most backbreaking tasks on the farm and spring, as a whole, one of the busiest times.

Apart from three or four occasions when he had left on some mysterious business, Luc—she no longer thought of him as a *comte*—had been at the farm now for nearly seven months and she could hardly credit the change in him. He had put on weight, most of which she suspected was muscle, and his face already bore a healthy tan. His hair had grown and although he still

wore it short at the front, at the back it curled down to
touch his collar. Standing there in a mended shirt and
worn buckskin breeches, he looked every inch the
peasant or he did until he moved; then his bearing
proclaimed him for what he was. Even when he was
tired he did not slouch and she knew he would never
learn to deferentially lower his gaze.

Not only had he remained at the farm but he had
actually pulled his weight. In fact, there were times
when he seemed to be enjoying the life. It had been hard
for him in the beginning, she remembered, for in spite of
the regular fencing he did, his muscles had been soft.
Yet he had never complained, not even when his palms
had been raw with blisters which had won him the
grudging respect of all but Leon.

Not only had he worked hard but he had watched and
learned and, on more than one occasion, Monsieur
Lemieu had praised his quick understanding. This
showed too in the way that he had so rapidly learned to
speak fluent Breton.

A close friendship had developed between Luc and
Guy, surprising considering their differing ages and
backgrounds, but they both loved horses. When Luc had
allowed Charlemagne to service Guy's mare it had
earned him the younger man's undying gratitude. The
foal was due in late summer and the whole family was
curious to see the result.

Leon, however, remained mildly antagonistic towards
Luc. They differed greatly in their political views, Leon
being in sympathy with the Revolution, but Madeleine
couldn't help thinking there was more to it than that. As
for Luc's attitude towards her, Madeleine had to admit
that he had been a perfect gentlemen, treating her more

like a sister than a woman he desired. It was what she had wanted from him and yet she could not help feeling just a little sad.

Moreover, living in such close proximity had only increased the attraction she felt for him. Now she found herself constantly aware of him and of his moods. His strong lithe figure and handsome face drew her eyes like a magnet and whenever she saw him smile, she felt the strangest softening inside.

When Leon returned nearly an hour later, they were all ready for their meal. He was bursting with news and could not even wait until they had sat down to tell them it.

'Well,' he announced. 'The Assembly has finally done it. For the last seven days, France has been at war with Austria.'

'I was hoping it wouldn't come to that,' Luc replied, looking grim. 'With the army so ill prepared, the Austrians will be at the gates of Paris within days.'

Leon sniffed contemptuously. 'I'd have thought that would suit someone like you. It would most likely mean a return to the old regime.'

Luc stiffened at what he considered an insult. 'I am a loyal Frenchman. In spite of the way I feel about the Revolution, I have no wish to see Paris fall!'

'Well, none of it concerns us,' Madame Lemieu told them, setting a large pot of stew upon the table. 'The people in Paris can take care of themselves. Come on now, let's eat before the meat gets cold.'

Madeleine could see that Luc was surprised by her aunt's lack of concern. He had still not been in Brittany long enough to understand how divorced the majority of them felt from the happenings in Paris. During the meal he was unusually quiet, which earned him thoughtful glances from both Madame and Monsieur Lemieu.

'You're not thinking of enlisting?' the latter finally asked.

"No...but should things go badly...' Luc shrugged. 'It is not easy to decide what to do. My country or my king? It is a choice I hope I never have to make.'

'You'd be a fool to volunteer,' Monsieur Lemieu told him. 'Your rank would count for nothing these days and you'd likely find yourself nothing but cannon fodder.'

'Is there likely to be a levy?' Guy asked.

His father frowned. 'Possibly. Whatever, it won't effect you. We Bretons have only ever fought for France on a voluntary basis and that's not going to change. In fact, what happens in Paris has very little to do with us here.'

Leon snorted his disagreement. 'Quite honestly, Father, I think your separatist ideals are misplaced. You are forgetting that it was the government in Paris who gave us the right to buy our farm.' He glared at Luc. 'For the ordinary people it has done nothing but good.'

'And it is the government in Paris who dictates to our priests!' his father snapped. 'We owe that assembly no gratitude or obedience.'

'Your father is right,' Madame Lemieu put in. It was a most unusual occurrence for her to speak out on something political and only indicated the strength of her belief. 'The government in Paris is setting itself above God! As for their soldiers, they do not even have the manners of our pigs.'

Like many Bretons, the Lemieus had little time for the Republican soldiers billeted in the area. Their dislike of them was further fuelled the following week when Luc and Guy returned from a trip to Vannes. The latter's face was badly bruised and both of them had knuckles that were skinned. Apparently the recruiting officers had been in the town. They had beaten Guy and tried to bully him into enlisting. It was fortunate that Luc had arrived on the scene.

'You should have seen him!' the young man exclaimed as his mother bathed his face. 'Once he had hold of the officer's sword there was no stopping him! Then the crowd pitched in to help. The recruiting tables were overturned and the soldiers were driven from the market place.'

'There could be repercussions,' Leon warned.

Luc shrugged. 'No one was killed. The soldiers were merely made to look foolish which was less than they deserved.'

'Luc did what was necessary,' Monsieur Lemieu said, 'and for that we are grateful.'

Surprisingly Leon nodded. 'We are in you debt, Valori.' Then he smiled. 'In truth, I am sorry I missed the spectacle.'

The following week, when the ladies wanted to pay a visit to Vannes, Monsieur Lemieu suggested Luc drive them. Leon was busy mending harness and he thought Luc more able to take care of himself than his younger son.

On a lovely sunny Saturday morning, they set off as soon as it was light, wanting to spend as long as possible in the town. Even though the journey took more than two hours, it was still quite early when they passed under the ancient ramparts and into the town. They trundled through the narrow cobbled streets, bounded on either side by tall narrow houses, and down to the harbour. After leaving the wagon at an inn they split up, Madeleine and her aunt to do some shopping and visit Madeleine's brother and Luc to run some errands for Monsieur Lemieu.

Thierry Vaubonne had lodgings near the port. These were rather cramped so he took the ladies out to an inn on the waterfront. He was a slim young man with a shock of hair even fairer than Madeleine's and a face that had been reddened by the sun and wind. He was some eighteen months older than his sister, almost twenty-three, but he looked younger than that.

Although she had not seen him for so many years, Madeleine was already becoming fond of him. He was pleasant and hard-working and passionately in love with a girl called Janine who lived on the Quiberon peninsula.

Apparently Janine and he had met under the most romantic of circumstances. Having been swept from his own fishing boat during a particularly bad storm, Thierry had been rescued by her father, another fisherman, and taken home by him. Janine had helped to nurse him and the two young people had fallen helplessly in love.

When Thierry informed them that he was going to be married at the end of the month, Madeleine was not surprised. Her aunt was delighted and promised that the whole family would make the trip to the Peninsula for the ceremony.

After their visit with Thierry, the two ladies went to call on a cousin of Madame Lemieu. That lady, the mother of two lively young children, proved to be unwell so Madame Lemieu decided to remain for a couple of days. Consequently, Madeleine found herself making the journey back to the farm alone with Luc.

As they travelled, they chatted easily enough and yet she found herself uncomfortably aware of him, of his broad shoulder so close to hers as they sat side by side on the wagon seat. If he was reminded of their first journey together then he made no sign, which disappointed Madeleine somewhat. Her eyes drifted to his lean, brown hands so gentle on the reins and so capable looking.

He no longer wore any rings and she knew there were calluses on the soft pads beneath his fingers, yet he kept his nails trimmed and scrupulously clean. It was silly, she silently chastised herself, to find a man's hands attractive, but she could not help herself. In fact, she found every bit of him attractive, from his gleaming dark hair to the worn boots upon his feet, and she was not the only one. Whilst they had been in Vannes she had seen more than one young woman turn an appreciative glance his way.

Some distance out of Vannes on the road back to the farm, they came to a crossroads where a signpost that lurched drunkenly pointed the way to Kercholin.

Luc pulled up and frowned thoughtfully. 'Isn't that the estate that used to belong to Philippe, the one he never sold?'

'Yes.' She shrugged. 'I expect some distant relative lives there now.'

'I've passed here several times and wondered whether to take a look at the place,' he said, turning the wagon.

'What are you doing?'

'There's no time like the present,' he replied. 'I expect you'd like to see it, too.'

That was certainly not the case. She made a sound of protest but it was already too late. As a child she had lived in the village and her memories of it were not pleasant ones. In fact, she had known little happiness until Philippe had taken her away with him.

'It's a waste of time,' she told Luc, but he took no notice.

Some fifteen minutes later, they entered a small village made up of only a dozen or so houses clustered around a manor house. The manor itself was built around three sides of a courtyard. Cottages formed part of the fourth side, the remainder of which consisted of a high wall and an entrance way closed by two full-length doors. The whole thing was built of grey stone with a steep, slate roof broken by gable windows and tall chimneys. It looked bleak, devoid of colour and generally run down. The doors to the courtyard were weathered to a dull grey and the windows appeared desperately in need of cleaning. Although it was the early evening, there was no sign of life apart from a couple of scrawny chickens pecking and scratching in the dirt next to the manor wall. Luc could not for the life of him understand why Philippe had treasured the place so, unless it was simply because it had once been Madeleine's home.

'So this is where you were born,' he commented as he halted the wagon.

'Not here,' she told him tightly, 'but in a cottage a little way out of the village.'

'It's not an attractive place.'

'Philippe was very fond of it,' she defended.

He shrugged indifferently, giving her a glimpse of the old Luc. 'I can't for the life of me see why. Kermosten is more impressive and far more comfortable. As for the farms,' he turned his head to view the land around, 'the income they give must be negligible. Philippe did the tenants here no favour by keeping the place. He should have sold it to someone who had time and money to invest in it.'

'You didn't sell Châteaurange,' she reminded him.

She was angry because he had brought her there and had wanted to puncture his self-righteous arrogance, yet the moment she saw the hurt in his eyes she regretted her words. In any case, they were not true. In spite of his lack of interest, he had not allowed Châteaurange to become run down.

'You do right to remind me, I took little interest in Châteaurange and lost it because of that.' He gave a funny little laugh. 'Your uncle believes that the nobles hold the land in trust for the people, that the soil has not only to be worked but to be cherished if it is to yield well. It is romantic nonsense, of course, but these last few months...' He shrugged and the wry quirk of the lips became a fully fledged smile. 'I've actually known him talk to that pear tree beside the barn.'

Although he laughed, it was quite obvious how fond he had become of her uncle. Madeleine's heart missed a beat and she had to resist the urge to reach out and hug him. How could her anger at him evaporate so swiftly, she wondered? How could her annoyance change so quickly to a feeling of affection that made her feel warm and soft inside?

They were both quiet for a moment, then Luc asked, 'Is there no one here you would like to visit?'

Madeleine shook her head. He couldn't possibly understand how ambivalent she felt about the place. She may have been born there but most of the memories she had of it were bad. Together with her father and two brothers she had lived in a tiny cottage on the edge of the village. There had never been enough food, little warmth in the winter time, and no softness or love. Her mother had died before she was three and her father, a cold harsh man, had resented both the need to care for his children and the intense poverty.

Madeleine remembered the hunger and the loneliness. Thierry had been sent to work for an old couple who lived in another village and Reynard had quarrelled violently with his father and had left home a good two years before Philippe had taken her away.

'Shall we leave then?' Luc asked.

She shook her head. 'Drive on through the village.'

Flashing her a look of concern, he obeyed, stopping, when she directed him, near a tiny abandoned cottage set several yards back from the road.

'That's where I was born,' she informed him softly, hating the fact that she felt ashamed. 'It's very different from Châteaurange, isn't it?'

'I should not have brought you here.' Luc's voice sounded strange as he reached for her hand. 'Are the memories very bad?'

'No,' she lied. 'I was just wondering how any man could sell his child, because that's what my father did, Luc. I try to think of it as something else, but that's what it was.'

When he drew her into his arms, she did not resist. In fact, she welcomed his embrace. In that moment she felt cherished and wonderfully secure.

'Ah, Maddie...' he sighed, gently brushing his lips

across her hair. 'Your father must have been made of stone.'

She was surprised when he did not try to take advantage and kiss her properly, surprised and grateful. Instead, he offered her what comfort he could without condition or reservation. It occurred to her that he was showing remarkable sensitivity for a man who could not possibly understand what she was feeling, his natal circumstances being so far removed from her own. The warmth inside her expanded until it was almost an ache.

I like this man, she thought, more than anyone I have ever met, and his touch does the strangest things to me. Reluctantly, she drew away from him and, smiling her thanks, looked up into his face. She was surprised to see how sad he looked. Had the tales of her childhood moved him that much, she wondered?

In fact, Luc had come to an unpleasant realisation. He still wanted Madeleine, just as much as he had when he had first propositioned her, but now he knew she could never be his. He had become too close to her family, too aware of their ideals and their worth. He would never be able to insult them by making her his mistress.

It was comfortable and convenient at the farm. Already he had made a number of friends in the area who could help him in his cause. Moreover, the place had become his home. The trouble was, he didn't know how much longer he could remain there without trying to seduce her.

When Madeleine asked him what was wrong, he forced himself to smile. 'Suddenly I'm tired,' he told her. 'Let's go home.'

* * *

For the next few days Madeleine was kept very busy at the farm. With her aunt absent, she had many extra chores. Luc and the others helped where they could but the bulk of the work fell on her. At the end of the week, Luc drove into Vannes to collect Madame Lemieu.

Thierry's wedding was planned for the end of May and the whole family were hoping to attend it. Normally this would not have been possible as one of the men would have had to remain to take care of the farm, but Monsieur Lemieu had decided that Luc was now capable of doing this. Young Raoul would also be able to help, making it possible for the entire family to spend a couple of days on Quiberon. The wedding was to take place in a small fishing village situated on the eastern side of the peninsula and Thierry was going to take them all across in his boat. Madeleine was really looking forward to the outing but was a little sad that Luc was not accompanying them.

A few days before they were due to leave, Madeleine's oldest brother Reynard arrived at the farm. He turned up late one afternoon when the men were out working in the fields. Madeleine came back from feeding the chickens to find a dark bearded giant of a man leaning negligently against the kitchen doorway. She had no idea who he was and therefore was rather wary of him.

'Maddie?' he asked, a look of surprise on his face.

Before Madeleine could respond her aunt appeared at the door. 'Say hello to your brother,' she prompted.

For a moment, Madeleine stood dumbstruck.

The big man chuckled and held out his arms. 'I don't think she remembers me, Aunt Marie.'

'Of course I remember you,' Madeleine insisted,

regaining her wits, 'but not looking like that!' Feeling suddenly delighted to see him, she rushed forward to be enveloped in what resembled a bear hug.

With a chuckle, he swung her off the ground then, setting her down, beamed at her, revealing a set of strong but crooked teeth. 'Little Maddie! *Dieu*, how you've changed, but then you always did have the promise of great beauty. The Marquis would not have taken you if you had not.'

'You're so big!' she exclaimed, and he threw back his head and laughed.

Studying him again, she thought how healthy and prosperous he was looking. He was wearing boots instead of sabots and his horse was obviously expensive.

'You've done well,' she said with satisfaction. 'You must tell me all about yourself and what you do.'

'I travel a lot,' he replied vaguely, 'and I buy and sell certain commodities, but I do not wish to talk about myself, little sister. I want to hear about Paris and all the things you did there.'

An hour later, when the other men returned from the fields, Reynard greeted his uncle and cousins ebulliently. Then he surprised them all by turning to embrace Luc.

'I had no idea you were living here, Valori!' he exclaimed. 'What do you think of my little sister, eh?'

'Your sister is very beautiful,' Luc told him sincerely.

Later, when she asked Reynard how he and Luc had become acquainted, he was a little evasive. 'We have a mutual friend. He tells me your Luc is a comte. Is that true, Maddie?'

'It's true,' she replied.

She wondered if they were talking about the same

person when he added, 'I like him. Whether he is talking to me, Cadoudal or one of the other nobles, his attitude is just the same.'

This made Madeleine wonder what kind of company they were both keeping. Comtes and peasants did not mix and certainly not on equal terms. The way Luc had settled in at the farm was an exception.

The men seemed to view Reynard's arrival as an excuse for a celebration. Between them they got through an exceptional amount of cider and then, at Leon's suggestion, began on the spirit which he and Guy had distilled the previous spring. When the men began to sing, Madame Lemieu decided it was time for her bed. She suggested her niece retire, too, but Madeleine was not tired.

'I'll go for a walk, aunt, and then go up,' she said. 'I shall not go far, don't worry.'

After collecting her shawl, she went out into the farmyard. It was a lovely evening. The sky was bright with stars and a full moon bathed her surroundings in its pale light. True to her word, she did not go far, only down to the field in which the horses were kept. Charlemagne heard her approach and came trotting towards her, hoping for a titbit. With the moonlight shining on his light coat, he looked ethereal. He nuzzled her hand with his warm, wet nose and snuffled indignantly when he found nothing.

'He has forgotten his manners,' said Luc from close beside her. 'Guy has ruined him.' There was no rancour in his voice which was distinctly slurred. In fact, he sounded amused.

'He's lovely,' Madeleine said, rubbing the animal's neck.

'So are you.'

Madeleine tensed when she felt his hand touch her hair. She took a small step backwards and turned to face him.

'Look but not touch, eh?' He gave a wry smile and leant back against the rough fencing. Madeleine suspected it was the only thing keeping him upright. 'You must admit that since I came to live here, I've been very good. . .the perfect gentleman.'

'You're drunk,' she accused.

'Mmm. . .abominably.' His grin was lazy, a little lopsided.

Tonight he was wearing a fine lawn shirt as white as snow. The neck was unfastened, revealing the tanned column of his throat. When he swallowed, Madeleine wanted to lift her hand to trace the movement. He really was a most attractive man and under different circumstances she would not have been able to resist him.

'I still want you, Madeleine.'

She was surprised by his statement. For months his attitude towards her had been almost brotherly. 'Luc, I haven't changed my mind about you.'

'No, I don't suppose you have.' Slipping his hand behind her head, he drew her slowly towards him. 'Your voice says one thing Madeleine, but your eyes promise another. . . I've been very patient. I think I deserve a small reward. . .'

The only place he held her was with his hand at the back of her neck. She could have pulled away, but his kiss imprisoned her. She could taste the cider on his lips and smell the slightly musky scent of him combined with the clean fresh smell of his recently laundered shirt. Her heart was pounding and a strange floating sensation began in her insides. Of their own accord her hands crept up to his shoulders and her fists curled in the material of his shirt.

Before she was really ready for it, he drew away, releasing her so abruptly that she almost fell. His legs also appeared none too steady as he leant heavily back against the fence. In the pale moonlight his skin looked waxen, like that of a ghost.

He closed his eyes for a moment and sighed. 'You'd better go in whilst you can,' he told her huskily.

Madeleine found that she was trembling. She longed to reach up and touch his face, to press herself closely against him, and her heart ached for them both. More than anything she wanted to give in to him, to be his mistress, but she knew it would destroy her. I love him, she thought, with sudden clarity. This is love that I feel.

It was fear that made her say, in a voice that sounded much calmer than she felt, 'Don't do that again, Luc. It is a waste of time and effort. No matter what you make me feel, I will never change my mind.'

Anger flashed briefly in his dark eyes. 'You are a fool, Madeleine,' he said quietly.

She left him then, not caring whether he was capable of finding his own way back inside. In fact, she hoped he was not. Sleeping outside on the cold ground would soon cool his ardour. As for herself, she knew she would get little rest that night.

The wedding was a few days away when a stranger arrived at the farm on a tired, lathered horse. To Madeleine's surprise he asked for Luc, referring to him by the title he had not used in months.

Luc was working in the fields along with the Lemieu

men, Raoul and Reynard, so Madame Lemieu sent Madeleine to fetch him. He did not talk with the man in front of Madeleine and her aunt, but instead took him for a walk. After about ten minutes, the two of them returned and, in spite of Madame Lemieu offering hospitality, the stranger took his leave.

'Not bad news, I hope?' Madeleine's aunt asked, having noticed Luc's frown.

'Yes and no. . .' He smiled wanly. 'I'm afraid I have to leave. . .tomorrow.'

Madeleine was indignant. 'But you can't!' she protested. 'You have promised to look after the farm.'

He did at least have the grace to look guilty, but she could see that he was not going to change his mind. 'I have a prior commitment. Unfortunately, I had already promised someone else. I'm sorry, Madeleine. I had no way of knowing the two things would coincide.'

'But my uncle is looking forward to the wedding,' she insisted. 'You cannot let him down.'

'If Luc has something more important to do then we shall understand,' her aunt said, although she did not sound as if she meant it. In fact, she sounded hurt and upset.

'Well, I shan't! I can't believe this business won't wait.' Madeleine could not understand how he could be so ungrateful when her aunt and uncle had given him a home. So great was her anger and disappointment that she failed to notice how miserable he was looking.

'Perhaps it would be better if I went at once,' he said tightly.

'Perhaps it would!' She ignored her aunt's sound of protest and plunged on. 'I thought you had changed, but you have not. You are as self-centred as ever.'

'Madeleine!' her aunt chastised.

She shook her head and turned away from him. 'I can't believe he's being so selfish.'

'I have to go. That's all I can tell you,' Luc said tightly, moving towards the stairs.

Madeleine sat down at the table, feeling angry and somehow betrayed.

'You should apologise,' her aunt said quietly, breaking into her thoughts. 'You were very rude.'

She could only shake her head; she was beyond words. In fact she was very much afraid that she was going to cry.

When Luc came back downstairs some ten minutes later, he was dressed as a gentleman. Over his shoulder he carried a saddle bag which was almost bursting at the seams, and in one hand he held a pistol.

When he saw the ladies looking at it, he forced a smile. 'There are some rogues on the road, as I have already discovered.'

'You'll need some food to take with you if you're so determined to go now,' Madame Lemieu told him. Both her expression and tone of voice suggested that she was resigned and willing to forgive him.

Whilst he went to saddle his horse and take his leave of the men, she found him a loaf and some cheese which she put into a canvas sack along with a flagon of cider. When he came back to collect it, he gave her a kiss and she hugged him tearfully.

Releasing her aunt, Luc turned towards Madeleine. His face bore that look of hard inscrutability she had not seen for a long time. 'I see I am not forgiven.'

'Take care,' she said, but she did not move into his arms or even sound as if she meant the words.

Throughout the meal that evening, she was unusually quiet, brooding on what she saw as Luc's desertion. Her brother, in particular, glanced thoughtfully at her from time to time, and once the meal was cleared away, asked her to walk with him. Together they went out into the farmyard and turned towards the river. The sun was sinking below the horizon; soon it would be dark. Reynard took some flint from his pocket and, after puffing mightily, managed to light his pipe.

For a while they walked in silence, both wrapped up in their thoughts. It was very peaceful; the chickens had stopped their clucking and the handful of cows the Lemieus kept had settled for the night. The air was balmy and the scents of the countryside blended with the tang of tobacco smoke from Reynard's pipe.

'Don't be too hard on Luc,' he finally said and, when she made no reply, added, 'what he is doing is important.'

'Is it?' She didn't sound very interested which made him sigh.

'Maddie, he's gone to fight for de la Rouerie. The Marquis has at last decided to take up arms against the Republicans.'

She stiffened in surprise and horror. 'You mean that he has joined the Association Bretonne?'

He nodded seriously.

'Does my uncle know this?'

'He does, but it is not something to be talked about in front of the others. I don't trust Leon's politics and I think your aunt would worry.'

Madeleine's emotions churned. She was glad Luc had not left for some selfish and trivial reason, but that relief was tempered by a new anxiety. What he was doing was dangerous and he could easily be killed.

'We are allies, your comte and I,' he continued quietly, 'your uncle, too, although he does not play an active part. We would all like to see the Republicans driven from the west; Luc because it could help his king, your uncle because he wants an independent Brittany, and myself. . .' He shrugged. 'Well. . .I just don't like the rules and restraints the Republic has placed upon us. I don't like the way it interferes. After the wedding I, too, am riding to join de la Rouerie at his château near Rennes.'

Madeleine remembered their prolonged stay in the city and guessed the connection. Even then Luc must have been working to help his king. In a way, she admired his commitment but she still couldn't see why he needed to leave immediately. When she said as much, her brother sighed in exasperation.

'You still don't understand,' he complained, turning her to face him. 'He is one of our leaders. There are others who would not go without him!'

Madeleine paled, shocked by the depth of Luc's involvement. She had known he had changed but up until then she hadn't realised just how much. With all her heart, she wished that she could take back her angry words.

CHAPTER EIGHT

REYNARD's revelation concerning Luc gave Madeleine much food for thought. Had he ever been as effete and self-centred as she had first believed? She doubted it. She felt guilty about misjudging him and prayed that she would have the chance to set matters right.

At the end of the week the entire family set out for Quiberon and the wedding, Monsieur Lemieu having decided to risk leaving the farm in Raoul's care. The young Breton had agreed to sleep at Kermosten whilst the Lemieus were away and to keep an eye on things. In that respect Luc's leaving had not affected matters, which made Madeleine feel even worse about the way she had berated him.

The sun was sinking below the far side of the peninsula as Thierry's small fishing boat approached its destination. Ahead of them, both the sea and the sand edging the shore were painted blood red by the dying sunlight, whilst to their right a small fort rose up, dominating the isthmus.

'What's that?' Madeleine asked Thierry as he sat beside the tiller.

'Fort de Penthièvre... From the top of it you can see the coastline for miles in every direction. The view is quite spectacular.'

'Is it inhabited?'

He smiled ruefully. 'Oh, yes, by the soldiers of the illustrious new Republic. I believe they have changed its name but the locals still refer to it as Penthièvre. I only wish it was not so close.'

When Madeleine glanced questioningly at him, he continued, 'Father Monet is marrying us. He has known Janine since she was born. Unfortunately, he has lost the living. He refused to take the oath to the Republic and was ejected from his house a few months ago. If he's taken by the soldiers he'll be deported at the very least. I counselled against asking him, but Janine was insistent.'

Madeleine knew that the girl's attitude was shared by the majority of peasants throughout Brittany and the Vendée. In many instances, Republican soldiers had needed to use force both to install constitutional priests in their parishes and to remove those who had refused to swear. Their own priest had actually taken the oath, seeking to avoid confrontation, but there were many who thought he had been wrong. The Lemieus were amongst these and had not set foot in his church since — even Leon, whose Republican views stopped short of going against the church.

As Madeleine stared at the fort, a shiver ran down her spine. She felt a premonition, a sense of something bad about to happen. It was brief, intangible, and before she was able to really grasp the thought it had slipped away from her.

'Are you cold, Maddie?' Reynard asked, coming to join her and Thierry by the tiller.

'A little,' she replied, forcing a smile.

He left her for a moment then returned, carrying his jacket which he draped across her shoulders. Madeleine thanked him and he ruffled her hair.

'Don't worry about Luc,' he said.

In spite of that brief, uncomfortable feeling of fore-boding, Madeleine enjoyed her time on Quiberon. Janine turned out to be a lovely girl, dark and vivacious and her family made the Lemieus very welcome. For a while at least, concern for Luc was pushed to the back of her mind. It returned with a rush once they got back to the mainland and Reynard, too, took his leave of them. Madeleine hugged him and wished him luck then asked him to give Luc her best wishes.

'Only best wishes?' he asked with a grin. 'I will tell him that you have forgiven him for leaving so abruptly and I will give him your love.'

Madeleine's spirits were low as the wagon trundled towards Kermosten and no amount of teasing by Guy could lift them. She had enjoyed being with both her brothers; although she had spent the majority of her life away from them, she found that she loved them both. It was not the tempestuous, all-consuming kind of love she felt for Luc, but something akin to the deep fondness she had felt for Philippe. Now, with Thierry going to live on Quiberon, she did not know when she was going to see either of them again.

It was strange being at the farm without Luc and she missed him dreadfully. She missed his ready wit and thoughtful conversation. She missed his teasing and support, but most of all she missed the inexplicable excitement of having him near, the way her heartrate would increase and every sense would become height-ened in his company. She had to admit that without him life at the farm had become rather dull. Inevitably she began to question the life she had chosen for herself.

* * *

Slowly the weeks passed. Guy's mare had her foal at the end of June. It was a lovely animal that strongly resembled Charlemagne and Guy was delighted.

'I wish Luc could have seen the birth,' he confided to Madeleine as they both leant across the side of the stall watching the leggy creature as it suckled from its contented mother. 'Do you think he will come back?'

Madeleine had been assuming that he would. It was only then that she realised he had made no such promise. There had been no word from him since he had left and news of the affairs of de la Rouerie was sparse and unreliable. Apparently the man had turned his château into a kind of military camp.

'I really don't know,' she replied.

'Father thinks de la Rouerie might march on Paris.'

'Sometimes our father is a fool.' Leon had just come in to the stable to collect some feed and had obviously heard something of their conversation. 'The authorities will never allow it. Mark my words, his optimistic little army will not even be allowed to leave Brittany.'

Madeleine's stomach contracted with anxiety and she wished with all her heart that Luc and Reynard had not become involved in the venture.

It was several weeks before they received any more definite news and then it was even worse then Madeleine had feared. Her brother Reynard arrived at the farm one evening looking exhausted. The Association Bretonne was finished. The authorities had found out about de la Rouerie's plans and had attacked his château, destroying his supplies. They had either driven off his men or had taken them prisoner. Reynard himself had been lucky to escape with his life.

'And Luc?' Madeleine immediately asked.

Her brother shrugged. 'I asked him to leave with me, but he seems to feel a duty towards de la Rouerie. The old gentleman is in hiding and Luc and some others are with him. If they have any sense they'll make for England. I told Luc he was a fool, that he could come back here and no one would be the wiser but he has this misguided sense of honour.'

Reynard stayed at the farm for several days. In that time, Madeleine was unable to prise any more information from him but she could tell that he was badly shocked by what had occurred.

Summer turned to autumn and autumn to winter. Life on the farm followed the seasons: harvest, cider-making, the turning of the land ready for planting in the spring. Like the rest of the family, Madeleine had little spare time and she was thankful for that. During the day she had no time to wonder about Luc but it was a different story at night. Then she would lie in the darkness, wondering just where he was and what he was doing. She did not even know if he was alive or dead.

As Noël approached the weather became extremely cold and Madeleine awoke each morning to a world white with frost. On the eve of Noël when they were returning from mass, secretly performed at a neighbouring farm, it began to snow. With the ground so cold, the snow soon began to lay, creating a thick, white carpet that appeared luminous in the fading light. After the men had seen to the livestock, checking that they had enough feed, the family gathered around the fire in the kitchen to drink mugs of hot spiced cider. It was a cosy setting and after a while Monsieur Lemieu began to tell stories.

Outside all was quiet, the kind of soft, deep quiet that accompanies snow. When they heard the neigh and snuffle of a horse in the yard, it sounded unnaturally loud in comparison.

'Who on earth would be visiting on such a night?' Madame Lemieu asked.

'No sane man, that's for sure.' Monsieur Lemieu set down his mug and climbed to his feet. 'Fetch me a lamp, Leon, and we'll find out.'

Leon lifted the lamp from its hanger on the wall and lit it from one of the kitchen candles. Both he and his father slipped on their coats and, opening the door, stepped out into the farmyard. Curious, Madeleine followed to stand in the half-open doorway, her arms wrapped around herself for warmth.

A rider had pulled up a wagon's length from the door. His coat and wide-brimmed hat were covered in snow. Both horse and rider looked exhausted and it seemed to take the latter a moment to gather the strength to climb down. Removing his hat, he dusted it against his thigh and turned to face them. The yellow light from the lantern picked out his features and, with a cry of joy, Madeleine recognised Luc.

A tired, uncertain smile lit his face as he glanced in her direction and her stomach gave a strange little lurch. Heedless of the way her slippers sank into the soft snow, she ran past the men in order to greet him.

Luc took her in his arms and, after swinging her off her feet, kissed her soundly. His action seemed the most natural thing in the world and made her want to cry out with happiness. The joy was short-lived, though. His lips were unnaturally cold and his lean cheek felt like ice. In concern she pressed a hand against the side of his face.

'You're frozen!' she exclaimed.

'I've certainly been warmer!' He grinned as he turned to embrace Monsieur Lemieu and grasp Leon's hand.

'Come inside, lad,' the farmer commanded, turning and calling for Guy to come and help his brother with the horse.

The young man grabbed his coat and, giving Luc's shoulder a welcoming squeeze, hurried to do his father's bidding. Madame Lemieu pulled a chair closer to the fire; after helping Luc off with his cloak, the farmer gestured for him to sit down in it.

Resting his head back, Luc glanced from the farmer to his wife. 'You do not mind me descending so precipitously upon you?'

'Of course not!' Madeleine's aunt exclaimed. 'You will always be welcome here.'

Madeleine stood back a little, suddenly shy. His eyes sought her out and he smiled at her, warming her to her toes. It was a tired kind of smile, though, and his eyes looked unusually dark in his pale face. Madame Lemieu plunged the poker in to a tankard of cider and wordlessly passed it to him.

He thanked her and cradled the drink between his hands. '*Dieu*! I don't think I've ever been so cold!'

'What you need is a warm bed,' she said, frowning. 'I will get it ready for you.'

'I've no wish to trouble you. I can. . .'

'It's no trouble,' she insisted, patting his hand as if he was seven years old. 'We have kept it aired in readiness.'

Madeleine knew that was true for she had regularly run the warming pan between the blankets. Luc, she could see, was pleased by the revelation.

Leon and Guy returned. After shaking out their coats,

they hung them beside the door. Immediately, they began to question Luc, eager to find out exactly what he had been doing.

'I was with the Marquis until last week,' he told them, 'but when he went to stay with friends at a château near Saint-Brieuc, I decided to come home. I doubt he will need me again; he's been advised to make for Guernsey.'

The fact that he referred to Kermosten as home pleased Madeleine immensely. It felt right to have him there; it was as if a great weight had been lifted from her shoulders. She could scarcely take her eyes from him and thought again what an attractive man he was. He seemed willing enough to talk and yet she sensed that there were times when he was holding back. From what she could judge, in company with the Marquis, he had been virtually living the life of an outlaw, unpleasant enough in the summer but unbearable in the winter when the weather was as harsh as it was.

As he talked she saw that his eyes were a little too bright, his conversation a little too rapid. In the warmth of the fire two pink spots had appeared like brands on his cheeks. He was not well although he was doing a good job of concealing it. When Madame Lemieu came back downstairs, she let him talk for a little longer then suggested he might like to go to his bed. Like Madeleine, she had noted his weakness.

When Guy protested she rather curtly silenced him, saying that anyone could see that Luc was worn to the bone.

'I am tired,' Luc admitted. 'And cold.' Standing, he turned to Madame Lemieu and again offered his thanks.

'It is nothing,' she told him and she gave him a hug. 'We are glad to have you back.'

Madeleine marvelled at the way he seemed to have wormed his way into the hearts of her family, Leon excepted. They did not love him as she did but they were certainly fond of him and he of them. Eighteen months ago he would not have let her aunt get so close, either mentally or physically.

She slept better that night than she had for weeks, relieved to know that he was safe. But it was a relief that was to be short-lived. By the morning he had developed a high fever that once again made her fear for his life. In his more lucid moments he insisted it was only a cold though his head hurt and there was a pain in his chest when he breathed. Taking it in turns, Madeleine and her aunt spent long hours at his bedside until, three days after his return, he fell into a deep but healing sleep.

In fact, he slept a great deal over the next few days. Even talking seemed to exhaust him and he became frustrated at his weakness. It was nearly ten days before he finally made his way downstairs. Then he surprised Madeleine by appearing quietly in the kitchen, wearing a clean shirt and breeches that he had found in his trunk. He had still not bothered to shave and the dark growth of beard only served to heighten his pallor. Madeleine was quite shocked to see how much weight he had lost and she was not the only one.

That evening when Luc asked Monsieur Lemieu about helping out again, he was firmly but kindly told that it would not be considered for some time.

'With Raoul coming over, we can manage well enough without you, lad,' the older man said. 'At the moment you are nothing but skin and bone. Rest for a couple of weeks and let Mother fatten you up. Then if you wish to stay on I'll be willing to accept your help.'

For the next few days, Luc kept to the farmhouse, which meant he was rarely out of Madeleine's sight. Often she would find him watching her, a dark and brooding look in his eyes. When she finally asked him what was bothering him, he rather sharply told her that there was nothing and that she was imagining things.

It was another couple of weeks before Monsieur Lemieu agreed to accept Luc's help about the farm and then only for limited periods. The weather remained bitterly cold and finding enough wood to keep the farmhouse warm became a continual battle.

Early one morning, Guy and Leon brought home a tree limb that had been blown off in the wind and Luc set to work chopping it into logs. Madeleine went outside to feed the chickens and was horrified to find that he had stripped off his coat and was working in his shirt sleeves. When she chided him about it, he curtly told her that he was quite recovered and not a child.

Madeleine returned to the kitchen and rather irritably began preparing a meal. Her aunt had gone into Vannes with Monsieur Lemieu and so the task had fallen to her. With more force than was needed she chopped a carrot and after dumping it into the stew pot, reached for another.

'Are you wishing that was me?' Luc asked quietly.

Madeleine looked up. She had been so intent on her task that she had not heard him come in. There was a wry, almost self-deprecating smile on his face, but his eyes were serious.

When she made no comment, he continued, 'I'm

sorry, Maddie. I did not mean to bite your head off just now.'

'It doesn't matter,' she told him, the words coming out more sharply than she intended.

'I think it does. I've been acting like a bear with a sore head.'

'That's an understatement.' Madeleine began work on another carrot. 'What I don't understand is why.'

'No,' he said flatly. 'I don't suppose you do.' He was quiet for a moment, then asked, 'Do you have some tweezers or a needle or something? Somehow I've managed to get a splinter under my fingernail.'

Putting down the knife, Madeleine fetched her aunt's workbox from beside the fireplace. It only took her a second or two to find a needle.

'Sit down and let me see,' she told him.

With a long-suffering sigh, Luc obeyed, perching one hip on the table. Madeleine winced when she saw the size of the splinter embedded under the middle fingernail of his right hand.

'How on earth did you manage that?' she asked.

He shrugged, stiffening slightly but making no complaint as she probed with the needle. She was so intent on her task that she did see the soft look that stole over his features and she started when she felt his left hand slip up and under her hair.

'I don't suppose you realise that being near you and not being able to touch you has been driving me insane,' he told her huskily.

Madeleine made no reply and, with great effort, centred her concentration on the splinter.

'It was bad enough before but since I've been back. . . I seem to be losing what little restraint I had. . .'

Her heart was racing and she was intensely aware of his touch. After a moment, the splinter came free.

'You really ought to wash that,' she told him.

He made no reply to that but said, 'I can't sleep for wanting you, Madeleine.'

She glanced up at him, then wished that she had not. He looked so sad and sincere. 'I won't change my mind. I won't become your mistress,' she heard herself say.

Luc sighed and gently rubbed his hands up and down her arms. 'Then marry me.'

'Marry you!' Her heart soared only to plummet like a stone. 'Now you are playing with me.'

'No, I'm not.' He did look exceptionally serious. 'Even if you would allow it, I can't simply bed you. I hold your aunt and uncle in too much regard.'

'You are being ridiculous,' she replied tightly, pulling away from him. 'A comte does not marry a woman like me.'

He sniffed derisively, not taking his eyes from her as she returned the workbasket to its place by the hearth. 'According to our government I am no longer a comte.'

She shrugged. 'If one assembly abolished titles, then another assembly can bring them back.'

'Quite possibly,' he replied with haughty indifference. 'In any case, it does not signify. I have always done as I pleased.'

Madeleine smiled at the momentary return of his old arrogance. She could at least cope with that. When she tried to return to her task at the table, he reached out to grasp her hand.

'I asked you to marry me, Madeleine,' he said, sounding a little peeved. 'You do at least owe me the courtesy of a reply. You are attracted to me, you know you are.'

Crossly she snatched her hand away, turning so that he should not see the indecision on her face. 'There is much more to consider than that. It's time you learned you can't have everything you want!'

Softly he came to stand behind her. Although he did not touch her, she was aware of him with every fibre of her being.

'Look at me, Maddie,' he commanded.

She did and was surprised by the degree of longing she saw in his face.

When he reached for her she did not pull away. Then he kissed her so softly, so tenderly that she felt she would die from loving him. If he had been rough or demanding, she would have pushed him away, but the sweetness of his kisses beguiled her, giving the illusion of safety and comfort. Slowly her arms crept up around his neck, burrowing beneath the curling hair at his nape. She knew she should stop him, but she just didn't have the willpower.

Luc knew how to arouse a woman. He knew all the slow subtle moves calculated to seduce, yet with Madeleine so pliant in his arms, he failed to remember them. The feel and taste of her excited him until it was he who was seduced, and he found himself crushing her against him without any semblance of finesse.

When he felt her begin to resist him, it was only by the use of sheer willpower that he was able to make himself draw away. Madeleine had no idea how difficult it was for him; all she saw was the knowing smile on his face.

'My answer is still no, Luc,' she told him with only an outward appearance of calm.

'No?' he repeated incredulously. 'By the saints! You are the only woman I have ever proposed to! Well, I won't accept your no, at least not yet. You can do me the courtesy of thinking about it for a few days!' Without further argument, he made for the door. With his hand on the latch he paused. 'Think about it!' he repeated. 'And, while you're at it, consider that no other man is ever likely to make you feel the way I do!'

Over the next few days, Madeleine though as much about his parting words as she did about his proposal. There was no denying the attraction between them but she did not think that it would be enough.

If only! If she thought that once then she thought it a hundred times. If only he loved her. If only they were of the same class. If only she was ruthless enough to take what he offered and never mind the future, but she was not. He would be marrying her simply to bed her and the novelty of that would soon wear thin. She could not bear to marry him and have him grow to hate her.

The following week, Monsieur Lemieu travelled to Vannes with a supply of potatoes. This time he was accompanied by his sons and Luc who, against Madame Lemieu's advice, had declared himself strong enough to make the journey on Charlemagne. Although the snow had long since cleared, it was still bitterly cold and the puddles remained frozen on the rutted road. Madeleine saw them off at first light and for once was glad not to be going with them. They returned in the middle of the afternoon, a full hour before dark, delighted with their success. Every single sack of potatoes had been sold and at a more than fair price. The Lemieus were in a mood to celebrate; such was not the case with Luc who declined a glass of calvados and instead proceeded to the stables to give both Charlemagne and the ponies a good rub-down. He needed no help, he rather shortly told Guy when the latter made to join him, and in fact would be grateful for some time on his own.

When Madeleine asked the others what was troubling him, Leon pulled a sheet of folded paper from his pocket and held it out to her. 'They were pinning these up in Vannes.'

Madeleine glanced down at it and her aunt peered across her shoulder. It was a drawing of the King's head. It was suspended by its hair and blood was shown dripping from the severed neck. Underneath it stated that the *ci-devant* Louis XVI had been executed on the 21st of that month at a quarter past ten in the morning. The act, it said, had imprinted a grand character on the National Convention and made it worthy of the confidence of the French.

Madeleine felt sickened. She had never met Louis but she could understand a little of how Luc must be feeling.

'It is murder,' Madame Lemieu said tightly and her husband nodded. 'Ah, poor Luc. I suppose he knew the King.'

'He did,' Madeleine replied, 'Well enough, I suspect, for it to be a blow to him personally as well as politically.'

Leon shrugged. 'Well, it does not affect us.'

'Such wickedness affects everyone,' his mother reproved. 'This king was a man like any other and I feel truly sorry for his wife.'

Luc did not return until Madame Lemieu was putting the meal on the table. Then it was only to say that he was not hungry and that he was going for a walk.

'A weak stomach?' Leon quipped

Luc turned towards him. A muscle tensed in his jaw and his dark eyes blazed. Quickly, Monsieur Lemieu cut in. He had not brought up two boys without being able to recognise when a fight was brewing.

'Hold your tongue,' he told Leon, then, turning to Luc, added, 'Take your walk, lad. There will be food available if you're hungry later.'

After collecting his cloak, Luc left and it was all Madeleine could do not to follow him. Every instinct urged her to go after him and offer what comfort she could, but her place was in the kitchen helping her aunt. She went through the motions of eating but found her own appetite affected both by the grisly picture and concern for Luc. Once the meal was over, she could contain herself no longer and, with her aunt's blessing, went in search of him.

She found him where she had expected, down by the river. He was leaning against the thick trunk of an old oak tree, staring down into the grey brown water as it swirled between the moss covered stones. He looked so solitary, so withdrawn and alone.

The love she felt for him rose up inside her, making it difficult for her to breathe. It was so much deeper than friendship, more enduring than mere physical attraction. She would love him, she realised, until the day that she died. How strange when there had been a time when she had not been able to stand the sight of him. Now she would do anything to ease his pain.

Slowly she made her way towards him, her feet sinking into the blackening leaves. It was their crunching that alerted him to her presence and he turned towards her, his expression bleak.

'It's too cold for you to be out here,' he said uncompromisingly.

She paused uncertainly. 'I though you might need a friend. If you still want to be alone, then I can leave.'

'I think I've had enough of being alone.' With a wry smile he held out his hand and she went silently into his embrace, slipping her arm around his waist, giving him a hug. After a moment, she heard him sigh.

'Were you very fond of him?' she asked.

'Of Louis. . .? I did not think I knew him well enough. Then the day before we left Paris. . .' He shrugged. 'In spite of everything, he had retained a quiet kind of dignity and he was hurt that his subjects should have treated him so. It was that more than anything that led me to pledge my support, my sword if need be. For all his faults he was a good man, a caring man. He did not deserve to die in such a manner. Our whole nation has been tarnished by the deed!'

'It must be the end of all hope of re-establishing the monarchy.' In a way Madeleine was grateful for that. A counter-revolution such as de la Rouerie would have initiated would surely have involved Luc.

'It will not be the end,' he replied, sounding quietly determined. 'Those of us who pledged our support to Louis now owe it to his son.'

'Will there be more fighting then?'

His jaw tensed and the hand that was moving comfortingly up and down her back stilled. 'I hope so. . . Our revolutionary masters have gone beyond reason.'

'Oh, Luc.' Madeleine was genuinely upset.

Using his free hand, he tilted her chin, forcing her to look up at him. The look of determination faded from his face. 'Do not worry, Maddie. Any violence will not reach you here.'

'It wasn't myself I was concerned about,' she replied sharply.

'Were you concerned for me?' When she did not reply he continued, 'Are you never going to admit the way you feel about me?'

'Luc, I. . .'

He silenced her with his lips, warm and demanding upon hers. He kissed her until she felt dizzy, until her heart was pounding in her chest and her legs had turned to water. When he finally drew his mouth away it was only so he could draw her even more tightly against him.

'Ah, Maddie,' he groaned into her hair. 'If you only knew how much I need you.'

Need, not love. It wasn't at all the same and yet, held so closely in his embrace, it seemed enough.

'Marry me, Maddie?' he asked again and this time she could only answer.

'Yes.'

The following week Luc received more bad news. Armand Tuffin, Marquis de la Rouerie, had died at his friend's château in northern Brittany. Exposure and deprivation had affected him as it had Luc, only he had not been able to recover from it. Before the body was even cold Republican soldiers had discovered it; severing the head, they had placed it on a spike in the château grounds.

Luc's face became set when he heard the news. 'He was a good man,' was all he said.

He made no outward show of emotion and yet

Madeleine knew that he was feeling it dreadfully. He would not cry for he had been brought up not to show weakness in that way, but that did not prevent her going to her room and crying for him.

CHAPTER NINE

MONSIEUR and Madame Lemieu accepted the
announcement of Madeleine's impending marriage with
a certain amount of ambiguity. Luc went through the
process of asking her uncle's permission to marry her,
but the older man knew that in reality it was a *fait
accompli*. Both he and his wife liked and admired Luc,
but they were doubtful about the consequences of so
unequal a match.

The idea of planning a wedding in part made up for
this, at least on *madame*'s part, even though there were
difficulties involved. Because he had taken the oath to
the civil constitution, their local priest was not considered suitable to perform the ceremony. In fact, in the
eyes of the church, Madeleine would not be properly
married should it be done by him. However, the problem was not insurmountable. The same priest who had
performed the Christmas mass was still in hiding in the
area and Madame Lemieu was confident of being able
to persuade him to perform the service. Unfortunately,
in the interests of secrecy, the wedding would have to be
small. This suited Luc well enough as he had no
particular friends he wanted to invite; in any case, he
wanted to maintain his anonymity. Madeleine under-
stood this but could not shake the notion that he was
ashamed of her.

'He has offered you marriage,' her aunt said, seeking

to reassure her. 'He must love you very much to do that.'

Madeleine wished that he did. There were times when Luc was so warm, so caring, that she could almost believe it, but in spite of this he never said the words. Each night she prayed that her own love would be enough.

'In the old days, such a match would have been unheard of,' her aunt continued. 'He may have lost his home and his title, but he is still very much above us and is probably a great deal wealthier than we can imagine.'

Up until then Madeleine had not really considered Luc's financial situation. She had assumed he had money for he regularly purchased feed for his horses and, in other small ways, he did not go without. Of course, he would have the income from his house in Paris and from his land, but she doubted it was enough for him to purchase another estate, otherwise he would not be staying at the farm. However, between the two of them she was convinced they could sustain a comfortable standard of living.

The next few weeks proved to be some of the sweetest and most frustrating of her life. There were times when Luc was both impatient and high handed, but he was also wonderfully tender. They quarrelled dreadfully about her wedding gown, Madeleine insisting that she and her aunt would sew it and Luc protesting that there was no need. There were competent dressmakers in Vannes and he saw no reason why they should not employ one. In the end, he all but dragged her off to the town and talked her into ordering a dress that was far more lavish than she had intended. When he wanted to pay for it she steadfastly refused; in that, at least, he did not get his way.

They were turbulent times, too. Even as Luc and Madeleine adjusted to each other, discontent abounded in the countryside. The war was going badly for France and, at the end of February, the convention declared a levy of thirty thousand men. Each province was to provide its quota, even Brittany. It was not yet full conscription, but any shortfall in the number of men who volunteered was to be made up by a lottery and from this no single man or childless widower between the ages of eighteen and forty was exempt. Needless to say, there was a spurt of marriages and Madeleine began to wonder if the date of her own nuptials should be brought forward.

Luc, however, was not registered in the province, which was just as well. After the affair with de la Rouerie, he viewed the French army as an enemy and confided to Madeleine that he would now join the *emigrés* rather than become part of it. Madame Lemieu fretted in case one of her sons should be forced to enlist, Guy having just reached eighteen, and the latter's assurance that he would become an outlaw rather than do so did little to help her peace of mind.

The peasants' discontent finally found an outlet in mass riots. There were numerous incidents like the one Luc and Guy had been involved in the previous year. Recruiting officers were beaten and their tables smashed. In some places Republican officials were murdered and their families threatened as the young men of Brittany and the Vendée made it clear that they would not be forced from their land.

Neither Luc nor Madeleine approved of the riots for they brought back all too forcibly the memories of what had happened in Paris. The mindlessness and the brutality was exactly the same, Luc rather sharply told Guy, albeit for a different cause. Gradually, however, some of the rioters began to form into more organised bands, roving the countryside and attacking the Republicans in the towns.

In the end, neither of the Lemieu boys were taken by the levy and they both remained at the farm. In Guy's case this was with reluctance. Several of his friends had joined the rebel bands but he had not the confidence or the heart to defy his father and follow them.

Another matter that caused discord between Madeleine and Luc was his deepening friendship with Georges Cadoudal. Cadoudal, the eldest of ten children, was a man of impressive stature and quick mind. He had studied humanities at the college in Vannes and it was his ability to converse on many subjects that had originally drawn Luc to him. He was heavily involved with the rebels and she was afraid he might influence Luc. When her brother Reynard next visited the farm, she spoke of her worries in that regard.

Reynard laughed. '*Dieu*, Madeleine! I have already told you that your Luc is a leader. He is not being influenced by Georges. More like it is the other way around. He is already involved; you can't change that. If you want a domesticated husband who is only interested in the work on the farm, then you are marrying the wrong man.'

Luc refused to discuss matters with her, merely insist that there was no danger and that he knew what he was doing. He also possessed the ability to kiss her senseless and drive all thoughts of the matter from her mind.

May approached, the month they had chosen for their wedding, and they had still not decided on a place to live. Madeleine suggested that they rent a small house in Vannes. Her aunt and uncle, however, cautioned them to do nothing in a hurry. They were welcome to stay at the farm, at least for a while. Surprisingly, this seemed to suit Luc.

'When we are ready, setting up on our own will present no problem,' he told her. 'At the moment, times are unsettled and it might be best to wait. In any case, we will need to take your dowry into account.'

Madeleine had forgotten all about Philippe's dowering of her and was surprised that Luc had not. From his knowing smile she concluded that he knew a great deal more about it than she. It was logical, of course, considering he had been so close to Philippe.

'Do you know how much is involved?' she asked curiously, thinking that, if it was a substantial amount, she would feel better about marrying him.

They were sitting together in a patch of spring sunshine down by the river and his mind was more occupied with her than with her dowry.

'Don't worry your pretty head about it,' he said, running his finger down her nose. His smile was full of blatant male appreciation as he added teasingly, 'It's not your dowry I'm marrying you for.'

His attitude irritated her and when he tried to embrace her, she pushed him away. He looked hurt and genuinely perplexed. Having finished work for the day, he had changed into a clean shirt and a pair of buckskin breeches. His face was deeply tanned, which might not have been fashionable in the drawing-rooms of Paris but which Madeleine found incredibly attractive. With his dark hair lifting in the slight breeze she thought him more handsome than any man had a right to be. Suddenly found that she did not want to quarrel with him. She could learn to live with his high-handedness.

Smiling ruefully, she apologised. 'I'm being a shrew, Luc. Wedding nerves, I suppose.'

He pulled her into his arms and, after kissing her, held her close whilst he buried his face in her hair.

'I don't think I shall survive until our marriage,' he said huskily. 'By then I think I shall have died of frustration.'

There were times when Madeleine came close to alleviating that frustration but, with the wedding date drawing nearer, she determined to make him wait. In her heart she was afraid, afraid that if she gave herself to him then he would not marry her after all. It was ironic, but having finally consented to be his wife, she found she did not have the courage to test his commitment to her in such a way.

About a week before the wedding, she and her aunt were in the kitchen and Luc was outside chopping wood when two dark-coated strangers arrived at the farm. They were sober, hard-faced fellows with shrewd eyes and an abrupt manner of speaking. Authority sat belligerently upon their shoulders in the manner of men not long accustomed to it. They were unaffected by Madeleine's gentle manners or her aunt's open hospitality and proceeded to question the two ladies in a rude and slightly threatening manner.

'We are told you know the *ci-devant* Comte de Regnay?' they demanded of Madeleine.

Her stomach turned over. Her first instinct was to lie then she changed her mind, aware that a mixture of truth and falsehood would be more readily accepted.

'I know him,' she replied, sounding a good deal more composed than she felt. 'He was a friend of my protector—Philippe, the Marquis de Maupilier. After Philippe died, the Comte brought me here.'

The taller of the two men frowned. 'We are aware of that, citizeness. Have you seen him since then?'

Madeleine shook her head. 'I assume he went back to Normandy. There was nothing for him in Brittany.'

'Nothing but revolt and sedition!' one of the men replied. 'De Regnay was involved in the Association Bretonne. He is also believed to have acted as a courier for the late king, although nothing has been proved in that regard. The man we sent to check on the matter disappeared. I don't suppose you know if he was carrying any letters when he was escorting you.'

Madeleine did not make an outright denial. 'I don't believe so. Apart from the various inns, the only place we stopped at was Châteaurange. I don't see how he could have delivered a letter to anyone, at least not whilst he was with me.'

The taller man grunted in disbelief. He then proceeded to ask her some other questions about Luc's activities in Paris which she answered as vaguely as she could, keeping to the truth whenever possible.

Finally they turned to Madame Lemieu. 'Should you hear from de Regnay then we want to know. We are aware that here in Brittany there is a great deal of sympathy for such miscreants. Such sympathy is treason!'

'What will happen to the Comte if you catch him?' Madeleine asked.

'He will lose his head. His estate has already been sequestered.'

Madeleine was shocked. She did not know how she was going to break the news to Luc. He had already lost so much. It did not register that the Comte's loss was also hers. Her primary concern was for his safety and his happiness.

Without properly taking their leave, the two men moved to the open doorway where they paused to observe Luc. Madeleine's heart returned to her mouth and she found it difficult to breathe.

'Who's that?' the shorter, stockier man demanded.

'His name is Jean-Luc,' she lied. 'He lodges and works here.'

At that moment Luc looked up. He touched his forelock to the two gentlemen and slouched across to the wood pile to collect another log. It was the first time Madeleine had seen him look at all ungainly. When she glanced at the visitors' faces she saw that they had already dismissed him as being of no account.

'He's a little simple-minded,' she confided.

'A pity,' the tall man commented as he walked towards his horse. 'A strapping fellow like him would do well in the army.' Once mounted, he glanced back towards the ladies. 'Remember, if you see or hear anything of de Regnay, then we want to know of it. You can contact us through the Hôtel de Ville in Rennes.'

As soon as the the men were out of sight, Luc put down the axe and, laughing heartily, went to hug Madeleine.

'Simple-minded, eh!' he said, giving her a kiss.

She was in no mood to join in with the joke. 'You are an outlaw! I cannot see how you can make so light of it!'

He shrugged. 'My only worry is that I might place the rest of you in danger.'

Madame Lemieu was not concerned about that. 'Half the young men in Brittany will be outlaws before long. Monsieur and I approve of what you are doing and are glad to help.'

'They have sequestered your estate,' Madeleine told him.

'I've known that for weeks,' he replied, surprising her. Then, with a grin, he added, 'It was always on the cards. Don't worry my dear; we shall be far from destitute.' Suddenly serious, he asked, 'Do you mind marrying an outlaw, Maddie? I know you did not bargain for that when you accepted me.'

'I am concerned for you,' she replied, 'but I have not changed my mind.'

Towards the end of May, on a day that was full of sunshine and promise, Madeleine and Luc were married. The ceremony was conducted at Kermosten and included only the family and a few of the Lemieus' close friends. With the spring planting completed, there was a comfortable air of satisfaction about the men that stemmed from the knowledge that they had earned their relaxation.

Madeleine clasped Luc's hand and thought how much she loved him. She could feel the calluses beneath her palm and was proud of the manner in which he had earned them. She had no idea how lovely she looked, how possessive and proud he felt of her. She watched him moving amongst her family, teasing her aunt and

laughing with her brothers and realised how completely
he fitted in. He was taller than Guy and Thierry and,
although he lacked the girth of Reynard and Leon, he
was somehow not dwarfed by them. It was more to do
with his presence than his size, she realised. When she
remembered what Reynard had said to her about Luc
being a leader, she felt suddenly inadequate and afraid.

Towards the end of the afternoon Luc came across to
her. He kissed her lightly on the mouth and gave a smile
that was full of satisfaction.

'Go and fetch your cloak, wife,' he told her. 'It's time
for us to leave.'

'Leave?' At first she thought she had misheard him,
for they had no plans to go anywhere. As far as she
knew, they were going to spend their wedding night in
her bed. 'I don't want to go for a walk,' she told him.

'Not for a walk, Maddie. I have somewhere to take
you.'

'Everything you will need has been packed,' her aunt
informed her, joining them with a conspiratorial smile,
'and Guy has already gone to harness the horses.'

'Trust me,' Luc said, grinning from ear to ear. 'I have
been happy here at the farm but I think our wedding
night should be spent in more privacy.'

Madeleine experienced a number of conflicting
emotions—pleasure that he should want her to himself,
excitement and apprehension, but she also felt annoyed
because he had not consulted her. If it had been
Philippe, then she would not have questioned matters,
but she found that she did not trust Luc in quite the
same way.

'Where are you taking me?' she demanded as he

placed her cloak across her shoulders, but he only replied that she must wait and see.

Everyone else seemed to have been let into the secret and they obviously approved. In the face of their happy smiles Madeleine did not feel that she could make a fuss. Outside, a small carriage was waiting with Luc's own horses between the shafts and Charlemagne tied behind. The carriage was obviously new; when she glanced questioningly at Luc, he confirmed the fact.

The sun was sinking as they headed along the road towards Vannes. She assumed they were going to put up at an inn there and, glancing at the small trunk lying behind her, hoped that her aunt had packed the right things.

'Sit closer to me, Maddie,' Luc commanded, lifting his free arm and drawing her firmly against his side.

She sighed more with acceptance than pleasure and he lightly kissed her hair. She loved Luc and wanted to be his wife in every sense of the word and yet the further they travelled from the farm, the more apprehensive she felt. He had only offered her marriage because he wanted her in his bed and she was very much afraid that she would disappoint him.

When they reached the crossroads leading to Kercholin, she was startled to find him heading that way. 'Luc, what are you doing?'

He grinned. 'Be patient a while longer, there's a good girl. You will be pleasantly surprised, I promise you.'

Surely he hadn't done anything as foolish as buy and rebuild her old home? That possibility was too awful to contemplate.

By the time they pulled up outside Kercholin Manor, it was almost dark. Madeleine was surprised to see that not only were the gates open, but the weeds had been cleared from the patch of ground in front of them. Behind them stretched a vast courtyard with the dark stone walls of the manor house bounding it on two sides and a stable block along the third. It was not a pretty place; it had been too long neglected for that. There was no porch, no decorative pillars. In fact, there was a starkness to it that was almost eerie.

'Luc,' Madeleine asked, 'just what are we doing here?'

'We are going to spend the night here,' he said, driving through the gates.

Madeleine sighed and, leaning forwards, peered into the fading light. The only sign of welcome was a light showing through a narrow window beside the door.

'Do you know the owners, then?'

'You could say that. It's ours, Madeleine. It is the dowry Philippe settled on you. . . I hope the servants have everything in order. I warned them to expect us at this time.'

Madeleine could hardly believe what she had heard. Philippe had willed Kercholin to her; well, not exactly to her, but to her husband. She found that she was not thrilled with the idea. The ancient old house looked dark and forbidding; she would have much preferred to live on a cosy farm. In fact, the idea of being mistress of such a place was decidedly daunting. She would feel awkward and out of place particularly as her family had once been peasants on the estate.

'How long have you known about this?' she asked Luc in a small, tight voice.

He dismissed her question lightly. 'Since before Philippe died. . . I just hadn't given it much thought.'

He smiled. 'Not until I began to consider where we might live.'

'And you never thought to mention it to me?'

He paused then in the act of climbing down from the wagon, for the first time aware that something was wrong. 'I thought I'd surprise you.'

When she made no response to this, he walked to the manor door. After plying the knocker briskly, he came to give Madeleine his hand. She climbed out slowly, a little stiff from sitting so long. A brighter light appeared in the side window. There was the sound of a bolt being drawn back and the door swung wide. A middle-aged woman in a dark-coloured dress peered at them, then warily smiled a welcome. Her face looked gaunt and hard in the yellow light of the candles she was carrying. At the back of the hall, another door creaked open and a man came into view. He too was of middle age. Drawing himself up to his full height, he straightened his waistcoat and came forward.

'Monsieur and Madame Lebrun, this is your mistress Madame Valori,' Luc said.

It was a shock for Madeleine to hear herself introduced in such a way. Thank God, he had not referred to her as his *comtesse*. She forced herself to acknowledge the couple, determined that they should not know how awkward she felt.

'Your room is ready,' Madame Lebrun told Luc. 'Would you like me to show it to you now or would you prefer some refreshment in the drawing-room?'

'We will go to our room,' Luc said, reaching for Madeleine's hand. Then, turning to Monsieur Lebrun, he ordered, 'See that our trunk is brought up, would you, Jean, and make sure the horses are well cared for.'

Madame Lebrun guided them up a wide stone staircase that led up from the back of the hall. Dingy oil paintings of various solemn-looking gentlemen stared down at them, ancestors of Philippe. Memories came flooding in on Madeleine. How uncertain and afraid she had been the first time Philippe had led her up those stairs. Ironically, she found it difficult to separate those old fears from the emotions bubbling inside her now. She was just as apprehensive, felt just as insecure.

When they reached the first floor, their guide turned right down a dark hallway, its polished floor covered in places by faded rugs that showed a disconcerting tendency to slide underfoot. From the smell of polish that permeated the general muskiness, Madeleine concluded that it had only recently been waxed. On one side of the hall, high windows overlooked the courtyard. On the other there were four doors, wide spaced because the rooms were large. Madame Lebrun opened the third door, then stepped back for Luc and Madeleine to enter.

It was an old-fashioned room, low and dark with heavy beams running across the ceiling and faded tapestries hanging from the walls. There was a heavy bed draped with some kind of dark red fabric, a tiring-table with a little mirror and a pair of delicate, velvet-covered chairs. Here was none of the elegance of Philippe's apartment in Paris.

In fact, none of the furniture seemed to match, as if it had been gathered from various parts of the house. It was, however, quite clean and a fire burned welcomingly in the hearth. Madeleine was glad of that for, in spite of the sunshine during the day, it had grown quite cold.

'All is as you ordered.' Madame Lebrun gestured to a

door that obviously led to the next room. 'There is also a fire in the dressing-room and wine and brandy should you require it.'

Luc dismissed the woman and Madeleine turned away to stare down at the fire. In the silence of the room she could hear the flicker and hiss of the flames devouring the green wood. She felt disappointed and somehow betrayed. Luc had discussed none of this with her.

'Madeleine, is something the matter?' he asked.

'Yes!' She took a deep breath before turning to face him. 'Luc, I shall feel awkward here.'

'Awkward?' He sounded surprised. Such a notion had obviously never occurred to him. 'You will be mistress here.'

'The peasants will remember me!'

He grinned. 'You have changed, Maddie, believe me. They will not recognise you. As far as they are concerned, you are Madame Valori. They will not question the matter further.'

'But if they do; what then?'

'I do not want to discuss this,' he grated, his eyes narrowing. 'You are my wife. *Dieu*, you are a *comtesse*!'

It annoyed Madeleine, the way he used or discarded the title whenever it suited him. 'What about the Lebruns?' she asked tightly. 'How long have they been in the house?'

Luc sighed. 'The Lebruns are new here. The old couple, who were in charge of the house when I first came over, were happy enough to retire to their daughter's in Vannes. It is not a good idea to keep such established servants.'

'You could have discussed it all with me,' she answered hotly. 'You could have told me the extent of the dowry!' Angrily she removed her cloak and threw it across a chair.

'Sit down, Madeleine,' he told her calmly. 'I'll fetch you a drink. I think you are becoming overwrought.'

Overwrought! Madeleine could have throttled him. She had known he was arrogant and overbearing but this was beyond anything. Nevertheless, she obeyed, sitting in stony silence whilst he disappeared into the dressing-room.

He returned a few minutes later, carrying two goblets of white wine. He pressed one into her hand and placed the other on the mantelshelf. Moving behind her, he began to massage her shoulders. Angry as she was, Madeleine could not help responding to his touch. She sighed with pleasure and was scarcely aware of Monsieur Lebrun entering with the trunk. After a moment, Luc bent to press a kiss on her neck, his lips burning her like brands.

'You must be tired,' he said quietly. 'I'll leave you to get ready for bed.'

Collecting his glass, he glanced at her once more before taking a hefty swig of the wine. It did not occur to Madeleine that he was as nervous as she, that he was just as apprehensive. He had planned for this moment so carefully, yet had the uncomfortable feeling that it was all going awry. Madeleine seemed as prickly as a hedgehog when he wanted her to be all soft and loving.

Sitting in front of the fire in the dressing-room, he poured another glass of the wine and tried to convince himself that he was not drinking it to boost his courage. Always he had used women. He had loved them and left them and felt totally in control. Yet with Madeleine it was different. He felt as unsure as a schoolboy and it irritated him beyond measure.

As soon as Luc had left the room, Madeleine rose from the chair. In a few minutes he would be returning and he would expect her to be ready for him. She experienced a strong desire to run. He had married her for what would happen that night and she was very much afraid that he would not find it worth the price.

She did not want to be there in that house, in that room and another fear was surfacing, buoyed up by her lack of confidence and self-worth. Kercholin seemed so important to Luc. Had it been the weight to sway the balance in favour of marrying her? He had, after all, been an aristo without an estate and he had stepped into the role of master at Kercholin with disconcerting haste and ease.

When Madeleine reluctantly opened the lid of the trunk, she was surprised to find an ivory silk nightgown lying on the top of the other clothes. Had Luc purchased it, she wondered? It was too expensive for her aunt to have bought. Bowing to the inevitable, she shed her clothes and put it on. That accomplished, she unpinned her hair and, rummaging for her brush, quickly tidied the shoulder-length tresses. She was on her way to the bed when Luc entered the room. He had removed his coat and boots and his ruffled shirt hung open at the neck. In his hand he carried another glass of wine.

Feeling awkward and embarrassed, Madeleine paused, her movement halted by the glow of desire she saw in his eyes.

'*Dieu!*' he muttered breathlessly. 'You have to be the most beautiful woman alive. I have nearly died from wanting you.'

Moving towards her, he drank half the wine in his glass, then offered the remainder to her. 'Go on. It will relax you.'

Slowly she complied, her eyes never leaving his. When she had finished, he took the glass from her and placed it on the bedside table. Then, taking her in his arms, he lowered his head to kiss her wine-dampened lips.

'So sweet,' he whispered in her ear.

Madeleine tensed at the hoarse note in his voice. He sounded like a stranger. She tried to draw away but he held her to him.

'No, Maddie. You can no longer deny me. You are mine now.'

The finality of his words frightened Madeleine. They made her sound like a possession, a thing. That, plus the apprehension she felt about her ability to satisfy him, drove her to test the regard he had for her.

'Luc,' she whispered. 'I'm tired. Must we. . .?'

He smiled knowingly as he trailed his fingers down the small of her back. 'You are frightened, my sweet, and there is no need for it. I will be gentle. I know how to please. . .and the answer is yes, we must!'

His uncompromising answer was like a shower of cold water, chilling her to the bone. There was no love in it, no tolerance. He was simply demanding what he considered his due.

When he kissed her again the magic was gone and she remained stiff and unresponsive in his arms.

'What now?' he demanded, giving her a gentle shake. 'Just what are you playing at? You've always been responsive enough before.'

'I'm beginning to wonder,' she said quietly, 'just why you married me.'

'You know why I married you,' he snapped, angry and confused. 'I married you because I wanted you and you would settle for nothing less. I've made you a *comtesse*, Madeleine. Is that not a fair trade?'

She had known it, but the blunt reply still hurt. 'And my dowry?' she asked. 'Are you telling me that did not enter into it?'

'Your dowry?' Suddenly he laughed. 'What maggot have you got in your brain now? Surely you do not think I married you for your dowry?'

When she did not reply, his expression hardened. 'My God, you *are* serious!' He studied her for a moment whilst the changing light in his eyes indicated his deepening anger, shaking her confidence.

With her heart in her mouth, Madeleine took a step away from him. 'Can you promise that you did not?'

'I'm damned if I will!' Her unfair accusation, flung at him when he was swamped by the need to make her his own, was fast pushing him beyond control. 'You should know me well enough not to have to ask.'

'Then perhaps we should sleep separately,' she said.

She had not meant the words to sound like a threat; the moment she had said them she would have taken them back had she been able. Luc's eyes darkened still further until suddenly his built-up emotions burst through his usual composure. He felt cheated and unbearably hurt; his pride, too, was stung. Whatever else, no one who knew him had ever accused him of being acquisitive and underhanded. If Madeleine hadn't done so in fact then it had certainly been implied.

'We shall not sleep separately, wife,' he snapped,

moving forward and forcibly lifting her chin. 'I will have you and tonight!'

Madeleine's gasp of hurt and anger was smothered the next moment as he took her mouth in a harsh, bruising kiss. She was amazed by his strength as he forced her down on to the bed. Within seconds her nightgown was gone, closely followed by his shirt. Luc was rough at first, angry and uncertain, and for a while Madeleine fought him—only for a while. Soon she began to feel that strange melting inside herself, that empty longing that only his closeness could fill.

Immediately he felt her response, Luc gentled. Now at last he would not be denied. But he would not be rough with her, he would not, could not, bruise a body he so cherished. She was silk and softness, warmth and sweetness, more beautiful than any painting or statue he had ever seen. Tenderly he smoothed her from neck to thigh then, with a restraint he did not know he possessed, he used all his experience to make her want him more. She too would have pleasure from this night, he thought grimly; she would at least think of him kindly for that.

All his experience, however, had not prepared him for the effect she had upon him. When the climax came he closed his eyes, lost to everything but the feel, smell and taste of her. Everything was sensation and yet never did he lose the sense of her identity as he often did with other women. Even as his passion broke through the iron control he had placed up on it, he was vividly aware of her and knew with a feeling of despair that it would be that way with no other woman.

CHAPTER TEN

WHEN Madeleine awoke, a narrow strip of sunlight had pierced the heavy drapes to fall across the bed in a golden bar. She felt well-rested, languorous and filled with a sense of well-being—until she remembered, and then regret and a troubled mixture of hurt and guilt descended on her like a dark cloud. Luc had been coldly ruthless in admitting why he had married her, but she too had played a part in the quarrel. How could she have let her doubts and insecurity make her into such a shrew?

Turning her head she looked for Luc, not knowing whether to be relieved or sorry that he was no longer there. When he had first begun to make love to her, he had frightened her with his roughness but then he had become so gentle, so tender, that he had almost made her believe that he loved her after all. She had experienced such pleasure and only a little pain. The entire experience had been far easier and more enjoyable than her aunt had led her to expect and she knew that Luc's patience and expertise was responsible.

'I love you,' she had wanted to cry out when he had collapsed exhausted upon her, but she had kept the words securely locked in her heart.

They had not spoken or even touched after that but had fallen asleep together, drained by their lovemaking and the turbulent emotions that had preceded it. Now he was gone and only the indentation in the pillow beside her told her that it had not been a dream.

What should she say to him? What should she do? She bit her lip to stop the tears. In the cold light of day, her actions the night before seemed childish, her accusations unjust. His pride if nothing else would have made it impossible for him to act in such a mercenary manner. In retrospect, she was honest enough to admit that she had been trying to push him away. She had wanted to hurt him, to make him angry, to put off the moment of their coupling, the moment when he would discover that she was no different from any other woman.

She had not been disappointed by their lovemaking, but had he? She adored him with every beat of her heart, but marriage involved more than that. It involved trust, sharing, mutual respect. Was it unrealistic of her to want more than a burning passion on his part? He had never pretended to be in love with her, had never whispered any words of love, and she had chosen to ignore the omission; she had loved him and wanted him so much. Now her pride lay in tatters and she found herself tied in marriage to a man who did not care.

She bit her lip as she stared up at the beamed ceiling. Could she make him love her? Had her accusations last night ruined any chance of that? For nearly an hour she lay there reluctant to face him, fearing his anger, his rejection. She had just decided that she could no longer put off the meeting when there was a knock on the bedroom door. Madame Lebrun asked permission to enter and then approached Madeleine, carrying a tray on which a light breakfast had been arranged.

'The master is up and is waiting to speak with you,'

the woman said, her expression one of faint disapproval. 'He seemed most impatient.'

That piece of information did not help Madeleine's confidence at all. She picked at her breakfast and, after she had dressed, spent an inordinate amount of time fussing with her hair. Nearly an hour had passed before she eventually made her way downstairs to join Luc.

As soon as she entered the drawing-room, she caught sight of him. He was writing something at an ancient writing-table and he drew her eyes like a beacon. Sunlight streamed through the square-paned window behind him, gleaming on his dark hair and throwing his handsome profile into clear relief.

It was all she could to not to rush to him and confess her love and only pride held her back. She was inclined to do anything, say anything, that would make him happy. Suddenly it seemed silly to have resented the way he had handled her dowry when, had she been able, she would have given him the world.

Taking a deep breath, she moved forward to stand before the desk. 'You wanted to see me?' she asked more calmly than she felt.

Obviously he had not heard her come in for he started. For a moment he just stared at her, then he sighed. There was no warmth in his gaze, which remained dauntingly impersonal.

'I have made some arrangements that I need to tell you about. Firstly, I have made it possible for you to draw money in Vannes.' He pushed a piece of velum across to her. 'The details are all there. Secondly, some horses of mine will be arriving over the next couple of weeks. I removed them from Maurice's care last year and had them stabled in Rennes in case I had need of them. I have asked Lebrun to employ a suitable man to take care of the stables and deal with the horses' feed.'

Madeleine swallowed. 'Luc, I do not need money. I still have a little of my own and my needs are simple. As for what happens in the stables, I really do not care. . .'

'You are mistress here, Madeleine!' he snapped, rising from the table. 'You will need to exert some authority.'

'I don't see why,' she replied, forgetting all her good intentions. 'Up until now you haven't consulted me at all! As far as I can see I'm just a possession to warm your bed.'

Luc sighed heavily and moved to stare out of the window. When he turned back to face her, Madeleine thought he looked as miserable as she.

'I think we need some time apart,' he said bleakly. When she did not immediately answer him, his hand lifted and he rubbed his fingers wearily across his brow. 'I can't seem to think logically when I'm around you. I'm going away for a while.'

For the first time Madeleine realised that he was dressed for riding, in buckskin breeches and top boots. His cloak, she now noted, was thrown in readiness across the back of one of the chairs. Sickness churned in her stomach and an unconditional apology rose in her throat, but she forced it down. She might have acted like a bitch, but by leaving he was showing her just how little she meant to him.

'Oh,' she managed to say with a feigned lack of concern. 'Am I to be told where?'

A muscle tensed in his jaw. 'Georges Cadoudal and others are riding south to fight for the Vendéan army. Your brother Reynard has decided to join him and so have I. I believe the grandly named Royal and Catholic Army has a good chance of clearing both the Vendée and Maine of Republicans.' He shrugged. 'Who knows? De la Rouerie's plan of marching on Paris may yet come to fruition. It could depend on men like me.'

At his words, Madeleine's heart sank still further. She wanted to tell him that he was a fool; instead she asked, 'Just when did you decide this?'

'It does not matter when I decided it. The cause is dear to me and we need time apart. Perhaps when I return. . .'

Bitterness welled up in Madeleine and fear for him made her speak more harshly than she intended. 'You may not find me here when you return! You wanted this house, Luc, and you can keep it! I would far rather live at the farm.'

Close to tears, she made for the door, but he swiftly intercepted her, holding it closed with his left hand while he loomed over her.

'You are my wife, Madeleine!' he snapped, his eyes blazing. 'If you are not here when I return then I shall come after you. You are mine now and your place is here in our home. Furthermore, if you so much as look at another man. . .'

For a moment she thought that he would hit her. Instead, he stepped away although fury still radiated from him.

'You need not worry on that last score,' she told him tightly as she reached for the door handle. 'I have had quite enough of men!'

'Madeleine!' Once more he stayed her although she did not turn to look at him. His voice was as cold as steel.

'There is something else you should know. For more than a year I have been withdrawing funds from Châteaurange and investing them in various accounts around here and in Guernsey. I also sold my house in Paris, which made a pretty penny. When I began to work against the Republic I was aware of what could happen. Believe me, I could buy this place two or three times over. I did not need to saddle myself with a peasant girl who does not have the sense to realise when she has the best of a bargain!'

Peasant girl! The two words registered in her brain louder than all the others. She didn't reply to that; she couldn't without completely breaking down. Instead, she pulled the door closed behind her and walked regally to the stairs. Luc was never going to know how much his leaving had hurt her.

From a gallery window, she watched him ride away. In all her life she didn't think she had ever felt as lonely and wretched, not even when Philippe had died. She regretted her accusation concerning the dowry and knew she should have apologised but overshadowing everything was the knowledge that Luc had only married her because she would not consent to be his concubine. Obviously he had been disappointed by their lovemaking; indeed, how could she have satisfied him when the price he had paid for bedding her had been so high?

About a week after her marriage, her cousin Leon called at Kercholin. Apparently a friend of his in Vannes had seen Luc riding out with Cadoudal and he had come to see for himself if it was true. When Madeleine admitted that it was, he let forth such a tirade against Luc that perversely Madeleine found herself defending her husband and in doing so became more appreciative of his point of view. He could not help not loving her; furthermore, the quarrel on their wedding night had been of her making.

When her aunt arrived the following day she was ready to accept the older woman's advice. Luc was wrong, Madame Lemieu said, to leave without settling their quarrel, but she doubted the marriage was damaged beyond repair. Madeleine must have hurt him or he would not have reacted so extremely and that was a good sign. God willing he would return and then it would be up to her to show him that she could be a caring and supportive wife.

'This is your home now,' her aunt said, looking around at the dingy furniture and tapestries. 'You could do what you can to improve it. That will at least demonstrate to Luc that you are committed to remaining here and are not staying simply because he has commanded it. I know you love him, child. If you can't bring yourself to tell him, then show him it in other ways. You are man and wife now in the eyes of God and our church and you will both have to make the best of it.'

The following morning, Madeleine had Monsieur Lebrun drive her into Vannes where she ordered fabric to replace the curtains in the main sitting-room and purchased two expensive Persian rugs for the floor. She bought pottery and silver candlesticks, heavy silk brocade to make cushions and a new tapestry to hang above the serving table in the dining-room. All this she extravagantly paid for with her own money, although she did draw on Luc's account to finance the additional help she needed with the cleaning and sewing.

For the next few weeks the house was a hive of activity. Floors were rubbed down and repolished, walls scrubbed, furniture waxed and the tapestries that were not soiled beyond repair taken down to be beaten and then sponged clean. Madame Lemieu and Guy brought over the trunks containing some of Madeleine's possessions from Paris; with these in place, she really began to think of Kercholin as home. Luc's horses arrived, five in all, together with two of his trunks which had also been stored in Rennes. Pre-empting Lebrun, Madeleine hired a young man called Jean-Paul to take care of the stables.

News from the Vendée was sparse and often conflicting. There was heavy fighting at Saumur, and later at Nantes where the Vendéan leader Cathelineau was killed. Breton soldiers were involved in both conflicts and Madeleine did not doubt that Luc had played his part. A letter from him would have eased both her anxiety and the ache in her heart but none arrived.

By the end of the summer, the refurbishment of the downstairs had been completed and, with waning enthusiasm, she turned her attention to the bedrooms. She had no idea whether she was a widow or merely a neglected wife and she began to doubt that Luc would ever return to view her efforts.

It was not until the middle of October that she finally received a letter from Luc. Her first reaction was an overwhelming sense of relief that he was alive. This quickly faded, however, to be replaced by a smouldering anger. There was no apology for not writing before, no words of endearment or any conciliatory phrases. If the

letter had shown the slightest warmth, then she would
have been prepared to forgive his long silence. It was,
however, disappointingly impersonal, full of facts and
points of general interest but there was not one mention
of affection, let alone love. After passing on greetings
from Reynard who was still with him, and asking to
be remembered to the family at Kermosten, he had
signed the missive simply, 'Luc', and dated it the 16th of
October.

It was several weeks before Madeleine learned that
the letter had been written on the eve of an important
and rather bloody battle, a battle in which the Vendéan
army had been defeated and forced to retreat north,
across the Loire. This knowledge, however, did little to
dampen her growing anger. He had made it quite clear
how little he thought of her; on several occasions she
considered packing her things and returning to the farm,
but her aunt's words stayed her—that and the reluctant
love she still felt for Luc.

Guy arrived at Kercholin at the beginning of November,
having met two *chouans* in Vannes who had previously
been with the Grand Royal and Catholic Army.

'Apparently, Cadoudal is still with the Vendéans,' he
told Madeleine. 'It's likely, then, that so is Luc.'

He had other news, too, sad news, to pass on.
Thierry's father-in-law had been lost at sea.

On the day before Noël, Leon rode over to drive
Madeleine to the farm. It was freezing and, as she pulled
her cloak more closely around herself, she thought of
her husband. She remembered how ill he had been the
year before and hoped that he was keeping warm. She
did not want to care so deeply about him, but found that

she could not help herself. Since their leaving Paris, it
had become as natural to her as the need to breathe or
draw near to a fire in winter time.

It was bitterly cold in the small town of Savenay and the
breath of men and horses looked like white steam in the
chill air. The woods surrounding the town, once peaceful and unspoiled, echoed with musket fire and the
crunch of booted feet as the Republican army tightened
their circle around the Vendéans. The Grand Royal and
Catholic army of the Vendée would not exist for much
longer.

After weeks of hard fighting, the Vendéans had
wanted to return home. They had met with defeat at
Angers and, unable to cross the Loire there, had tried
again at Ancenis. With the river swollen in winter and
the Republicans having requisitioned all the boats, this
had proved difficult; only the generals Stofflet and
Jacqueline, together with a few hundred men, had been
able to find a way across.

Tired and dispirited, believing their generals dead,
the remainder of the army had followed the river west
through mist-shrouded marsh land into the wooded area
around Savenay. They had arrived there the day before,
two days before Noël; a Noël that few would live to
celebrate.

Luc struggled to control his nervous horse and
glanced back at the houses where many of the Vendéans
had decided to make a last stand.

Beside him, Reynard Vaubonne swore savagely.
'We'll never make it,' he growled, referring to
Cadoudal's proposed attempt to break out.

'It is death to stay,' Luc replied. 'This way at least we have a chance.'

Then they were off, following the giant Cadoudal as he spurred towards the enemy lines. Muskets rattled and the man next to Luc fell amid hooves and flying dirt. Mercifully they were almost into the trees before the next volley cut into them. Luc drew his sabre and laying about him, charged into the Republican line. Charlemagne reared up, all but decapitating a man with his flying hooves and Luc felt the jar all the way up his arm as his sabre connected with bone. In a matter of seconds the sleeve of his jacket was red with Republican blood. Then they were through the line, through the trees and riding hard for freedom across a low-lying meadow.

A musket ball whistled close to him, almost knocking his hat from his head and, glancing sideways, he saw Reynard fall. As the other men raced on, Luc turned back. Reynard was on his feet although he was decidedly unsteady and blood was pouring from a wound in his shoulder. Reaching down an arm, Luc used all his strength to hoist the injured man up behind him.

Charlemagne was a fine horse but with his double load he could not keep up with the others. Eventually Luc drew up and, helping his brother-in-law from the saddle, bound up his wound. The pistol ball was still embedded in his shoulder and it was obvious that he was going to need more competent help. Reynard was lucid enough to tell Luc of a family he knew in the area who would be willing to take him in.

'They used to help me with some of my trading ventures,' he explained.

In spite of their desperate situation, the euphemism

made Luc smile. He knew quite well that Reynard made his money from smuggling salt. After helping the big man back on the horse, Luc began leading it westward towards an isolated farm in the Marais. As he trudged along, it struck him most forcibly that he would rather be going home. Regardless of all that had passed between them, he was desperate to see Madeleine again, to hold her in his arms and take comfort in the soft, welcoming warmth of her body.

In the months that he had been fighting he had often regretted his hasty departure. He knew he would have joined the fighting eventually—his honour and commitment to the King would have made sure of that—but in leaving so abruptly, he knew he had been running away. Madeleine's accusations had hurt and that was not an emotion he was accustomed to feeling. He liked her company and he wanted her in his bed, but, he reminded himself, that was all. Years of women courting him for his rank, of matchmaking mothers trying to ensnare him for their daughters, had made it impossible for him to believe that Madeleine could want him for himself. As far as he was concerned, she had traded her body for marriage and position, yet on their wedding night had been blatantly unwilling. At least, she had at first; the culmination of their lovemaking had been all he could have wished for. Although she had undoubtedly been a virgin, her sensuality had delighted him. She had surpassed his expectations, so why then did he feel so cheated and unsure?

It wasn't until the second week in January that Madeleine learned of the crushing defeat at Savenay. Cadoudal and several other *chouans* had returned, but of Luc or Reynard there was still no word. Towards the end of the month, the weather worsened. The road into Vannes became a quagmire and it was impossible to travel either there or to the farm in a wagon. Madeleine felt as if she was living in a prison and determined that as soon as the weather improved she would learn to ride.

The following Sunday when Guy came to call she asked if he would teach her. He thought it an excellent idea and, the weather having temporarily improved, insisted on giving her the first lesson that afternoon. His mare was well trained and placid and Madeleine achieved enough success to boost her confidence and to make her eager for another lesson.

That evening, tired after the unaccustomed fresh air and exercise, she retired to bed early and, after reading for a short time, drifted off to sleep. How long she slept, she did not know, but the candle beside the bed had burnt quite low when she was awakened by someone moving across her bedroom.

When her eyes opened, the first thing she saw was a pair of mud-splattered breeches. Slowly, her gaze travelled upwards and she found herself staring into her husband's beard-roughened face. For a moment she thought she was dreaming, then he spoke to her.

'Hello, Maddie.'

'Luc?' She sat up sleepily, struggling to come to terms with the various emotions she was feeling—relief, pleasure, apprehension, but most of all anger that he should so suddenly appear and then act as if it was the most natural thing in the world. She wanted to hug him, to assure herself that he was unharmed. She wanted to kiss him and at the same time she itched to slap him and wipe the smile from his handsome face.

'How did you get in?' she finally managed to ask with applaudable calm.

Luc's smile changed to a frown. 'Madame Lebrun was just on her way to bed. . . You don't seem very pleased to see me.'

'How can you expect me to be,' she parried, 'when you haven't seen fit to send word to me. One letter, Luc, in God knows how many months!'

'I could not get in touch with you before,' he replied, hiding his guilt behind a show of annoyance. He could not explain the hurt and the anger he had felt every time he had picked up a pen, the feeling that to write would somehow be a weakness on his part. 'Reynard and I had to lay low. After the battle there were Republican soldiers everywhere.'

Tossing his damp cloak across a nearby chair, he sat down on the edge of her bed. Madeleine watched helplessly as he removed one of his boots and tossed it across the floor.

'Just what do you think you are doing?' she demanded.

'Undressing.' The second boot followed the first.

'I hope you don't intend to sleep here. Your own room is ready and aired.'

'Your brother is using it,' he replied, removing his jacket and beginning to unbutton his shirt, 'and even if he was not, then I would still choose to sleep here.'

'But you're filthy!'

'That's right.' He did not even turn to look at her. 'A little dirt never hurt anyone, Madeleine, and I'm too tired to do anything about it now.'

She could hardly believe this was the same man who had strutted so elegantly around the salons of Paris. 'I have no wish to sleep with you and you have no right to expect it! You disappeared without word for months. I haven't known whether you were alive or dead, or whether you intended to come back at all!'

He turned at that, his eyes bright with anger. With his shirt hanging open and his hair tousled, he looked wild and more than a little dangerous. 'I never said I wasn't coming back. As for sleeping with you, I have every right, or had you forgotten?'

She could have shaken him for his arrogance and turned away in angry disgust as he stepped out of his breeches and then his underclothes. She felt the mattress shift as he slipped between the sheets and crossly decided that she would go and sleep elsewhere. Before she could swing her legs over the edge of the bed, he reached out to grasp her arm.

For a moment he maintained his grip then, with a tired sigh, released her. 'As I've already said, Reynard is in my room and by now Madame Lebrun will have gone to her bed. You might as well stay here. God knows, I'm too tired to bother you. It's a cold night and at least you'll be warm.'

Gazing into his face, Madeleine saw that he was being perfectly honest. He looked exhausted and undeserved concern welled up inside her. Reluctantly, she settled back against the pillows.

Reaching out, he snuffed the candle then settled back with a tired groan. For several minutes she lay quietly beside him, wishing with all her heart that there was a greater closeness between them. How wonderful it would have been to know that he loved her and to be able to welcome him back as a wife should. She tried to relax, but even so it was a long time before she drifted back to sleep. In spite of everything, she found that she felt safer and more contented than she had for weeks. Luc was alive and whole and that meant everything.

When she awoke the first thing she became aware of was the heavy weight lying across her stomach. Cautiously she turned her head to look at Luc. During the night he had rolled towards her and was lying on his side, one strong arm draped possessively across her. She could feel the heat he was generating through the fabric of her nightgown and became aware that his thigh was nestled snugly against her own.

She took a deep breath, her nostrils filling with the pleasantly musky scent of a sleeping man as she cautiously tried to edge away from him. The arm across her waist tightened and he made a sleepy sound of protest. When she glanced at his face she saw that his eyes were open. As she watched, the shadows of sleep cleared from them and he smiled.

'Why so eager to leave me?' he asked in a voice still husky from sleep.

'I have things to do,'she replied tightly.

'What things? Come, Maddie, you are mistress in this house. There is nothing you have to do.'

He pushed himself up on one elbow so that he could look down at her, and the arm that had been imprisoning her slid up her side to play with the strands of blonde hair that lay spread across her pillow. When his knuckles brushed her skin, she stiffened. Beneath the soft fabric of her nightgown, her heart was pounding so hard that she was convinced he would notice its beat. His bare chest brushed against her breasts as he lifted a leg across her, pinning her to the mattress. His lips covered hers in a gentle kiss that became harsher when she failed to make any response. Where his leg was draped across her, she could feel the growing evidence of his arousal.

'Luc, I don't want this,' she protested.

'Yes, you do,' he answered arrogantly, turning her face back towards him. 'Oh, yes, you do,' and then he kissed her again until all thought of refusing him had fled from her mind.

Somehow that morning seemed to set the pattern for the next few months of their marriage. By day Luc was decidedly aloof, maintaining a distance between them, yet at night he would take her in his arms and make love to her as if there was no tomorrow. He never spoke of love, though, or whispered the endearments she so wanted to hear, and Madeleine kept her own feelings hidden.

She had wanted so much to marry him, but what joy was it when he only shared his body, never his heart? The irony of the situation was not lost on her. She had refused to become his mistress, his concubine, yet in spite of their marriage vows, that was really all she was.

Reynard stayed at the manor for almost a month, long after his wound had healed. A closeness had developed between him and Luc, not surprising in view of the way Luc had saved his life and later helped to nurse him. Madeleine was glad of it, but she also found that she wes jealous. Luc no longer talked to her as he did to her brother.

Even after Reynard had left them, he often returned. Sometimes he and Luc would ride off together and be gone a number of days. Although Luc never actually told her, Madeleine knew they were riding with the *chouans* who were carrying on a kind of guerrilla war against the Republic, and she suspected that arms and ammunition had been stored on the estate.

Georges Cadoudal was captured by the authorities and imprisoned first at Auray, then at Brest, and she feared for Luc, knowing that if he was taken he would suffer a far worse fate. Fortunately the authorities seemed to have lost track of him and he was careful not to draw attention to himself. He continued to forgo his title and was known to all in the area as simply Luc Valori, a distant relative of Philippe de Maupilier.

He had another name, too, a pseudonym that was used by the *chouans*. She discovered this one evening when she was talking to Reynard. They called him *le loup noir*—the black wolf—and she could not help thinking how well the name suited him. At the same time she was hurt that he should have kept such an important part of his life a secret from her. Although she was not a fervent Royalist, she did favour an independent Brittany and she would have liked to help. She said nothing to Luc although she was frustrated and hurt at being shut out of everything but his bed.

Such of the *chouans*' activities that were general knowledge she soon came to hear about. They entered the towns and freed the prisoners from gaol; they raided the Republican army's pay and supply convoys, terrorised their garrisons and crept into town and village squares to chop down the liberty trees. When the Republicans tried to hunt them down, they disappeared into the forests or back to their homes. When Luc was

away from Kercholin, Madeleine worried dreadfully
and learned to sleep lightly, subconsciously listening for
his return.

In spite of his commitment to the *chouans*, Luc still
seemed to find time for Kercholin. He put into use all he
had learned at Kermosten and, under his informed
management, the farms on the small estate began to
prosper. The peasants respected him and that respect
also encompassed Madeleine. If they did recognise her,
nothing was said, and they continued to treat her with
the deference due her position.

Noël came and with it heavy snow. It lasted into
January which the revolutionaries had named Nivôse.
Old people shook their heads and declared it the
harshest winter they could remember. Rivers and har-
bours froze and hot stones had to be dropped down to
melt the ice in the well. Even travel to the farm was
impossible and, for a while, all *chouan* activity ceased.
For her part, Madeleine was glad to have Luc at home.

It was not until the end of the month that the thaw set
in and grass that seemed impossibly green began to
appear in rapidly expanding patches.

During the second week of February the *chouans*
again rode out. Madeleine was awakened one clear,
frosty night by the slamming of a door on the floor
below her. As the Lebruns had already gone to bed, her
first thought was that it must be Luc. She lay quietly
waiting for him to come to her and when he did not,
decided to go downstairs and investigate. She did not
want him falling asleep in a chair, not with the weather
so cold, and furthermore was concerned that he might
be hurt.

Climbing from her warm bed, she put on her robe and

by the light of a branch of candles made her way downstairs. She saw a light coming from below the door of the small room that served as a library, and cautiously opened it. To her surprise, Luc was not alone. Her brother Reynard was there, together with a well-built, dark-haired stranger.

Madeleine's first reaction was to apologise and take her leave. Then she noticed Luc's frown. He was obviously not pleased by her presence. Perversely, that made her stiffen her spine. It was her home, too, and yet he had not mentioned that he was bringing home guests.

'You did not tell me you would be entertaining,' she mildly chastised him.

'I did not expect to be,' he replied tightly.

'I beg you to forgive the intrusion,' the dark-haired man said, coming forward to bow with courtly grace over Madeleine's hand. 'Georges Cadoudal at your service, Comtesse.'

So this was the infamous Cadoudal, the giant of Morbihan. He was extremely tall and broad as well, with a heavy-featured, almost handsome face and an air of absolute assurance. His presence surprised Madeleine; she had thought him to be in prison.

Cadoudal glanced over his shoulder at Luc, and teased, 'It is a shame to hide such beauty away, my friend. We should all be able to feast our eyes on such a lovely lady.'

That the big *chouan* was an accomplished flirt soon became apparent as he set about charming Madeleine. To her shame, she encouraged him, in spite of Luc's thunderous expression. She had been starved of every-day affection, of compliments that were not hoarsely whispered in the bedroom, and she did not think it would not hurt to try and make him a little jealous. After a short while, however, she decided that she had pressed her luck far enough and, making her excuses, returned to bed. She was, after all, hardly dressed for entertaining.

When Luc joined her a short while later, she could tell that he was angry. The bedroom door shut sharply behind him, not quite a slam, and she thought it best to feign sleep. Behind her closed eyelids she could make out the glow of candlelight as she heard him undress and felt him slip into bed beside her.

'I know you're not asleep,' he grated, catching hold of her chin and forcing her to look at him. She could feel his anger in the tension of his fingers and, when she opened her eyes, could see it in the hard set of his jaw.

'If I had any sense I'd beat you,' he hissed. 'You will never again encourage a man to fawn over you like that. You belong to me! You are my Comtesse and you will learn to act in a manner befitting your station!'

Then he kissed her, a bruising, punishing kiss that crushed her lips against her teeth and made it almost impossible for her to breathe. When he made love to her it was with an anger and passion that surprised her. It was as if he wanted to set his mark upon her, to remind them both that she was his and his alone, and that she no longer had any choice in the matter.

CHAPTER ELEVEN

MADELEINE stood at one of the windows in the upstairs gallery, staring out across the countryside. In the distance she could see Luc riding hell for leather, his figure picked out by the pale winter sun. She watched him as he turned back towards the manor house. He disappeared behind the cottage roofs then passed through the arched gateway and into the yard below her vantage point. This was the third day in a row that he had ridden Charlemagne so hard.

She was certain that something was bothering him and had been since Cadoudal's visit. At first she was inclined to blame her own behaviour for his restlessness, but she soon became aware that there was more to it than that.

Turning from the window, she made her way downstairs. She collected her lace-making cushion from the side-table and settled down in front of the fire. She heard Luc come in and was surprised when, instead of going upstairs to change, he came into the drawing-room to join her. She watched as he circled the sofa she occupied and flopped down in a chair before the fire, stretching his long legs out in front of the blaze. For a moment he stared into the flames, his expression sombre.

'Madeleine,' he said quietly, without looking at her. 'I'm going to England. It will be for some time.'

Nothing he could have said would have surprised her

more. Always he had declared his determination to
remain in France.

'Emigrate?' she demanded. 'Have the authorities
discovered your whereabouts, then? Are you in danger?
If you are, then of course I will come with you.' She
paused uncertainly. 'That is, if you want me to.'

Her tirade elicited a rare smile. 'The visit is to further
the royalist cause... The Comte de Puisaye has gone to
London to try and persuade the English Prime Minister
to help us, to support our army with British troops if
necessary. There are those who think I can aid his
efforts.'

'But you are not a politician or a diplomat.'

'No, but there was a time when I used to visit England
regularly. I have friends there and some of them are in a
position to help us... I also have a letter that might be
of use in rallying the *émigrés*. It's from the late king
himself. It is of less significance since his death but it
may move those who will not act in d'Artois's name.'

Madeleine was a little shaken by that revelation; she
found the depth of his commitment to the Royalist
cause, in particular his involvement at a creative level, a
little frightening.

'I don't particularly want to go, Maddie,' he continued. 'God knows, I'm not even truly convinced that
it's the way to proceed. English troops on French soil!'
He grimaced. 'The idea is anathema to me yet those like
the Comte de Puisaye are convinced it is the only way
we shall succeed. Certainly it is the only hope we have
of marching on Paris to free the dauphin. De Puisaye
has had vague promises of financial aid from the British
but needs something more concrete.'

In that moment, Madeleine felt closer to him than she

had since their marriage. He was really talking to her
again, sharing his hopes and his fears. Privately, she
thought that the boy who should have been Louis XVII
was already dead. The last news they had of him was
that he was ill and being kept in terrible conditions. Luc
had been most upset.

'Perhaps the English won't have to send soldiers,' she
said. 'Perhaps money and arms will be enough.'

He shrugged. 'Whatever, I feel that I must go.'

'When?' she asked quietly.

'At the end of the month.

Madeleine realised then that she did not want to be
parted from him again. In fact, she was not sure their
marriage would survive another long separation.

'Take me with you,' she blurted.

Luc was silent for a moment and she was sure he was
going to refuse.

Then he surprised her. 'Very well, Maddie. I suppose
it can be arranged.' At her look of pleasure, he lifted his
hand. 'I must warn you though; I will have little time to
spend with you.'

'That will not matter,' she assured him. 'I am used to
my own company.'

He still looked doubtful and she realised that
although he had agreed he was not completely convinced of the wisdom of it.

'You won't be sorry,' she told him, and determined to
give him no reason to change his mind.

Over the next week, they were both busy preparing for
their journey and Madeleine was glad of it. When she
was idle, doubts about the wisdom of accompanying Luc
played on her mind. What if she let him down? What if

one of their acquaintances from Paris was there? She did not mention her fears to him, though, for she knew he would be quick enough to tell her that she need not go.

One morning, Luc drove the wagon into Vannes and returned with a shy, young woman called Lisette Montcalm whose parents owned a dressmaker's in the town. In his usual high-handed manner, he informed Madeleine that he had taken on the girl to travel with them and to act as her maid. Madeleine was a little annoyed that he had given her no say in the appointment, but it soon became obvious that Lisette would suit admirably. She was nimble fingered and artistic and was able to dress Madeleine's hair to perfection.

In spite of the war between the two countries, travelling from France to England proved surprisingly easy. They crossed Brittany using a route set up by the *chouans* and then sailed on a fishing boat to Guernsey. From there it was a simple enough task to find a ship to take them to England. They travelled with what Madeleine considered an inordinate amount of luggage. Luc had insisted that she pack a number of gowns she had not worn since leaving Paris; it was imperative that they both look their best.

They arrived at Tilbury on a cold and misty day towards the end of February. Madeleine shivered beneath her thick cloak and looked apprehensively around at her dismal surroundings. At first sight England looked a bleak and unwelcoming place. The way the people spoke sounded strange, and although she had learnt a little English under Philippe's direction, it bore little resemblance to what she heard. Luc, however, experienced no problem and was inclined to forget that Madeleine's English was so limited.

They put up at a hotel for a few days and then moved into a suite of rented rooms in Curzon Street. Luc took on not only a cook but also a man to act as a general servant, rather as Jean-Paul had done. The fellow was called George Bates and a greater contrast to Jean-Paul could not have been found. He was portly and stolid and very much aware of what he referred to as 'his place'. He was kind to Madeleine, though, and seemed not to notice her smiles of gentle amusement.

The rented rooms were large and airy and, according to Luc, in a desirable situation. No sooner had they settled in when a trail of expatriate Frenchmen called to see them. Madeleine was surprised how poor some of them looked. Luc confided that many were in a desperate situation.

'They did not expect to forfeit their estates,' he told her. 'Most, too, had not planned on being away from France for so long.'

Madeleine enjoyed her first two weeks in England. Luc was prepared to spend time with her and seemed to enjoy showing her around. They visited Ranelagh Gardens for tea and went to see the waxworks and the British Museum. Luc was relaxed and more open than he had been at any time since their marriage and she began to hope that he had at last forgiven her for the things she had said to him on their wedding night. Unfortunately, he had come to England for a purpose and he could not continue to dance attendance on her.

As the days passed, he spent less and less time at the rooms in Curzon Street as he met with like-minded Frenchmen and visited the various London clubs. He insisted that this was not for pleasure. Madeleine knew that the social aspect was important in rallying support but she began to grow resentful of his absences. With no tasks to occupy her nor company other than the servants, she soon became bored.

Luc moved in the highest circles whilst Madeleine remained on the sidelines. She made no complaint, for it was she who had asked to come, but the neglect was hard to bear. At least at Kercholin he had spent the nights making love to her; now he was often out late, sometimes not returning until dawn, and, at his suggestion, they slept in separate rooms. Ostensibly it was so that he would not disturb her but she began to wonder if that aspect of their marriage had finally begun to pall with him.

They had been in London just over a month when their first English visitor came to call. She did not wait for Bates to announce her, but entered the drawing-room like a small whirlwind and, going straight up to Luc, kissed him full upon the lips Then she stood back, still holding his hands, whilst he continued to smile at her like an idiot.

'Ah, Lucian, dear! Had I known you were in London then I would have returned sooner. I have been with my late husband's mother in Bath—such a boring place.' Finally releasing his hands, she took another step back and surveyed him from head to toe.

'You're looking good,' she pronounced.

'And you are as beautiful as ever,' he told her.

Madeleine stood silently for a moment, not quite sure how to react to the raven-haired beauty. She was both surprised and annoyed by the way the woman had thrown herself into Luc's arms—not that he had complained. He had enjoyed every minute! She wanted to voice her displeasure, but was wise enough to know she would only sound like a shrew.

Then the woman caught sight of her. Dainty black brows arched in surprise. 'And who is this, Lucian?' she asked.

'My wife.' Still smiling, Luc gestured to the woman. 'Madeleine, this is Lady Edith Roseberry, an old friend of mine.'

'Wife?' Lady Edith repeated, scrutinising Madeleine quite openly. 'She is beautiful, Lucian. As always your taste is impeccable.'

Madeleine knew then that it was going to be difficult to dislike Lady Edith. Vitality radiated from her and there was both frankness and intelligence in her startlingly blue eyes. Rather hesitantly and in what she hoped was correct English, Madeleine offered refreshment. Lady Edith accepted and then somehow contrived to find a seat next to Luc.

'When I found your card yesterday, I was delighted,' she told him. 'With such dreadful things happening in France, I have been so worried about you.'

'There was no need.' Luc settled back in his chair, smiling at her concern. 'Madeleine and I left Paris before the Terror. We are living in Brittany now.'

'Not at Châteaurange?'

A shadow crossed his face. 'Châteaurange was burned and the land sequestered. I have thrown in my lot with the Royalists, you see.'

'Oh, Lucian, I'm so sorry.' Lady Edith had the temerity to pat his hand. 'I am extremely wealthy now. Should you need. . .'

'We are well enough provided for,' he hastily assured her. 'Châteaurange was not my only asset. However, in your capacity as hostess you could be of immense help to me.'

'You know I will help you in any way I can,' she told him, and there was no doubting her sincerity. Turning to Madeleine, she asked, 'Where did you and Lucian meet?'

'In Paris. My... guardian died and Luc was kind enough to escort me to my aunt's home in Brittany.'

Fortunately Lady Edith did not seem to notice the hesitation and Madeleine was spared the need to go into further detail by the arrival of the tea. As she poured it, Luc and Lady Edith chatted with the familiarity of close friends. Madeleine felt left out and a little awkward. During her time in Paris she had mixed easily with gentlemen, but had been allowed no contact at all with real ladies. Moreover, they had reverted to English and some of what they were saying was unintelligible to her.

'I am giving a ball next month,' Lady Edith said as she accepted her tea. 'You must both come. Before that, I am taking a group of friends to the theatre. My box will accommodate two more and I would very much like you to join us.'

It was Luc rather than Madeleine who replied that they would be delighted.

After their visitor had left, Madeleine asked Luc more about her.

'She is an old and very dear friend,' he said and from his tone it was obvious how much he thought of her. 'Her late husband was a politician and she retains a number of friends in that field. She is also extremely wealthy.'

Obviously Lady Edith was one of the influential friends he had come to seek out.

'Were you more than friends?' Madeleine asked.

For a moment she thought he would not answer her. 'Yes,' he finally replied. 'At one time we were lovers.'

Madeleine remembered Philippe telling her about an affair Luc had once had with an Englishwoman. The affair had continued on and off for several years until the distance between London and Paris had finally put an end to it. In spite of what Luc had said, she could tell there had been more to the relationship than a simple affair.

'She's very nice,' was all she said.

Over the next few weeks they were often in Lady Edith's company. Madeleine wanted to dislike her, but found that she could not. As a person she was warm and full of vitality. She had a well-developed sense of fun and was able to draw Luc out of himself and make him laugh in a way Madeleine had never managed.

They went with her to the theatre and the ballet and, on horses that she provided, went riding with her in Hyde Park. Thanks to Guy's instruction Madeleine had become quite a proficient horsewoman and was able to keep up with the rest of the party. Eventually, however, the riders began to split off into pairs. Madeleine found herself accompanied by a young, fair-haired friend of Edith's, Sir Daniel Wrayford.

Wrayford's French was good and, in spite of his rather fulsome compliments, Madeleine enjoyed herself. At least, she did until she saw Luc and Edith. They were laughing together and there was an air of intimacy between them, like that of two lovers. As they

approached Madeleine, Edith said something to Luc
then appeared to tease him for his response. Leaning
across, she squeezed his hand.

When Madeleine saw the gentle, almost intimate
gesture, she felt her stomach knot with jealousy. The
woman was obviously still in love with Luc and
Madeleine did not see how he could fail to respond to
her.

As the days passed, Madeleine watched Luc and
Edith together and became more and more convinced
that they were having an affair. It was a notion supported by the fact that he no longer shared her bed. It
caused her to lose sleep and affected her appetite,
making her look so wan that Luc eventually noticed and
made comment on it.

'If London does not suit you,' he told her, not
unkindly, 'I can easily make arrangements for you to
return home.'

During the second week of April, Lady Edith held her
ball. It was quite a small one by the standards of the
London *ton*, but a number of important people were
invited. Luc insisted that Madeleine have a new gown
for the occasion; when she protested at the expense, he
coldly told her that she was his wife and as such had a
position to uphold. She had almost forgotten how
imperious he could be and felt like slapping him for the
set down.

The gown was of the palest cream, only a shade
lighter than her hair, with a bodice studded with tiny
freshwater pearls. She knew she looked good in it, more
regal than she would have thought possible, but in spite

of the satisfaction she felt when she looked in the mirror, she found that she did not want to go.

When she joined Luc in the sitting-room where he was ready and waiting for her, she nearly refused to accompany him. He looked so splendid in his silver grey coat and satin knee-breeches, so aristocratic and some-how right, that she was reminded once more of their differing backgrounds. Luc stared at her for a moment, then slowly smiled.

'You look lovely,' he said and he meant it.

A warm wave of pleasure swept through her and for a moment, she forgot her fears. His approval meant everything and she vowed that she would not let him down.

Lady Edith's house was in Grosvenor Square, not far from Hyde Park. It was in the middle of a splendid terrace and some four storeys high. The small ballroom was on the first floor, at the top of wide, gently curving stairs. Lady Edith was standing beside a set of mirrored double doors to welcome her guests. Ignoring protocol, she gave Luc a hug and then swiftly brushed her lips across Madeleine's cheek.

The ballroom was full of splendidly dressed people. The pastel-coloured silks and organdies of the ladies were no more colourful than the satin evening coats of the men. Overhead hung two enormous chandeliers, the hundreds of candles in them making the glass shine like mammoth diamonds. Madeleine had never been any-where so grand.

The ball began with a country dance and Luc led her out on to the floor. Thanks to the instructor he had hired for her, she was able to perform her part with a certain amount of expertise. After that, she danced with an array of partners who attempted to converse with her in excruciatingly bad French until, shortly before midnight, young Sir Daniel came to claim her hand. That dance proved to be an energetic one and she enjoyed it immensely. Her pleasure was somewhat dimmed, however, when, towards the end of the dance, she caught sight of Luc dancing with Lady Edith. The latter was laughing up into his face and he was smiling fondly at her.

The dance over, Madeleine's young admirer went off to procure her a glass of lemonade. For a while, she stood fanning herself, absently listening to the hum of mainly unintelligible conversation around her, then from somewhere to her left she heard a person speaking in French.

'De Regnay seems to be very taken with our hostess,' said the voice. 'I can't for the life of me see why, not when he has such a beautiful little wife. She has the looks of an angel!'

Any pleasure Madeleine might have felt over such an analogy was swiftly dispelled by the reply that followed.

'Angel! Her looks could not be more deceiving. She was de Maupilier's whore! God only knows why de Regnay of all people should marry her.' The man chuckled, then coarsely added, 'She must have attributes that are not visible. According to gossip she was pleasuring the old man up until the day he died. Too much for his heart, I daresay!' Then both men laughed.

Madeleine felt the colour drain from her face. She was so humiliated that she wanted to run and hide. She glanced frantically around looking for Luc and, turning, almost bumped into him.

'I want to go home,' she said.

'No.' His expression was thunderous and she realised that he too had heard what had been said. 'You are my Comtesse. You will not run away!'

Apprehensively, Madeleine glanced towards the speaker. 'Who was it?'

'De Brunnière,' he replied tightly. 'He was an acquaintance of Philippe's whom I never did like. I would call him out, but I think it unwise. He has no influence here, Madeleine. Little credence will be given to what he says, particularly with Edith standing our friend.'

All the time he was speaking to her he had hold of her arm as if he was afraid she would bolt.

'You can let me go,' she told him. 'I am not going to run away.'

He nodded and glancing over her shoulder, smiled tightly. 'Young Wrayford is returning. Drink your lemonade and let him have another dance. Forget de Brunnière. He is of no account!'

Madeleine did as he commanded, dancing again with Sir Daniel and then letting him lead her in for refreshments. After that she danced with him again and then with Luc's friend, Comte de Puisaye. Finally Luc came to claim her hand.

'You're looking pale,' he commented.

'I have a headache.' It was an outright lie. She just felt totally sickened by what she had heard.

'I'll take you home. We can go now without causing comment.'

'You can stay if you wish,' she told him.

He shook his head, looking genuinely concerned. 'No, I'll come with you. I have completed my business here.'

Slipping his arm around her, he guided her towards the door. 'If you get your cloak I'll make our farewells.'

They were both quiet on the way home, neither of them referring to de Brunnière's vile comments. When they arrived at Curzon Street, Luc walked Madeleine to her bedroom door then kissed her briefly on the cheek.

'If you have a headache, I won't bother you tonight,' he said, turning and heading for his own room.

It was all she could do not to call after him. More than anything, she wanted the comfort of lying in his arms. Unfortunately she was not sure enough of his regard to ask it of him. Miserably she wondered what chance their marriage could have of success when he was so insensitive to her need of him. She had never felt more lonely or unloved in her life.

For the next few days life followed its usual pattern. Luc was out a great deal. Madeleine had little chance to talk to him, although he did confide one morning over breakfast that a truce was to be signed in Brittany.

'But that's wonderful!' she exclaimed. 'Now you will not need English help.'

'The fighting is not over,' he answered sharply, sobering her. 'The Republicans offered little. Many of our people will sign but simply for the respite. Once the spring planting is over they will take up arms again. Georges, however, says he will not put his name to the treaty.'

'You will not sign, then?'

He shook his head. 'I will not put my name to something I have no intention of keeping. In any case, the authorities have lost track of me and I am certainly not going to bring myself to their attention.'

Madeleine felt bitterly disappointed. Peace could mean amnesty and guarantee his continuing safety. 'Perhaps you should consider signing,' she said.

'You know nothing of it!' he snapped, rising from the table, intending to go upstairs. At the door, he paused. Without turning to look at her, he made an awkward apology. 'I'm sorry, Maddie. At the moment I have a lot on my mind.'

Later that day she discovered just what that was. She had just finished her afternoon tea and Bates had collected the tray, when Sir Daniel Wrayford came to call. Luc was at White's and she was glancing idly through some fashion plates.

'I have come to offer you my support,' he blurted as soon as he had been shown into the room. 'I do not know how your husband can be so careless of your feelings.'

'I do not understand you,' Madeleine answered calmly, gesturing for him to sit down.

'It is all over town!' he exclaimed, settling beside her on the sofa. 'Your husband is to fight a duel over the honour of Lady Edith Roseberry. People are saying that they are lovers!'

Madeleine's stomach sank and for a moment she felt quite sick. Drawing on all her pride and self-possession, she determined to act as a comtesse should, supporting her husband in public no matter what she thought of him.

'Then they lie,' she replied calmly. 'Lady Edith is merely an old friend; indeed, she is close to both my husband and myself.' She forced a laugh. 'In any case, my husband is too busy at the moment to have time for a mistress!'

'He would have served you better by ignoring the insult to her,' Sir Daniel continued with a pitying look, reaching for her hand.

'Oh, I daresay, but Luc is always loyal to his friends.'

When the young man protested at her tolerance, she brushed it aside. 'You may tell those who will listen that I applaud my husband's actions!'

'Oh, dear lady, you are too good, too kind!' Still holding her hand, Sir Daniel slid to his knees in front of her. 'I am your devoted servant. I know you can never return my love but you can always rely on my support, my utmost support!'

'You are making an ass of yourself, Wrayford.' Luc spoke coldly from just inside the door. 'Get up before I decide to put my boot to your backside!'

How long he had been there and how much he had heard, Madeleine could not tell. He had not raised his voice and his expression remained unreadable but the glow in his dark eyes revealed his anger.

The young Englishman scurried to his feet. He swallowed hard. 'If. . .if. . .you want satisfaction, de Regnay, I am willing to give it.'

Luc's jaw tightened as he tossed his gloves and cane upon the side-table. 'Don't be ridiculous! Now get out so that I can talk to my wife!'

Wrayford turned back to Madeleine. 'Your servant, ma'am.' Then he left with almost comical alacrity.

'You should not encourage him,' Luc grated.

'You are a fine one to talk!'

He, of all people, had no right to criticise her, not after what she had just heard. He was to fight a duel, and on Edith's behalf! Not surprisingly, she found herself torn between anger and anxiety. Whoever Luc's opponent was, he was unlikely to choose swords, so Luc's expertise would count for naught. Pistols were notoriously unreliable and he could quite easily be killed.

Dieu! How could he be so foolish? How could he be so crass, flaunting his affair before everyone? How could he hurt and humiliate her so? He had not thought it wise to challenge de Brunnière over her honour, yet when someone had made uncharitable remarks about Edith, had been only too eager to leap to her defence.

'Ah,' Luc said with a sigh as he poured himself a brandy, 'You have heard about the duel, then.' His air of long-suffering superiority made her long to slap him.

'It is no great thing. It happens all the time.'

'Word has it you are fighting to preserve Lady Edith's good name.'

His face settled into a stony mask. 'Among other things.'

Madeleine began to feel her temper rising and was glad of it, for it blotted out the pain. Did he think her a complete fool? 'It is all over town, Luc. They say she is your mistress!'

'What they say or think does not matter,' he replied tightly. 'There is no need to concern yourself about it.'

'Not concern myself!'

There was an edge to his voice as he continued, 'Whatever, the duel will go ahead. I would not withdraw now, even if I could do so with my honour intact.'

'But by fighting it you are admitting to everyone that she is your mistress!'

Luc set his empty glass down upon the side-table with a force that made it crack. 'She is my good friend and I will let no man insult her!'

'Even if it means making a fool out of me?'

'You will not be made to look a fool,' he snapped, 'not in the eyes of those who matter, anyway.'

Madeleine felt herself trembling. Weeks of neglect had taken their toll and she was angry and upset. She had to know for sure, had to ask him outright. 'Is she your mistress, Luc? Can you deny it?'

Luc's temper, too, was boiling. He was tired after too many late nights and he did not appreciate being questioned and judged.

'*Dieu!*' he grated. 'I will not deny it! I will not justify myself to you! If I take a mistress, then it is my own business. A well-bred wife does not question her husband on such a matter!'

It was tantamount to a confession. She had suspected it but oh, how she had hoped that she was wrong. The aching hurt expanded inside her, fuelling her anger. 'If you fight this duel, then I shall not be around to hear about it. I shall return to France!'

'An ultimatum, Madeleine?' he sneered. 'Well, I shall not beg you to stay. You were the one who wanted to come with me, remember?'

His words caused her stomach to turn over. Obviously he did not care what she thought, what she did; he did not care about her! In fact he would rather have her out of the way so that he could pursue his relationship with Edith.

'I shall leave for France in the morning,' she said, wanting more than anything for him to argue the point, for him to swear that Edith meant nothing to him and beg her to stay.

'You will have to put off your departure until there is a suitable ship,' he said coldly. 'I will arrange it for you.'

'There is no need. . .' Madeleine began, but he sharply silenced her.

'You are still my wife!' he snapped. 'I will make sure you are escorted safely home.' A muscle tensed in his jaw; then he added, 'It is probably for the best. I know now that I should never have brought you with me.'

Two days later Madeleine and Lisette set out in a hired coach for Dover, there being no suitable vessel sailing from Tilbury until the following week. They were accompanied by an aged Breton noble, a supposed friend of de Puisaye's, who had agreed to accompany Madeleine all the way home. Luc was not there to say goodbye; he had already left for Hampstead Heath where he was to take part in the duel.

Madeleine felt miserable and, much as she tried to suppress it, dreadfully worried about him. She had to force herself to get into the coach and, at the last minute, nearly blurted out that she would stay. Luc had made all the arrangements, however, and couldn't have more clearly said that he wanted her gone.

In the middle of the morning, she ordered the coach to turn back. If Luc wished it then she would still return to France but not until she had satisfied herself that he was unharmed.

It was past luncheon by the time Luc returned to Curzon Street. He was tired and sickened by what he had done. His opponent was dead, shot through the heart, but he felt not the slightest satisfaction. In fact, he felt empty and more than a little guilty. As Bates helped him off with his cloak his eye was drawn to the tear in his jacket sleeve. The pistol ball had come close, very close.

Bates tut-tutted at the damage, and after rather sharply telling him that it was of no consequence, Luc went into the drawing-room to pour himself a drink. With his glass more than half filled with brandy, he flopped down in the chair. He had known Madeleine would be gone when he returned, but the reality still hurt and angered him. Contrary to opinion, he had not resumed his affair with Edith although he had deliberately fostered the misconception. He had his reasons and could have explained them to Madeleine but he was not used to justifying himself and, moreover, didn't feel he should have to.

He swirled the brandy around in his glass and smiled sardonically. As usual, she had been too quick to judge and condemn him. He should never have married her; a woman of his own class would have been far more understanding. By the time Lady Edith arrived he was more than a little drunk. Even so he managed to stand and execute a courtier's bow. This was sufficiently unusual to betray him.

'You're foxed, Luc,' she accused.

'Abominably so. . . Won't you join me?'

'Your wretched countryman is dead, I hear. I hope you are not drowning your sorrows on his account.'

'No,' he replied.

Edith frowned. 'Where is Madeleine?'

'Boarding ship about now,' he replied. Then, with a bitter smile, added, 'She took exception to the duel—more accurately, she took exception to what the duel was about. She thinks you're my mistress.'

'It is all over town, Luc.' She shrugged. 'I do not mind.

I am used to being gossiped about, but I can understand how Madeleine must have felt.'

When he got up to pour yet another brandy, she moved forward to stay his hand. More than anything, she would have liked the gossip to be true. She had been a little puzzled by Luc's readiness to challenge the Frenchman on her behalf, but it had flattered her none the less and given her some encouragement.

'You've had enough, you know,' she said gently, laying her palm against his cheek. 'Ah, Luc, I would do anything to ease your pain.'

Her eyes were very blue, full of warmth and desire. Her face was lifted expectantly, and setting his glass down upon the table, Luc took her into his arms. She was soft and scented and he was inordinately fond of her. Why, he asked himself, should he concern himself with a wife who thought so little of him, a wife who obviously didn't care whether he lived or died? Men in his position had always taken mistresses.

Dipping his head, he kissed her hard. He put his heart and soul into the kiss, silently praying that he would feel the same aching excitement that he did when he took Madeleine in his arms. The result was disappointing but he did not give up, pressing on with renewed intensity. It was only when he at last lifted his head that he caught sight of Madeleine, standing like a statue in the door-way. His first reaction was one of pleasure at her return, but that swiftly abated as he became aware of her anger and his own compromising situation.

'Madeleine,' he began, 'It's not—'

'I came back to make sure you were all right,' she grated, her face mirroring her anger and hurt.

'Obviously you are!' Turning, she walked quickly from the room, her head held high.

'Madeleine!' he snarled, hurrying to the front door. 'Madeleine, wait, damn you!'

He caught up with her as she reached the roadway and placed a restraining hand on her arm.

'Let me go!' she snapped, her temper rising. 'I find you totally loathsome! Oh, how I wish I had never married you!'

He released her then, as if her flesh burned him, and his expression turned from anger to stone.

'I see,' he said when he did not see at all. 'Run back to Kercholin, then, but if you do, I shall not follow you there. I have other matters to occupy my time.'

'Like Lady Edith?'

'Your origins are showing, my dear,' he sneered, 'when you become so put out by a kiss.'

His demeanour and bearing reminded Madeleine of the time he had propositioned her. He was just as insensitive, just as arrogant, every inch the inflexible and self-centred aristo who did not perceive what he had done wrong. He did not care about her. To him she was nothing more than an object to warm his bed and lately, he had not even wanted that from her. He did not seem to feel he owed her fidelity or consideration. He thought he had a right to take a mistress!

'Sometimes,' she grated, 'I think the Jacobins had the right of it!' Then she was gone, into the coach and away before he could react to her final words.

When Luc went back inside his face was as white as chalk. He wanted to strike something and only Edith's presence prevented him from smashing his fist into the wall. It was an urge he had never experienced before.

Furiously, he wondered why Madeleine was capable of doing that to him. She was the one woman who made him lose the detachment he had always possessed.

'Will you go after her?' Edith asked and he shook his head. He would not pursue a woman who thought so little of him, a woman who had always questioned his motives and his honour. She could rot at Kercholin for all he cared. He was well rid of her and her ability to tie his emotions in knots.

Edith frowned and, going across to him, ran her hand soothingly down his arm. 'Come down to Oxfordshire with me this weekend, Luc,' she coaxed. 'I am staying with some friends...William Windham will be there.' When he did not answer at once she added, 'I could even arrange an invitation for your friend de Puisaye.'

Windham was the Secretary for War and a chance to meet him socially was too good to miss. When Luc agreed, Edith could not prevent a smile of satisfaction. He was hurt and angry but in a few days he would be ready to accept the comfort she intended to offer.

CHAPTER TWELVE

MADELEINE reined in her little mare and gazed out
across the budding countryside. The spring sun was
warm on her back and a soft breeze tousled her hair. It
was a beautiful day yet her spirits remained low. Since
returning to Kercholin she had received no word from
Luc. He had not written or tried to contact her in any
way. She should not have felt so hurt or surprised. He
had married her to bed her and she had always known
the novelty of that would pall.

Many wives turned a blind eye to their husband's
affairs but she knew she could not be like that. She'd
had enough of living on crumbs of affection, of trying to
make him love her, and her pride was in danger of being
damaged beyond repair. She tried to convince herself
that she no longer wanted him, yet images of him with
Edith intruded on her sleep and she felt sick with
jealousy.

On more than one occasion, she had considered
returning to the farm. Kercholin was now Luc's and she
did not want to be there if he returned. She had not yet
confided in her aunt, however, and dreaded having to do
so.

Kicking her horse into a canter, she determined to
shake her mood of bitter melancholy. She arrived back
home in the middle of the afternoon and was surprised
to find Thierry waiting for her. She was delighted to see
him but could tell at once that something was wrong.

'It's Janine,' he confided when Madeleine asked him what the trouble was. 'Her mother died last month and she is taking it badly. Coming on top of what happened to her father, it has been more than she can bear. . .and she's pregnant.'

'I'm sorry about her mother,' Madeleine told him, 'but surely a child will take her mind off her grief?'

'Perhaps.' He went on to explain that Janine's pregnancy was causing her dreadful sickness. Her spirits were low and she had become so weak that he disliked leaving her in order to fish. 'But I have to,' he continued. 'It's our living. If you could visit us, even for a short while, then it would be such a help. I know Luc is away just now so it will not matter to him, and I really am desperate.'

Of course Madeleine agreed. In fact, she was glad to have something to take her mind off her own misery. When she told him that she would go with him the following day, he hugged her and told her she was the best sister any man could have.

They set out the following morning in the wagon Thierry had hired. Lisette accompanied them as far as Vannes and her parents' home. She would have liked to continue on with her mistress but Madeleine knew there would be no room for her at Thierry's. Moreover, she would have felt totally out of place there with a maid.

In spite of the small inconveniences, Madeleine found that she liked it on the peninsula. Her brother's cottage was simple and the work she did hard, but it felt good to be useful. Gradually Janine's sickness eased. She began to put on weight and became more cheerful and optimistic. Sometimes Thierry took his boat out at night and sometimes in the daytime, depending on the tides. It was demanding work but, as his wife's health began to improve, the lines of tiredness and strain disappeared from his face. It was not long before Madeleine came to realise that she was staying on more to please herself than because she was still needed.

A few days after Midsummer's Eve, the English fleet was seen cruising off Port-Haliguen. The following day, Thierry returned with the unsettling news that a large landing of *émigré* troops and arms had been made at Légenès, close by on the mainland. The *émigrés*, supported by a contingent of British marines, were joined by a thousand *chouans* under the command of Georges Cadoudal, and when the Republicans advanced against them, some heavy fighting occurred.

Madeleine immediately thought of Luc. He and de Puisaye had obviously been successful in England and she wondered if he had been able to tear himself away from Edith in order to take part in the venture. Surprisingly, she hoped he had not. It was more comfortable to think him safe in England. She knew that if Cadoudal was present then so was her brother Reynard and she worried about him as she listened to the sound of the guns rumbling across the sea, like thunder above thick cloud.

On the fourth of July, a further landing took place at the southern end of the peninsula itself. Red-coated *émigrés* were seen tramping across the woods and fields, converging on Fort Penthièvre where they easily ousted the Republican garrison there. On the mainland, however, their army had no such success. The Republicans, commanded by the brilliant General

Lazare Hoche, moved against them in force and, in spite of their attempts to counter-attack, managed to push them back to their original landing place.

In the dead of night, the retreating Royalists crossed the mudflats to Pen-er-Le and were reported retreating along the peninsula to join their compatriots at the fort. A fisherman who had witnessed this was astounded by the number of civilians in their ranks, peasants of the area with their families, animals and wagons, all heading for the small fort.

'Do you think Reynard will be there?' Madeleine asked when Thierry brought them the news. She did not mention Luc, although thoughts of him had again come into her mind.

'I'll tell you what, Maddie, we'll both walk over there this afternoon after I've had a rest,' Thierry suggested. 'I've no wish to get involved in the conflict myself, but if Reynard is there we can take him some baked fish and some of Janine's bread. There has been no gunfire for quite some time. I think it will be safe enough to go over, at least for a while.'

It was really hot by the time they set out. The sun beat down from a cloudless sky and there was no breeze at all to cool them. It was a walk of about an hour to the fort which was situated halfway down the peninsula at the southern end of a narrow isthmus. It had been built on a rocky outcrop on the western side but, because the isthmus was so narrow, completely commanded the landward approach to the southern end of the peninsula.

From the direction Thierry and Madeleine were taking, the land sloped gently up towards the fort and, even from a distance, they could see the moving collage of men, horses, wagons and camp followers that had gathered around it. Slowly they threaded their way between the motley assortment of people. Most of them looked tired and there were several who had been wounded. Nearer the fort, a group of green-coated *chouans* was making camp in a hollow. Approaching them, Thierry asked for Reynard.

'A big bearded fellow, is he?' a young soldier asked, and when Madeleine nodded, gestured towards the mainland. 'He's down there, I think, helping to dig out our guns.'

They followed the hill around then climbed down on to the isthmus. On their left, a sandy beach curved away from the rocky base of the fort in a golden swathe, whilst to their right, the coast was more rugged and white topped waves tumbled on to dark-coloured pebbles.

About two hundred metres along from the fort, a heavy cannon appeared to be bogged down in the sandy road. They recognised Reynard immediately; he stood a head taller than the men around him. As they watched, he lowered his shoulder to one of the wheels and pushed with all of his considerable strength. Slowly the cannon began to inch forward. The horses strained against the harness and then, as the wheels hit firmer ground, it moved freely. The impetus of his push carried Reynard to his knees and his curses made Madeleine's ears burn.

Thierry grinned. 'Your language has not improved, brother.'

Reynard looked up from dusting off the knees of his breeches. His coarse shirt was damp with sweat and open to the waist, revealing a chest that was almost as hirsute as his jaw. He looked formidable indeed.

'What are you two doing here?' he asked, not sounding best pleased.

'We thought you might be with the army and came to see if you were all right,' Thierry said brightly. 'We brought some fresh bread.'

More astute than he, Madeleine asked, 'Aren't you pleased to see us?'

'Of course I am.' He did not sound convincing. Gesturing about him, he added, 'It's just that this whole business is such a mess. We are in retreat, you know.' Taking the basket from Madeleine, he hugged her and sheepishly offered his thanks.

'What happened?' Thierry asked.

Reynard made a sound of disgust. 'The powers that be could not agree on who should command. Whilst they squabbled, the Republicans moved against us. We only escaped by crossing to the peninsula at low tide. George, Luc and I were among those acting as rear-guard.' He smiled wryly. 'We almost got our tails wet!'

Madeleine's stomach contracted painfully. So Luc was there; deep down she had known it.

Reynard frowned at her. 'I do not understand what is happening between you and Luc. He has not discussed matters with me, but I know he has not been home. The two of you should talk. Now is not the time to be holding grudges.' When she did not reply, he added, 'He's a good man, Maddie. We have fought side by side and I have never found him wanting.'

'Being a good soldier does not necessarily make him a good husband,' she replied. 'I am not sure I want to see him.'

As it was she was not given the choice. When she looked up, the man that she saw riding purposely towards them was heartrendingly familiar.

'What the devil are you doing here, Maddie?' Luc

grated as he pulled his horse to a halt beside them. He
was no more pleased to see her than Reynard and took
even less trouble to conceal it.

'I am staying at Thierry's,' she replied, although she
did not feel she owed him any explanation. Anxious that
he should not think she was chasing after him, she
added, 'I did not expect you to be here. I thought you
would still be in England.'

A muscle tensed in his jaw as he stared coldly down at
her. She was dressed like the other peasant women,
even down to the lace cap, and she knew it would
displease him. Soon after his return from the Vendée he
had asked her not to wear black and she had been
willing enough to comply. Living with Thierry, however,
she would have felt out of place wearing anything else.

'You're looking better than you did in London,' Luc
commented. Madeleine could not say the same for him
and she hated the concern she felt. His face looked grey
with fatigue and he was badly in need of a shave. His
green uniform coat was covered in dust and there was a
small tear in one sleeve. When he dismounted there was
a stiffness to his movements that denoted a man who
had spent too long in the saddle. Madeleine felt a
quickening inside herself accompanied by a deep aching
yearning. Even now, after the wretched way he had
treated her, she could not help responding to him.

'That was the last of the stranded guns,' he told
Reynard. 'We couldn't shift the one near the forest so
we had to spike it.' Turning to Thierry, he added, 'We've
been digging them out since late yesterday. The ground
is too soft, more sandy than we expected.'

He took a deep breath then touched Madeleine on
the shoulder. The contact was brief, no more than a

second, but his fingers seemed to burn through the thin fabric of her dress. 'You should not be here,' he said tightly, 'but now that you are, there are things we need to discuss. Walk with me for a while.'

It was an order rather than a request but she did not feel she could refuse him, not without appearing unreasonable. There was no warmth in his voice or his expression—in fact, he was like a glacial stranger, as if he had never shared her bed.

When she reluctantly agreed, he handed Reynard his horse and led the way down from the rough road and on to the wide, sandy beach. The track was a little rough, but he did not touch her or aid her in any way although he waited politely for her at the bottom. With a sigh he removed his green jacket and slung it across his shoulder. His shirt was damp and clung to his broad shoulders and well-shaped back like a second skin.

Together, they made their way back towards the fort, Luc walking beside her but being careful not to get too close. After a while, Madeleine stopped to remove her sabots.

Luc dragged his eyes away from her ankles and, glancing over his shoulder towards the mainland, commented, 'Hoche is up there somewhere, probably at Sainte-Barbe. It won't be long before he moves against us.'

'Will there be more fighting?'

'Yes.'

To Madeleine, it seemed hard to believe. The scene was so beautiful and, apart from the men clustered around the fort, incredibly peaceful. They were the only two people on that stretch of beach. For once there was a lack of seagulls and even the sea was calm, very blue and shining like cut glass.

Anxiously she studied the fort. It looked reassuringly square and solid, as though it had grown up from the rocky cliff it sat upon. The cliff was exposed now because it was low tide and the smooth, golden sand led right up to its base. In fact, she could see some soldiers sitting on the rocks that formed its lower reaches. She suppressed the urge to tell him to take care.

'You were obviously successful in England,' she said after a while.

He gave a funny little laugh. 'Oh, yes. I only hope it has not been for naught.'

It was the first sign of emotion in him. He sounded tired, depressed, perhaps even a little bitter. Madeleine's heart went out to him. If the Royalists failed, then she knew it would not be from lack of effort on his part. She bit her lip to hold back words of sympathy, knowing he would not welcome them from her. She could not bear that they had come to this. They had been so much closer when they had only been friends.

'How is Edith?' she asked after a moment, hoping anger would help to wash away the hurt.

'She was well enough when I left her.' She thought he was going to say something more. Instead, he turned to stare out across the bright water, hiding his face from her. 'Did you get my letter?'

Madeleine shook her head. 'I've been with Thierry for several weeks now.'

'I've deposited a large amount of money in your name. The details are in the letter I sent to Kercholin.'

When she began to protest, he held up his hand to silence her. 'I can afford it and if you don't take it, then I shall only end up spending it on the war. I've also signed

Kercholin over to you. It was yours morally; now it is by right. Our marriage may have been a mistake but I do not want you to suffer for it.'

He was buying her off, she realised, making sure she was comfortable so that he could do as he pleased. Why could he not see that the only thing she wanted from him was his love?

· 'Money is not the answer to everything,' she told him, more sharply than she intended. 'I have enough for my needs. I do not want yours.'

'*Dieu*, Madeleine!' he growled in quiet exasperation. 'However you feel about me, you are my wife and I have a duty to take care of you whether we live under the same roof or not!'

Tears sprang to her eyes. He made her sound like a maiden aunt, an impoverished dependant. He may not love her and had tired of having her in his bed, but his pride would demand that he looked after her. He was treating her as he would his horse or his dog. She had never meant any more to him than that.

'I don't want your money,' she snapped. 'I am not even sure I want Kercholin.'

Suddenly she found that she could no longer cope with the conversation. Emotion was bubbling up in her, threatening to choke her, and she did not want him to see how upset she was. Their marriage was over, in fact if not in law, and she could almost hate him for it. There would be no other husband for her, no children. Eventually they might be able to divorce but to her family, to her friends and neighbours, she would always be married to Luc.

Turning away from him, she began walking briskly back towards the road. She knew that he was following her but she did not look back. When he reached out a hand to steady her as she climbed back up the bank, she dragged her arm away from him as if he had something unpleasant and contagious. Reaching the road, she glanced around for her brothers. They were some distance away, back where she and Luc had begun their walk.

Behind her, Luc swore with a ferocity that made her turn. When she did, she was surprised to find his attention centred not on her but on a group of nearby *chouans*. Georges Cadoudal was standing like a colossus in their midst, arguing hotly with a smaller man who appeared to be wearing rather a lot of gold braid.

'It's D'Hervilly,' Luc explained tersely. 'Most of our problems stem from his insistence on command. He refuses to accept orders from de Puisaye until he has had confirmation from England. I shall have to go and mediate; it's what I've been assigned to do.'

He took a couple of steps away from her then, all of a sudden, turned back. His eyes flashed with anger and something more that was disguised before she could name it. 'Only you could condemn me for wanting to make sure that you were well taken care of,' he grated.

Then, before she could reply, he was striding away from her and crossly shouldering his way through the narrow circle of *chouans* to join the two commanders. He had actually sounded hurt, Madeleine reflected with a mixture of anger and surprise. Surely he had not expected gratitude, not after the way he had behaved?

'It is ridiculous!' she heard D'Hervilly say as he gestured irritably towards a group of civilians. 'They are hampering our work and overcrowding the fort. Get rid of them!'

'I cannot,' Cadoudal replied hotly. 'They have fled before the Republicans, forsaking their homes and farms. They have nowhere else to go and are looking to us for protection! Would you have the sea swallow them up?'

'Bah!' growled the general. 'I do not understand what kind of army you men are running. You are amateurs!'

'It was not us who wasted five days disputing over who was in command,' the big *chouan* snarled. 'In truth I am sorry that I committed my men to such a farce.'

'You committed your men to free Brittany,' Luc told him quietly. 'We may yet make a success of the venture if we work together.'

When two pairs of angry eyes turned towards him he did not flinch but calmly mediated between the two of them, deflecting D'Hervilly's accusation that he was de Puisaye's man and quietly insisting that they must put aside their personal feelings in order to do what was best for their cause.

'And does your own commitment stretch as far as leading a sortie to verify Hoche's position?' D'Hervilly demanded. 'We need someone to do just that.'

'If it is judged necessary.'

'It is, my friend,' Cadoudal told him seriously.

Luc shrugged. 'Then I am willing enough.'

The big *chouan* grinned and clasped him on the shoulder. He said something that Madeleine could not quite hear, then the three of them began walking up the hill towards the fort. Luc did not glance back and Madeleine suspected that he had already put her from his mind.

There was nothing of the courtier in him now, he was lean and tanned, every inch the rugged *chouan*. His jacket was once again slung across his shoulder and he looked unapproachable and hard. For the first time since she had journeyed with him from Paris, Madeleine found herself wondering if he was capable of the kind of love she had sought.

'Don't worry, little sister,' Reynard said, totally misinterpreting her frown. 'I will look after your husband for you.'

When she glanced questioningly at him, he added, 'For this, Luc will need his own men. We have done such work before.'

'Perhaps I do not care what happens to him,' she snapped, but she knew that she lied. His welfare would always be of concern to her and she found herself wishing with all her heart that he had not volunteered for the mission.

She was quiet on her way back to the cottage and, when Thierry questioned her about her marriage, refused to discuss it with him. That night she lay tossing and turning in her small bed. It took her an age to drop off to sleep and when she did it was only to dream, a nightmare in which she saw her husband lying dead upon the dark grass.

The following morning, she determined to return to the fort. She would get no peace, she realised, until she knew that both Luc and Reynard had returned safely from their night's work. This time she made the journey alone. Thierry was out fishing and Janine was not up to making the walk on what had turned out to be another scorching day. Again, she took bread and fish. She would not linger, she vowed, or even seek Luc out; she just needed to assure herself that both he and Reynard were safe. As soon as she approached Penthièvre it became apparent that a number of soldiers had already moved out, further along the peninsula, she supposed. The *chouans* were camped closer to the fort with their horses penned against the side of the hill. Madeleine glanced around for her brother and finally caught sight of him talking to two other men.

The moment he saw her, he stood up and began walking towards her, his face breaking into a relieved smile.

'I was hoping you would come,' he said. 'Luc made me swear not to send for you and I was close to breaking my word.'

The concern she saw in his eyes caused fear to curl like a snake in the pit of her stomach. 'He's hurt, isn't he?'

Reynard nodded. 'He took a pistol ball in the shoulder during our mission last night. The surgeon removed it earlier this morning. I doubt he will die, Maddie, but he has need of you now.'

Madeleine felt a tremendous sense of predestination as she walked with Reynard up the steep path to the fort.

'We had found out what we wanted and were on our way back when we met up with a Republican patrol,' he explained. 'There was some fierce fighting. For once, we had the best of it but Luc was hurt.'

He led her in through the tall gateway, briefly acknowledging the sentry on duty there, then turned left, towards one of the outbuildings. Inside the single-storey structure, it was dark compared to the bright sunshine outside. When her eyes became accustomed to the gloom, Madeleine saw that a number of straw pallets had been set out on the floor.

Luc was lying propped up by a pile of blankets, on the one furthest from the door. His shirt was gone, but someone had draped his tattered green coat across his shoulders. Beneath it, thick white bandages swathed his chest and left shoulder. He was dreadfully pale and his dark lashes lay in sooty semicircles against his cheeks. All the love Madeleine had tried to suppress came surging back in an overwhelming tide.

'He passed out whilst the doctor was working on him,' Reynard confided. 'We have no laudanum and he refused to drink the *eau-de-vie*.'

'He hates the stuff,' Madeleine choked, remembering the night so long ago when all the men at the farm had overindulged.

Heedless of the dirt on the floor, she knelt down beside her husband. It didn't matter what had happened between them, she couldn't walk away from him when he was like this. She smoothed back his sweat-dampened hair, then gently touched his lip where he had bitten it in his efforts to hold back the cries of pain.

It was typical of him, another example of his colossal pride, and yet at that moment it made him seem even more vulnerable.

You idiot, she thought fondly. I don't suppose anyone would have minded, had you screamed your head off.

Reynard watched her with an expression of sad satisfaction. 'I assume you'll be staying.'

She nodded. 'Can you get a message to Thierry?'

'Yes.' He smiled approvingly and patted her head where it rested across Luc's. The movement was just enough to disturb the injured man and he opened pain-

filled eyes. When he recognised Madeleine those same
eyes flashed with anger and he glared accusingly at
Reynard.

'I did not send for her. She came on her own,' the big
chouan said quietly. 'It is for the best. She can help take
care of you.'

'The devil she will!' Luc spoke with obvious effort. He
tried to sit up then fell back with a hiss of pain. 'Why the
sudden wifely. . .concern?' he demanded from between
clenched teeth. 'Yesterday you couldn't even stand for
me to touch you. I don't want. . .you. . .here!'

Madeleine tried to ignore the hurt his words caused.
He may not want her but he was not going to be given
the choice. When he was well it would be a different
matter; then she would not force herself upon him.

'I'm staying and there is nothing you can do about it,'
she told him determinedly.

A bead of perspiration trickled down his beard
roughened cheek. 'Bossy. . .' he grated, then he sighed,
obviously too ill to argue the point further. 'Stay if you
must. I can't. . .stop. . .you.'

For the rest of the day, Madeleine sat next to Luc,
occasionally bathing his face and neck and helping him
to drink. He was obviously in pain yet he made not the
slightest complaint. She ached to see him suffering and
was relieved when, towards the evening, he fell into a
feverish sleep.

Reynard turned up just as darkness was falling,
bringing blankets and a jar of cider. He stayed with her
for a while and shared the fish and some of the bread
from her basket. After he had gone, Madeleine curled
up on the floor and dozed fitfully only to be awakened
shortly after dawn by his return. Mercifully, Luc still

slept and they spoke in hushed voices so as not to disturb him.

Frowning anxiously, he watched her nibble at the remains of the bread. Finally he said, 'I've been talking to Georges, Maddie. We both think you should take Luc away from here.'

After washing down the bread with a mouthful of cider, Madeleine shook her head. 'He's too ill to be moved. Surely you can see that.'

'I think it's a matter of necessity.' He lowered his voice still further before continuing. 'Look, it's not common knowledge but we are going to mount an offensive. As part of that, George and the rest of us are leaving for the mainland as soon as it is dark. The British Admiral, Warren, is providing boats and we have some fishermen willing to help us. When D'Hervilly advances, we *chouans* are to take Hoche in the rear. I didn't mind you being here as long as I could protect you and as long as the fort was well manned. Unfortunately, that will not be the case. *Dieu*, Maddie! I do not trust the competence, even the loyalty, of those who will remain once D'Hervilly rides out. He has accepted turncoats into our ranks and men who have changed their colours once will do so again. Should his attack fail. . .' He grimaced. 'I really think you should leave. I can get hold of a wagon to take you both to Thierry's.'

Much to his exasperation, Madeleine refused to give him a answer. 'I will see what the doctor says,' she replied.

Doctor Horlage, who examined Luc later that morning was quite definite. 'If you move your husband, the wound will likely open and he will bleed to death,' he told her, and that settled the matter.

Madeleine refused to leave either with or without Luc and eventually Reynard bowed to her wishes. He was dreadfully worried though and, when he came to take his leave of her that evening, he brought her a small, loaded pistol.

Glancing at Luc, who had lapsed into something between a sleep and a swoon, he sighed resignedly. 'I doubt he will ever forgive me for allowing you to remain here.' Then he handed her the pistol. 'I hope you will not need it, my dear.'

When she wished him good luck, he smiled gently. 'You, too, little sister.'

For the next few days Madeleine had little time to think of the war as her whole attention was centred on nursing Luc who tossed feverishly. He obviously needed her and just as obviously resented the fact.

'I don't want you here,' he told her one evening when she had finished changing his bandages. 'Go back... to...Thierry's.' But his fingers closed possessively around hers; even in his sleep he did not let her go.

His words suggested one thing and his action another. His relationship with her had often been like that and Madeleine was no more able to understand the contradictions in him.

The nursing of the other men was carried out by a peasant girl, Babette, and a young priest, under the direction of the physician. As Luc began to recover, Madeleine was able to help a little with the general nursing and she was dreadfully upset when one of the wounded, a young man no older than Guy, died. Then Luc forgot to be cool and distant with her. Ignoring his own weakness, he dragged himself from his bed so that he could take her in his arms.

'I would have spared you this,' he grated against her hair. 'You really should leave here.'

She would go in an instant if only he would accompany her, but she knew better than to ask. His wound was healing and he still believed he had a part to play in the fighting.

When she glanced tearfully up at him, he sighed. 'It is for your sake that I want you gone, Maddie.'

Hope rose up inside her. For a moment he seemed so like the old Luc, the man who had protected her and cared for her during their journey from Paris.

'You should have told me that before. I was beginning to think you such an ungrateful wretch,' she told him.

He did not respond to her teasing. 'Then you will leave.'

'In a day or two,' she replied.

On the 16th July, in the early hours of the morning, D'Hervilly and the other generals—including the young *émigré* de Sombreuil who had arrived from the Elbe only the day before—led their men out to engage the Republicans controlling the landward entry to the peninsula. From the fort they could hear the sounds of the guns spitting out death and destruction, Frenchman against Frenchman, peasant against peasant. Madeleine was swamped by the futility of it all and could almost have hated Luc for helping to bring it about. She could not understand how the restoration of a monarchy or the freedom of Brittany could be worth so many lives.

Dr Horlage took her up on to the ramparts. It was a fine clear morning and, glancing towards the mainland, they saw faint puffs of smoke. Madeleine watched for a while, feeling angry and impotent. She was surprised and concerned when Luc came to join her. He had pulled on his breeches and a clean shirt from his saddle bag, which he had neglected to button.

'You should not be up yet,' she immediately chastised.

'It's only for a while,' he replied tightly. 'I need to know what is going on.'

Slitting his eyes against the glare from the sea, he stared towards the mainland, his expression grim. Madeleine wondered if he was regretting the course he had chosen.

'I hope it will be worth it,' she said.

She had not meant to sound so bitter, so condemning. Luc's expression tightened. She could almost see the shutters come down behind his eyes. Over the last two days they had been drawing closer together; now, all that was undone in an instant.

'If we succeed it will.' He leant a hand against the parapet to steady himself. 'If not. . .' His throat worked. 'To tell you the truth, I do not want to consider that possibility until I have to.'

By the evening, they knew that the attack had failed. For some reason the *chouans* had not taken Hoche in the rear and the attempt to break out of the peninsula had turned into a rout. D'Hervilly had been seriously wounded and was later taken on board an English ship. Over all, the Royalists had lost more than fifteen hundred men. The survivors returned to the peninsula and a sanctuary they knew would only be temporary.

Against Madeleine's protestations and the over-worked doctor's advice, Luc refused to return to his bed. He was fit enough to carry out duties around the fort, he declared, and there were others in greater need of nursing than he.

For the next two days Madeleine hardly saw him as she helped to care for the influx of wounded and dispirited men. She knew he was busy helping to prepare the defence of the fort and she worried because he was doing too much too soon.

Their situation was dangerous, she realised; de Puisaye and de Sombreuil had led their men further south along the peninsula, leaving Penthièvre as their first line of defence. Luc's pleas for her to leave became more vehement and still she refused. She would leave before the fighting, she promised, but not until it was imminent. She said it was because she was needed but, in reality, it was because she wanted to spend as much time as possible with him. She had still not forgotten or completely forgiven him for what had happened in London, but with life so precarious, it didn't seem to matter anymore. She loved him desperately and was so afraid for him, knowing that, if the fort fell, then those remaining within its ramparts were destined to become either prisoners or corpses.

CHAPTER THIRTEEN

WHEN Luc came to the makeshift hospital on the
evening of the 20th July, his face was grey with fatigue
and Madeleine knew that determination alone was
keeping him on his feet. His expression revealed nothing
of what he was thinking as he rested his uninjured
shoulder against the doorway and watched her bandag-
ing a young man's leg. His green jacket was undone and
so were the top two buttons of his shirt. When he
regarded her with eyes made smokey by tiredness, her
heart gave a strange little lurch. With his jaw covered in
stubble and his hair dishevelled, he looked just like he
had the times he had woken up in her bed.

'You ought to rest, Luc,' she said, tying the two ends
of the bandage together and drawing the cover over the
young man. 'You look terrible.'

'You're a fine one to talk.' He pushed himself away
from the doorway with obvious effort. 'You have been
in here for hours.'

'I'm not the one who was shot,' she replied, walking
up to him and laying the back of her hand against his
cheek. His skin felt cool, thank goodness, in spite of the
sheen of perspiration she could see on his face.

Luc smiled tiredly and glanced over to where the
young doctor was tending another soldier. 'I am taking
my wife to my quarters to rest,' he told him. 'She has
done quite enough for today.'

When Madeleine opened her mouth to protest at his

high-handedness, he knew exactly how to silence her. 'I won't rest if you don't, Maddie.'

It was blackmail, of course, and he was quite aware of it, but she couldn't find it in her heart to be angry with him. He looked so tired that she would have agreed to anything in order to persuade him to lie down. Consequently, she allowed him to take her arm and lead her across the courtyard and into the main part of the fort. He opened a door on the ground floor and gestured for her to enter. It was a small, spartan chamber containing a chair and a single, narrow bed. Madeleine wondered what he expected of her.

'We both need to sleep,' he said flatly, reading her mind with disconcerting accuracy. 'If you prefer it, I will stretch out on the floor.'

Madeleine glanced at the dirt floor. It looked hard and uncomfortable, no place for a man with a sore shoulder, and besides, she wanted to be close to Luc. She had seen him struggle valiantly against his weakness, forcing his battered body to obey him and making not the slightest complaint, and her heart had nearly burst with love for him.

'There is no need for that. We can share the bed,' she said, slipping off her sabots and settling down on top of the blankets. It was too hot for covers and had been all day, a heavy, oppressive heat that heralded a thunderstorm.

Luc nodded. He seemed to relax a little although he did not smile. After removing his jacket, he sat down on the edge of the bed and for a moment rested his head in his hands. Madeleine resisted the urge to wrap her arms around him.

'Luc?' she queried instead.

'Mmm. . .?'

'Are you all right?'

'Yes,' he replied, but when he bent to remove his boots he gave a grunt of pain.

'Let me,' she said, getting up from the bed to help him. 'You will only hurt your shoulder.'

With the boots removed, she found herself kneeling between his thighs. She looked up into his eyes then wished she had not; the misery she saw momentarily revealed in their dark depths was like a knife turning inside her.

At once he tried to hide it, smiling gently as he ran a finger along the delicate line of her jaw. 'You know I won't force myself on you, don't you?'

'Yes.'

'But I need to kiss you. I need that much. . .'

Then, dipping his head, he kissed her with a soft persuasiveness that made her head swim. Madeleine felt the same old hunger, so deep it seemed to eat into her very soul, a hunger she knew she would only ever feel for him. She had not thought she was ready to make love with him, to completely forgive him for the way he had treated her, yet at that moment she could not have refused him, not after she had seen such pain in his eyes.

His hopes for a return of the monarchy lay in ashes and she felt such a need to make up for it. Moreover, in a matter of days, even hours, she knew he could be dead. England seemed far away and what had happened there almost irrelevant, as if it had happened to two different people. When she had left Luc, she had been so hurt and angry, had felt so betrayed. It seemed impossible, now, that she had come so close to hating him.

'Ah, Maddie, what time we have wasted,' he whispered, resting his forehead against hers in a gesture that combined a deep, soul-wrenching weariness with an element of capitulation. 'I never thought pride a vice but now I know that it is.' He gave a funny little laugh. 'It is true what the English say about it.'

Madeleine did not fully comprehend his words but she sensed a humility in him that she had not known before and she could not bear it. Then it was she who lifted herself and laid her mouth against his, entwining her arms around his neck. She felt him stiffen in surprise, then he was kissing her back in a way that only he could do. Her world was bounded by his touch, his taste, and her reason peeled away, layer by layer, until she was guided by senses alone. Her hands glided over his shoulders and she felt the tense, hard muscles there, felt the warmth and life in him.

Drawing her more comfortably against him, he lay back with her on the bed. The movement hurt his shoulder but he did not care. He had been aching to hold her, to bury himself in her softness and forget the horror closing in upon them. With one part of his mind he knew that passion alone could not set matters right between them, that they really should talk, but he needed her. Oh, how he needed her!

'Ah, Maddie.' Her name was a smothered whisper as a wave of emotion struck him, more intense than simple passion, softer than lust.

Almost reverently, his hands explored the contours of her body, caressing her, exciting her, releasing buttons and slipping inside her clothes to slide over her satin-soft skin. They released the silken curtain of her hair from its confining pins so that he could bury his face in it and smell the sunlight that even the stench of the hospital could not erase.

He had intended to be gentle but, laying her palm against his cheek, she turned his face to slant his mouth and kiss him more deeply. With surprise, he realised that she did not want gentleness, that she wanted to lose herself in their lovemaking just as much as he.

Madeleine throbbed with the passion of too many neglected days and nights. She thought of Edith and wanted more from Luc than he could have given the Englishwoman, more than he had given all the other women in his life before he had married her. She fed his demands with demands of her own, fuelling his passion and, against his intentions, sending him spiralling out of control.

'Damn you, Madeleine!' he grated from between clenched teeth, the moment before he took her. 'It has nearly killed me to stay away from you!'

For an instant she wondered about his words and then she ceased to think at all, giving herself up to sensation and the all-consuming love she felt for him.

She must have dozed because she awakened to feel Luc's hand softly caressing her, across her back and down her loosened hair. It was a strange contrast to their almost violent coupling, a gesture not intended to arouse further passion but to sooth and comfort her. When he was as gentle as that, she could almost believe that he loved her, almost, but she needed those simple words. If he would only say them and mean them, then she could forgive him anything. But he did not say them and a familiar sense of disappointment pierced her euphoria.

'Tomorrow you must go back to Thierry's,' he told

her, his voice husky with sleep. 'You have been here too long already. Hoche is bound to attack and I don't want you here when he does. I want you to promise me that you will leave, and at first light.'

'Perhaps.'

'Promise me!' he insisted, using the last of his strength to prop himself up and stare down at her. '*Dieu*, Madeleine! You have done quite enough to help. I want your word.'

'And if I refuse to give it?'

'Then at first light I will personally drag you back to Thierry's.'

He sounded determined and, although she could not see him clearly in the fading light, she knew the expression that would be on his face. He was the Comte again, the aristo who would brook no disobedience. It was oddly comforting.

'Very well, tomorrow I will leave.'

Settling back down, he pulled her against him again and his breath gusted out in a sigh. He slept then, a sleep of exhaustion, and Madeleine knew she would never be able to waken him. His right arm was draped across her and his pale face was turned into the hollow of her neck. Beneath her cheek, she could hear the steady beating of his heart. Staring up at the rough plaster ceiling, she tried to make sense of what was happening between them.

In that moment of intense passion, Luc had revealed more of himself than he had ever done and it had given her much food for thought. There were still questions to answer, grievances to salve, but she sensed that they were closer than at any time since they had married. A soft smile curved her lips. She had been wrong to think he no longer wanted her; in fact, the passion between them had been even greater than before.

But you want more than passion, she reminded herself, more than his kind concern. You want his fidelity and his heart.

Overhead, a crack of thunder split the air, making her start.

Instinctively, Luc's arm tightened around her. Although she knew it was only an illusion, she felt more cherished and secure than she had in her entire life. She settled back down and wished with all her heart that she could encapsulate that moment, prolong it and lock it away so that, for them, the dawn would never come. It was her last coherent thought before she too drifted off to sleep.

They slept more deeply than either of them had for months, wrapped comfortingly in each other's arms. They did not hear the thunder as it raged with unusual ferocity or see the lightning that lit the cell-like room. As innocently as two children they slept whilst, the storm over, the Republicans slowly advanced.

In three columns the blue coated figures marched through the darkness, the one in the centre commanded by the brilliant General Lazare Hoche. With him were two commissioners of the Republic who were determined that the invaders, the cursed Royalists, should be taught a hard lesson from which others might learn.

The dawn had barely begun to chase away the shadows of night when the alert was given at the fort. The jarring sound of the tocsin jerked Luc rudely from sleep and he reached for his boots, hurriedly dragging them on. His shoulder protested but he ignored it. Beside him, Madeleine sat up, rubbing her eyes.

'It has begun,' he told her tensely as he straightened his shirt and buttoned his breeches. 'We are under attack.'

Gunfire sounded, rocking the whole building, and Madeleine fought the instinct to cover her ears. Her heart was pounding and she felt sick with apprehension, more for Luc than for herself. She watched as he pulled on his green jacket and picked up his sword. When he turned towards her, it was still too dark for her to see the expression on his face, but she knew he was torn between doing his duty and staying to protect her. With immense effort she managed to smile.

'Go,' she told him. 'I know that you have to. I am not afraid.'

It was a lie, of course, and he was quite aware of it, but he knew she would not break down. Madeleine heard him sigh. She longed to reach out to him, to plead with him not to go. More than anything she wanted him to remain with her so that he would be safe.

'Stay here,' he grated. 'If they breach the wall, it will be safer than the infirmary.'

Madeleine began to protest. If there were more wounded then the physician would need help and besides, she had no wish to be alone.

'Please!' Luc cut short her protest. 'Do this one thing for me. I'll be back as soon as I can.' He took a step towards the door then swiftly turned back to plant a brief, hard kiss on her lips. Before she could draw breath, he had gone, shutting the door firmly behind him.

The next hour seemed one of the longest in

Madeleine's life. Gunfire echoed through the fort and in the moments when it ceased she could hear the sharp crack of musket fire. There was shouting, too, and the sound of booted feet running along the passages and up the stone stairs. Madeleine had no idea what was going on and the suspense was almost unendurable.

Fighting on the ramparts, Luc had lost all sense of time. He loaded his musket, fired and reloaded, helping the small contingent keep up as rapid a fire as possible. For perhaps the first time since he had taken up arms for his king, he felt really afraid, not for himself but for his wife, and he wished with all his heart that he had been strong enough to send her away the day before.

He did not notice the beauty of the eastern sky as the sun began to rise above the ocean, nor see the shadowy figures climbing over the wall behind him. It was only at the last moment that some sixth sense caused him to turn in time to dodge the blade of a knife. Swinging the stock of his musket, he broke his assailant's jaw. The next few moments were hectic. Fighting raged around him as the intruders sought to subdue those who remained loyal. Luc drew his sword and used it to spit another Republican, then, seeing that it was hopeless, made for the stairs.

Madeleine had just decided that she could be of more use elsewhere and, regardless of Luc's instructions was going to search for him, when he came charging into the room. She knew at once that the news he brought was bad. He was dishevelled and out of breath and in his eyes she saw the shadow of defeat. Flying mortar had cut one of his cheeks and there were powder stains on the other.

'We are betrayed,' he grated. 'The enemy are inside.

Whilst we were still firing they somehow managed to climb the rocks. They have to have had help from the men on that side!'

Before Madeleine could properly assimilate the information, he had taken her hand and pulled her out into the corridor heading towards the outside door. Booted feet sounded on the stairs leading from the floor above and half a dozen Republican soldiers came into view. Three of them carried muskets and the other three, junior officers of some kind, carried swords. Luc protectively pushed Madeleine behind him and lifting his own blade, turned to face them.

Madeleine's heart was in her mouth as she watched them approach. Luc was only one man and the Republicans pressed forward eagerly, those with muskets not bothering to reload but lifting their deadly bayonets. They were certain that they could take him but they had reckoned without his skill with a sword, a skill that within seconds had become frighteningly apparent to them.

Anxious to strike the first blow, one of the Republican swordsmen lunged. With a lightning-swift movement, Luc parried, twisting his wrist and sending his opponent's blade flying before impaling him through the heart. Wrenching his sword free, he lifted his guard in time to block the thrust of a bayonet. Metal sparked against metal but Luc was the first to disengage and cut his opponent down.

The savage strokes of his sword seemed to ignite the air as he took on the other two swordsmen. A feint to the chest, a slice to the neck—Madeleine hardly saw the blow that dispatched the next man, so swiftly was it delivered. Then, with a graceful stroke that appeared featherlight in its execution, he cut another man from ear to jaw. Indeed, four of his six opponents had fallen beneath his rapacious blade before other Republicans arrived from the direction of the courtyard.

Madeleine tried to cry out a warning but before she could do so, rough hands had hold of her and she found herself pinned to the wall. Through the doorway to the courtyard she could see blue-coated figures swarming in through the main gateway. Luc backed into the doorway of the room they had occupied. He was breathing hard and blood dripped from the point of his sword.

'Hold, Royalist pig!' a Republican officer told him, resting the barrel of a pistol beneath Madeleine's chin. 'Surrender or you both will die!'

Behind him other soldiers levelled their muskets. The sun was up now, glinting off their bayonets, more than one of which was smeared with bright blood. It was the end and Luc knew it. For himself he cared little and would gladly have sacrificed his life in order to take more of his enemies with him. Madeleine's survival, however, meant more to him than revenge, more to him than the bloodcurdling rage that was keeping him on his feet.

'Lay down your sword and we will spare the woman,' the officer repeated.

The tip of Luc's sword wavered uncertainly and slowly he lowered his arm. Next moment they were upon him like a pack of wolves, beating him and knocking him to the floor; then, hauling him to his feet, they propped him against the wall. His lip was bleeding and already a bruise was spreading across his soot-smeared cheek. More ominous still was the bright patch of blood showing on the shoulder of his coat.

Madeleine, who had been struggling to go to his aid, finally managed to slip from the officer's grasp and hurtled forward to wrap her arms around Luc. Almost as soon as she touched him the soldiers were pulling her away.

'I love you, Maddie,' he said thickly yet quite clearly enough for her to hear. It was the first time in his life that he had ever said the words.

Grief and terror clouded Madeleine's mind and it was a moment before the meaning of Luc's words fully impinged upon her. Then, before she knew what was happening, before she could voice her own feelings, the soldiers had hustled her away.

She glanced back over her shoulder and knew that the image of Luc as he appeared then would haunt her for the rest of her days. He could hardly stand and yet he still managed to hold himself proudly. Anger blazed from his dark eyes, fierce and defiant, but it could not quite conceal the misery there. Madeleine's inability to help him tore into her like a knife.

Against her protestations, they dragged her away and shut her in what had once been a storage room near the gate. Three other women had also been confined there, Babette and another girl of about the same age. The third woman was older, well past forty. She had lingered to nurse her wounded husband but he had not recovered. She had intended to bury him and return to her relatives that morning. Now, she doubted the Republicans would let her do either.

Madeleine, at least, had the consolation of knowing that Luc was still alive, but she did not know for how long. She had heard horrific tales of the way prisoners had been dealt with in the Vendée and feared the worst.

The women were left alone, giving Madeleine ample time to consider Luc's parting words. He loved her! The pleasure she felt at that was overshadowed by the fear that she had only won his love when it was too late.

The fighting in the fort had been over for some time, although they could still hear the thunder of distant cannon, when they heard a sudden isolated burst of musket fire.

'*Dieu!*' gasped the older woman. 'The devils have put the prisoners before a firing squad.'

Madeleine forced back threatening tears and prayed as she had never prayed before. Had Luc perished? Irrationally, she felt that she would know it if he had. When a soldier entered, bringing a bucket of water so that they might quench their thirsts, she approached him.

'Please,' she asked, meeting his gaze squarely, 'can you tell me what has happened to my husband?'

He was a young man with the coarse, weathered features of a farmer who did not really look as if he belonged in the colourful blue uniform. As he gazed at her the look of compassion in his eyes was replaced by one of blatant, male appreciation.

'Come on, lad, get a move on,' a seasoned sergeant snapped from the doorway.

'The prisoners are under guard in another part of the fort,' the young soldier quickly confided. 'When the fighting is over, General Hoche will decide what's going to happen to them .

'And the shooting?' the widow asked.

'We have shot or put to the bayonet the traitors who went over to your side,' the sergeant snarled from the doorway. 'They thought they could redeem themselves by helping us take back the fort but Hoche has no time for turncoats. We were ordered to show them no mercy!'

Madeleine wanted to ask about the fighting, but could see that she had stretched her captors' patience far enough. In any case, she found herself less concerned with the defeat than with how it would effect Luc.

As the day wore on, the temperature in the small store room soared. Hot and uncomfortable, Madeleine waited and worried. The sun was past its zenith before the distant guns finally died away, leaving a silence that was ominous in its finality.

On a beach at the southern end of the peninsula, in the shadow of another, less impressive fort, the remnants of the recently arrived *émigré* regiments and a small number of *chouans* finally laid down their arms. They had been fighting and retreating since the early hours of the morning, some seven or eight hours, and they were exhausted. The warm sand was patched with blood, pitted with shell holes and littered with the bodies of dead and dying men.

The young Duc de Sombreuil, confirmed in command by de Puisaye before the latter had sought shelter with the English fleet, placed his sword into the hands of Hoche. To fight on, he knew, would have meant annihilation. In return for their surrender, Hoche had promised to treat the *émigrés* as prisoners of war. Necessity forced de Sombreuil to trust him, although he feared the pledge of leniency was beyond the Republican general's power to keep.

Later, as he rode towards Penthièvre, at the head of a column of prisoners under close guard, the young Duc allowed his thoughts to turn towards home. In his mind, he pictured the young bride he had left on the very eve of their wedding and he had the chilling premonition that he would never see her again. Overhead, the sun shone cruelly bright on the desolate and defeated column.

In the middle of the afternoon, Madeleine heard noises, signalling the arrival of a large contingent of men and horses. For some time, she and the other women listened to the various comings and goings, ignorant of exactly what was going on. Eventually, when the heat had gone out of the sun, the door to the storage room was thrown open and the women were herded outside.

The air smelt wonderfully fresh after the stench of their confinement and the sunshine seemed unnaturally bright. For a while they stood dazed and blinking, like miners who had just emerged from beneath the ground. Madeleine's sight sharpened and she found herself staring at a mound of bodies piled up grotesquely against the courtyard's outer wall. Dizziness nearly overcame her and she would have fallen had the widow not reached out to steady her.

'The traitors,' the same young man who had brought them the water confided kindly. 'Your husband is not amongst them.'

'Where have they taken the prisoners?' she managed to ask, realising for the first time that the fort was unnaturally quiet.

'They are being taken to the mainland, to Auray, where the authorities will decide what is to be done with them,' the sergeant put in. 'As for yourselves, you are being released. Think yourselves lucky that the general has decided to deal leniently with you. You will not be punished as long as you make your way home. If you attempt to follow your men, then you will be shot.'

A few minutes later, the four women were herded through the main gateway and the heavy gate was latched behind them. Turning around, Madeleine allowed her gaze to roam across the sea. The storm on the night the fort had fallen had cleared the air, leaving a profound and empty calm. To her right, the setting sun sparkled off waves that lapped gently against the golden sand, whilst across the bay, the mainland was receding into shadow. Overhead, the seagulls had returned to issue their melancholy cries as they dived and wheeled in the pink-tinged light. Now there was peace where, only hours ago, there had been chaos and hostility, but it was an empty, lonely kind of peace, as if the earth itself had been purged of vitality. As she stood in the shadow of the fort, Madeleine began to tremble, feeling chilled in spite of the warmth that lingered in the salty air.

'I suppose I shall do as they suggest,' the widow said dully.

'I have a sister who will welcome me, but what of you, Madeleine? Will you take the risk of following your husband?'

There was no question of Madeleine not following Luc. Already she was forming a plan.

'Of course I shall follow,' she told the other women, 'but not on foot. I have a brother who owns a boat and one way or another, I shall persuade him to take me to Auray. The town is on the river, I believe. I have to see my husband again.'

I have to tell him that I love him, she added silently as she watched the other women set off across the isthmus.

Whilst she had been imprisoned in the storage room, she had realised that she too had never said the words, but she would, she vowed. Luc loved her and yet he had not come to her at Kercholin and now she suspected the reason for that. She prayed that it was not too late, that the authorities would be lenient. Surely they could not execute so many men. But Luc was an officer and, apart from that, bore a greater responsibility than most for the landing. Moreover, he was already an outlaw; if they discovered his identity, he would surely die.

By the time she reached her brother's cottage it was almost dark. The lanterns, showing through the tiny window, drew her like a beacon and she quickened her tired steps as she made her way up to the door. As she entered, four pairs of eyes turned towards her, for her cousins were also there. Tales of the fighting had reached Kercholin and they had come specifically to take her home, and Janine too, should the situation require it.

'Thank God!' Leon muttered from his chair.

Suddenly Madeleine found herself choking back tears. Her legs turned to rubber and she would have fallen had Leon not hurried forward to take her in his arms.

'It's all right, Maddie,' he crooned rocking her as if she was a child. 'It's all right. You're safe now.'

Determinedly, she pulled away from him. 'No! It's not all right!' she insisted almost hysterically. 'Luc is a prisoner and I am very much afraid that he will be shot.

I have to find a way to rescue him. I just have to!' Rounding on Thierry, she continued, 'You have to help me. You have to take me to Auray.'

'You're being ridiculous, Maddie,' Thierry replied gently. 'There won't be anything you can do.'

'If you don't help me, then I shall go alone.' She could feel the hysteria bubbling up inside her but there was nothing she could do about it. 'I have to see Luc again. I love him, you see, and now I know that he loves me.'

'It's all right,' Leon repeated, giving her another hug. 'We'll help you find Luc, so you can see him at least. We'll even help you free him if it is at all feasible.'

Thierry sighed and rolled his eyes towards the heavens. 'It's a fool's errand. There will be hundreds, maybe thousands of prisoners in the town.'

Leon ignored his words. 'Guy, Thierry and I will go with you to Auray,' he said, and for once Madeleine did not resent his overbearing attitude. If anyone could help her save her husband, then it was he. It struck her, then, that he and Luc were very much alike. Too much alike perhaps, for them to ever get along well with each other.

CHAPTER FOURTEEN

Luc gritted his teeth against the burning pain in his shoulder and wondered how much longer he was going to be able to endure the forced march. In the rosy rays of the setting sun, the ground beneath his feet looked enticingly soft and he longed to lie down upon it, to turn his cheek into the dust and close his eyes. Only a strong sense of survival and his innate pride kept him going. He knew that to fall behind meant death; he had already seen more than one wounded man collapse and be shot out of hand.

The Republicans were nervous and he could understand why. Already his keen mind had noted the fact that there were too few of them guarding the long cohort of prisoners. He was surprised that no one had tried to escape. Had he felt stronger, he would have made an attempt himself, but he was experiencing the greatest difficulty just staying on his feet.

An image of Madeleine came into his mind and, in spite of his physical discomfort, he smiled. She had looked quite stunned when he had blurted out his love for her, but she could not have been any more surprised than he. Until he had actually said the words he had not realised it himself. He had married her because he wanted her and could have her no other way. He had not expected to fall so deeply in love with her.

He loved her body, worshipped it, in fact, but he also loved her. He loved her gentleness, her intelligence and compassion, and would do so, he realised, even when she was wrinkled and old and the fire he felt for her had burned away. He did not know when it had begun, only that it had crept up on him until he felt consumed by it. She had become his wife and she had given him her body but he had found it no joy to possess her only in bed. He knew now that he had wanted her heart.

He must already have been in love with her on their wedding night, he decided. That was why her accusation about the dowry had hurt so much. What a fool he had been to try and push her away, and what a coward. It hadn't changed the way he felt about her although it had nearly killed any chance he'd had of her loving him in return. He had not taken her into his confidence or deigned to justify himself and he had nearly lost her because of it.

Did she love him? There was a time when he had thought not, when he had been sure in his arrogant heart that she had only married him for his position. She had never spoken of love, but surely she had shown him, particularly over the last few days? Now he wished with all his heart that he had explained his behaviour in England. He had remained faithful even after Madeleine had left him, and last night had finally decided to sacrifice his pride and tell her what he had always felt she should have known. Unfortunately, the moment he took her in his arms he had forgotten his intention.

He smiled to himself. They should have talked but he could not regret their passionate lovemaking. It had been better than any time before, perhaps because they had both known it could be their last. Silently he prayed that she was safe. One of their guards had told him that the women were to be released, but he had no proof of it.

'Move along there!' commanded a harsh-voiced Republican, cutting into Luc's reverie. 'Close up on the men in front!'

Automatically, Luc quickened his stride. When he thought he could stand the pace no longer, a brief halt was called and the prisoners sprawled with relief on the yellowed grass at the roadside. Luc settled down with his back to a pile of stones that had once formed part of a dolman. He glanced around and for a moment wondered if he had the strength to make a break for it.

Unfortunately, it was some distance before the trees became dense enough to provide cover which was, he suspected, the reason they had been allowed a temporary halt there. Leaning back against the smooth stone, he ran his tongue across his parched lips. At that moment he would have given almost anything for a drink.

'*Dieu*, I wish I had a tankard of nice cool cider to drink,' moaned a young, red-coated soldier from close beside him.

'Cider!' joked another. 'If you are going to wish for something, wish for a mug of good English ale. I developed a taste for it whilst I was living in London.'

'Water would suit me well enough,' put in a third. His voice sounded weak, almost plaintive. 'Just water.'

They were very young, Luc thought, watching them from beneath half-closed eyelids, particularly the young man who had wanted water. For the most part they were the sons of aristocrats who had emigrated during the terror, old enough to fight yet scarcely old enough to understand the complexities of what they were fighting for. They had come willingly and optimistically and they had been betrayed by the petty vanity of those in command. It was the leaders who had sabotaged the landings yet it was not they who would pay the price.

The injured D'Hervilly had been taken on board an English ship and no doubt de Puisaye had already joined him there. And what of Cadoudal? Why had he failed to take Hoche in the rear? Had the Republicans intercepted the *chouans*, Luc wondered, or had the giant of Morbihan washed his hands of an affair he could only see ending in disaster?

Regret was a useless thing and Luc had never had much time for it. Now though, he found himself regretting the part he had played in helping de Puisaye procure English aid. The responsibility sat heavily upon him, making him feel sickened and weary beyond words. He was almost glad of the pain in his arm, of the ache in his head, for he felt it was little more than he deserved.

When it was time to move off again, the youngest of the officers complained that he was too exhausted to move. Sheer will-power brought Luc to his feet. For a moment he stood, looking down at the young man whose face was pinched and pale. Up close he looked even younger, too young. Luc wondered if he had lied about his age in order to join the army or whether he was late coming to maturity. He didn't even look as if he needed to shave.

Reaching down his hand, he offered it to the youngster. He could do that much for him. 'You will continue because you must,' he said quietly. 'We are all tired.'

It was well past midnight by the time the cavalcade of exhausted shambling men reached the town and port of Auray. They had been marching for hours and Luc did not like to think about the number who had fallen by the wayside. The young fresh-faced soldier was not one of those, although Luc and one of the other officers had been dragging him along for the last hour.

The prisoners were halted in the middle of the town in front of the impressive church of Saint-Guilda's. There, beneath the pale light of an almost full moon, they were separated, some *émigrés* to be confined in Saint-Guilda's and others, de Sombreuil and his officers amongst them, to be sent to the church of Saint-Esprit, not far away. Luc and the other *chouans*, who numbered considerably less than the *émigrés*, were marched through the town and down a narrow, cobbled street towards the river. They did not cross the stone bridge that spanned the inky current but were escorted on to two ancient boats that were tied up against the quay, downriver from the bridge. Half of them were directed on to *Du Père Éternel* and the rest on to *La Chartreuse*. Luc was amongst the latter and was just preparing to follow the other prisoners down a ladder into the hold, when a burly sergeant gestured for him to wait.

'We've got another officer here by the looks of it,' the fellow shouted. 'Better put him with the others.'

Another soldier grabbed Luc's arm and roughly propelled him to the companionway. A handful of steps led steeply downwards and exhaustion caused him to stumble. His left shoulder came into sharp contact with the wall and he bit back a grunt of pain.

'Move!' the Republican commanded, impatiently poking him in the back with the barrel of his musket.

A single lantern hung from a hook in the bulkhead. By its dim glow Luc could just make out another soldier standing on guard beside a door at the far end of the companionway.

'In there!' the soldier behind him commanded, as the guard opened the door.

Luc stepped in to what he thought was some kind of store room. He could not be sure for almost immediately, the door slammed behind him and it was pitch black. He felt dizzy and disorientated and when someone called out to ask who he was the voice seemed to be coming from far away.

'De Valori,' he managed to say. Then he did something he had not done in his life before. He toppled forward in a dead faint.

Madeleine stood at the edge of the quay close to the narrow stone bridge that spanned the river at Auray. The tide was in and the grey-blue water rubbed sluggishly against the bridge's ancient arches. Thierry had brought his boat up river with the tide; at present it was moored on the eastern side of the river not far from the small custom-house. He and Leon had gone into the town to see what they could find out.

The latter had a friend who was a sergeant in a regiment recently transferred from Vannes and was hoping to get some information from him regarding the prisoners and their placement. For once Madeleine was grateful for his Republican leanings, grateful too that he was willing to use his contacts to help Luc whose political views were so different to his own.

A supply wagon driven by two Republican soldiers came down the hill from the town and turned left along the quay, stopping beside a large ship that was moored some hundred metres downriver from where Madeleine was standing. She was surprised to see two other soldiers leave the boat, which appeared to be nothing more than a disused cargo vessel, and collect a sack of supplies from the wagon. After a moment, the wagon moved on to a second vessel and the process was repeated.

'Did you see that?' Guy asked from close beside her. 'There must be soldiers billeted on board those ships.'

'Or prisoners.' Madeleine echoed his thoughts. 'Shall we take a look?'

Her cousin nodded and reached for her hand. 'We'll play the part of a courting couple,' he said with a grin. 'If you smile at me lovingly, I might even give you a kiss.'

Hand in hand they walked along beside the water. To their right rose the castle-like walls of the old town, built centuries ago to protect the merchants of Auray against attack from the sea. There was a stiff breeze blowing and, in spite of the sunshine, Madeleine felt quite chilled. With a shiver, she drew the shawl Janine had lent her more closely around her shoulders.

Sauntering past the two cargo boats, they saw that neither of them was in very good condition. In fact, they looked likely to sink in the open sea. There were Republican soldiers on the decks of them both.

Guy gave Madeleine a knowing look and an encouraging squeeze of her hand. 'I think they are standing guard,' he whispered.

They continued on for about a quarter of a mile then began to retrace their steps. They had just passed the ship furthest downriver—*La Chartreuse*—when a particularly strong gust of wind tugged at Madeleine's shawl, almost dragging it from her shoulders. As she settled it back around herself she knew what she should do. Indeed, it was almost as if the wind had been the

hand of providence, telling her. Men seemed to think
her pretty; for the first time in her life, she intended to
exploit the fact.

'I have an idea,' she confided. 'If it doesn't work I
shall have sacrificed Janine's shawl but I can always buy
her another one... When I go over to the boat, you stay
here.'

Without giving her cousin time to answer or question
her, she released her grip on the shawl. At once the wind
took it, sending it swirling and flapping along the path
and out towards *La Chartreuse*. For a moment she
thought that she had miscalculated and that it would go
uselessly into the water, but at the last minute a
particularly strong gust caught it and plastered it against
the ship's bow.

Feigning dismay, she hesitantly approached the boat.
The two soldiers on deck were openly laughing at what
had occurred. Madeleine was relieved to see that they
were young and hoped that they would respond to her.

She flashed her most charming smile. 'I don't suppose
one of you would be kind enough to get my shawl?'

Her cheeks had been tinted a pale peach by the wind
which had tumbled her golden hair into appealing
disarray. In fact, she looked uncharacteristically wanton
and the two soldiers responded just as she had hoped.

'Only for a price,' the nearest soldier teased, smiling
at her in a self-assured manner.

Without waiting for her reply, he sauntered across the
deck to untangle the garment and, still smiling broadly,
took it to where she was waiting on the short, wooden
gangplank. He had long, dark hair and a drooping
moustache. He was good looking in a rather coarse sort

of way and obviously aware of the fact, certain, too, that
he could charm a simple peasant girl

'It ought to be worth a kiss,' he challenged, leaning
one hip against the ship's bulwark.

Madeleine forced herself to smile flirtatiously. Somewhere in the back of her mind, she wondered if he was
married.

'I am promised,' she told him, glancing over her
shoulder at her cousin and then wrinkling her nose, 'but
it is my parents' wish, not mine.'

He nodded towards Guy. 'Your fiancé?'

'I'm afraid so. His father is a friend of my own.'

He held out the shawl to her but when she reached for
it playfully drew it away.

'A kiss,' he insisted. Then, his smile broadening, he
added, 'You're not worried about what your fiancé
thinks, are you?'

Madeleine shook her head and, after pouting prettily,
went up on tiptoe to comply. She had intended it to be a
brief kiss, one that would promise him more, but
catching hold of her arms, he kissed her thoroughly—
and all Madeleine could think about was Luc, and how
much nicer his lips felt, how much sweeter his taste. This
man's kiss did not set off the same sweet ache inside her;
in fact, it did nothing but sicken her. As soon as she
could without revealing her distaste, she pulled away
from him.

'You are very forward, Monsieur,' she chided
although she smiled to soften her words.

'I am a Parisian,' he said, grinning as he handed her
the shawl.

'Then you are a long way from home.' She tied the
shawl around her shoulders then, standing with her hand

on her hip, glanced over at the ship. 'What are you doing here? I thought you were a soldier, not a sailor.'

'A sailor!' he laughed. 'Not me! In any case, this old hulk's not going anywhere. We're guarding prisoners, that's all.'

'Oh,' she simpered, ignoring Guy's call for her to join him. 'Is that dangerous?'

He shook his head and grinned over his shoulder at his compatriot. 'My friend and I are more than a match for a few ragged *chouans*.

'Phew! I have seen these *chouans* and they are not so ragged,' she said. 'In fact, their officers look quite smart.'

'Smart! You wouldn't say that if you saw the ones we have on board. They look like scarecrows. They have no manners either. They attacked the food we gave them like animals.'

Madeleine's heart began to hammer. She could hardly believe that it had been so easy. Could one of those officers be Luc? She wanted to question the soldier further, to ask exactly what the officers looked like, but dared not do so for fear of giving herself away. As it was, she was sure the soldier would be able to sense her excitement and, when Guy called out to her again, was glad of an excuse to turn away.

She walked to the bottom of the gang plank then glanced coyly over her shoulder. 'Will you be here tonight?' she asked.

He grinned. 'Until midnight, *chérie*.'

'Then I may see you again.' She followed Guy, turning once more to wave at the soldier.

'Hang on to your shawl this time,' he called cheerfully after her.

'They have officers on board,' she told her cousin excitedly. 'One of them could be Luc!'

'It's possible, but he could also be on the other boat, or anywhere else come to that,' he cautioned. 'Don't get your hopes up, Maddie. We shall have to wait and see what Leon has to say.'

He was right, of course, but somehow she could not restrain the bubble of hope that rose up inside her. They crossed back over the bridge and, looking down, Madeleine saw that the current was now flowing swiftly, the natural direction of the river combining with the retreating tide. When they returned to Thierry's boat, they found him already on board. He had found out little during his tour of the port, but when Leon joined them a little later, it was a different story.

'I was able to locate my friend and he was of some help,' he told the others as they sat in the shelter of a tarpaulin. 'Apparently they have the *émigrés* confined in the churches—the soldiers, that is. The officers were separated from them and taken to the prison yesterday morning. As far as my friend knows, they are still there, apart from the *émigré* leader de Sombreuil, who has been put into lodgings at L'Auberge du Pavillion where he is under heavy guard. My friend does not think there are any *chouan* officers with the *émigrés*, but he cannot be sure. There are more than three thousand prisoners in the town.

'He thinks that the most likely place for Luc to be is on one of the hulks moored on the other side of the river. Apparently most of the captured *chouans* are being held there. The big question is, which ship? The soldiers who escorted the prisoners to the boats are off duty at the moment, but my friend is going to speak with them. I am to meet with him again this afternoon when he hopes to have more information.' He paused and glanced seriously at Madeleine. 'This is going to be expensive. I've told my friend that you can be relied upon to come up with the money.'

'Promise him whatever you must,' she told him. 'I don't care what it costs if it will help us save Luc.'

'He will take some of it on trust, Maddie, but not all.' He named a considerable sum. 'He wants half of it before he will tell us anything more.'

Madeleine's heart sank. Auray was not that far from Vannes but she had never done business there. Neither the traders nor the bankers would know her and by the time they had sent to her own bank it would be too late.

'I don't think I can get it quickly enough,' she answered flatly.

'What about jewellery?' Leon asked. 'Surely you have pieces that Luc or even Philippe have given you. . .?'

'But not with me! I had no need of such things on the peninsula!' Hopelessness welled up inside her. Dear God! There had to be some way!

'I suppose there is no chance of the authorities pardoning the rebels?' Thierry asked.

Leon shrugged. 'De Sombreuil will be taken before a military tribunal tomorrow. It is expected that he and the other *émigrés* will be condemned to death. As for the *chouans*, the authorities may be more lenient towards them. They do not want to alienate the people here any more than they have already. Such leniency may not be extended to their officers, especially not to Luc who has already been declared an enemy of the Republic.'

Thierry sighed resignedly. 'We can borrow against the

boat.' When Madeleine hugged him, he smiled. 'Lord, I know you are good for it, my dear, and you have done a lot to help me.'

With the boat as collateral they had no problem raising the money. It still represented only half of what the sergeant wanted although it was a small fortune as far as Thierry and the Lemieus were concerned. The Republican was to collect the balance at a specific hostelry in Vannes; this regardless of their success in rescuing Luc.

Leon went into town again that evening to meet with the fellow and when he returned he was openly smiling.

'The authorities have not yet taken down the names of their prisoners so my friend could not say which ship Luc is on. However, he does know that all the officers are on the same one... It's *La Chartreuse*, Maddie. It has to be, and that being the case, I think we can do it. We can get him out!'

'Would they keep the officers separate from their men?' she asked, her heart filling with hope. She had bravely spoken of rescue but only now did she really believe they could do it.

'That seems to be their policy.' He glanced seriously at her. 'I want you to be sure about this, really sure. Even if Luc is on *La Chartreuse*, we could still fail, then things would go badly not only for us but for him as well. Although I consider it unlikely, I could be wrong. There could be an amnesty for him.'

Madeleine shook her head. 'They won't pardon him, not if they find out who he is. By calling himself Luc Valori he has not drawn attention to himself, but there are too many people involved in the landings who know him as the Comte de Regnay.'

Leon studied her face for a moment then nodded. 'Very well.' He smiled wryly. 'Now all we need to do is think of a plan, some way of boarding *La Chartreuse* without being seen.'

'From the river, using our rowing boat,' Thierry suggested. 'It would have to be at slack water, around eleven tonight. It will be dark by then and with a bit of luck this wind will blow in some cloud.'

'They'll hear us,' Leon complained.

'What we need is some kind of diversion.' Guy turned to Madeleine. 'Your idea with the shawl was an inspiration. Can't you think of something else?'

A diversion, a scene, a fight or quarrel of some sort, that was what they needed. The idea came to her and she almost laughed. 'I could sneak back to see that soldier. Guy, or someone pretending to be my father, could catch me and begin to beat me.' Her eyes brightened with enthusiasm. 'I'm sure that soldier could be induced to come to my aid. . . Once you are on board you can overpower them and release Luc!'

It was the best plan they could come up with. Guy thought a father, an older man, would make it all more plausible and Thierry suggested that they enlist the aid of a friend of his, an old fisherman whose boat was moored not far from their own. When the others agreed, he immediately went off to find the fellow, returning only minutes later with him in tow.

Roland Kalon was more than seventy years old. He had grizzled hair and a complexion tanned to the colour of leather by salt spray and sun. His step was surprisingly spritely for his age and intelligence and humour shone in his brown eyes. Fortunately, like the majority of his generation, he was a separatist at heart and had little love for the Republicans. He was more than willing to help them and, when Leon suggested payment, gallantly told him that the gratitude of a pretty woman would be quite enough. He quickly grasped what was required of him then laughingly confided that it had always been his ambition to become an actor.

Their plan was simple enough but Madeleine knew that there were a dozen or more things that could go wrong. Luck, however, seemed to be favouring them. The cloud they had hoped for began to thicken; by the time darkness fell, it had obscured most of the stars. There was still a chance that the moon would break through, but they dare not wait for perfect cover.

It was an hour before midnight when Madeleine, walking a little ahead of the old fisherman, made her way along the quay towards the two prison ships, a basket of fresh pastries on her arm. Her brother and cousins had set off some ten minutes before and although she could not see them she knew they would be approaching the stern of *La Chartreuse* in Thierry's small rowing boat. She could feel her heart beginning to pound and the palms of her hands felt damp with sweat. Was this how men felt before they marched into battle, she asked herself? Had Luc felt such fear? If he had, then he had never betrayed the fact. As they passed the first boat, Roland began to run after her.

He caught up with her as they drew level with *La Chartreuse* and she knew it was time to start screaming.

'Stop it! Stop it! How could you treat me so?' she wailed, her voice rising shrilly. 'No! No . . .! For pity's sake, stop it!'

'Tramp!' Roland shouted, beating her across the shoulders. 'Hussy! You have a good man waiting to marry you and yet you come sneaking down here to whore with the soldiers!' He spoke in a mixture of French and Breton. It sounded most strange but the soldiers needed to get the gist of what was going on.

Although he was trying not to hurt, the blows still stung and she did not need to fake her screams. Then he grasped her shoulders and shook her until her head began to swim. In the dim light from the lanterns set out on the deck of *La Chartreuse*, she could just make out his face. He appeared genuinely furious; indeed, had she not known he was acting then she would have been truly afraid.

'You little bitch!' He swung his arm back and pretended to strike her, sending the basket she was carrying flying across the cobbles.

'Oh, help me! Help me! He is crazy with drink!' she cried, glancing across at the boat. 'Stop it! For the love of God, stop it, Father. I meant no harm!'

Drawn by Madeleine's screams, the two sentries left their post to investigate.

'Help me!' she shouted, pulling away from Roland and running towards the side of the ship. He caught up with her before she reached it and swung her around, drawing his arm back to strike her again.

'Hey, fellow, there's no need for that! Leave her alone!' ordered the soldier Madeleine had spoken to that morning. 'Leave her alone, I say!'

'She is my daughter and I'll deal with her as I like,' Roland replied. 'I'll teach her to sneak out after dark!' Then he hit Madeleine again, hard enough to make her head spin.

The young Republican muttered an oath and, against

the protest of his companion, rushed across the narrow gangplank and on to the dock.

'Let her go, you drunken bastard,' he snarled, lifting his muskets.

It was then that several things seemed to happen at once. A third Republican, a burly sergeant, appeared by the ship's railing and demanded to know what was going on. As the soldier moved towards him, Roland pushed Madeleine, sending her flying. Then, obviously feeling that he had played his part, he took to his heels along the quay.

Slowly, Madeleine staggered to her feet. She could see that the sergeant was about to order the soldier back to the boat and she knew she had to keep their attention for a while longer. She took a step towards him then, with a soft groan, collapsed at his feet in a pretend faint.

CHAPTER FIFTEEN

THE hurried footsteps approaching Madeleine sounded unnaturally loud and she was glad of it, for they drowned out the frantic beating of her heart. She sensed the soldier bending over her, then felt him lift her up in his arms. For a moment it was as if all her senses had been heightened. She could feel his warm breath against her hair and the thick serge of his uniform beneath her cheek, and she could smell tobacco and a touch of garlic. Every fibre in her body urged her to pull away from him, and keeping her eyes shut and her body limp was one of the most difficult things she had ever had to do.

'You can't bring that woman on board,' she heard the sergeant complain.

'*Parbleu*, sergeant! I can't leave her lying on the floor!' the soldier protested.

She heard his footsteps echo across the wooden gangplank, then felt herself being laid down on the deck of *La Chartreuse*.

'Is everything all right over there?' The call came from the neighbouring ship.

'It's fine. Just two peasants creating a disturbance. We have it in hand,' the sergeant replied irritably then, turning to one of his own men, ordered, 'Bring that lantern over here so we can see how badly the girl is hurt.'

When someone began to rub her hands, Madeleine permitted herself a groan. Had Leon and the others had

enough time to board, she wondered? She desperately
hoped so for she did not think she could make her faint
last for much longer. When she eventually opened her
eyes, the three Republicans were bending over her.
Dazzled by the lantern, she blinked.

'Feeling better?' the soldier with the moustache
asked.

'A little.' Still she strove to delay her apparent
recovery. 'Has my father gone?'

The soldier nodded. 'What was all that about?'

'I was only coming to see you. . .bringing you some
pastries I had made.' She smiled her most charming
smile. 'My father is crazy. He would lock me up if he
had his way.'

Just behind the soldiers she thought she saw something move but the light was nearly blinding her and she
could not be sure. She tried to sit up then fell back with
a groan.

'Oh, dear! I do believe I have done something to my
ankle.' She lifted her skirt unnecessarily high in order to
examine the injury and three pairs of masculine eyes
fixed themselves on her bare thigh.

Leon Lemieu smiled grimly and, gesturing to his
brother, moved stealthily up behind the crouching
soldiers. As swiftly as a striking snake, he brought the
butt of his pistol down across the side of the sergeant's
head then turned to threaten the other two men.

'If you are silent and do as I say, then you will not be
harmed,' he told them.

The young soldier with the moustache turned to glare
angrily at Madeleine. Ruthlessly, she suppressed the
feelings of guilt, reminding herself that Luc's life was
at stake.

'I'm sorry,' she told him. 'We won't hurt you. We only want to release the officers you are guarding.'

'Are there any more of you?' Guy demanded and the soldier nodded, still staring reproachfully at Madeleine.

None too gently, Leon hauled him to his feet. 'Where?'

'We have another man standing guard in the companionway.'

Leon grunted. 'Tie these two up,' he told Guy.

When the younger Lemieu handed Madeleine his pistol, she stared at it uncertainly.

'You only have to point it and pull the trigger,' he told her with a grin. 'It's already cocked.'

This made the second soldier swear and he hastily lay down on the deck in order to aid Guy. Both soldiers were bound hand and foot and a handkerchief was shoved into the mouth of the second one. Madeleine was relieved when this was done and Guy reclaimed his weapon for she doubted if she could have brought herself to shoot either of the Republicans. They were young and, in a way, not so different from the Lemieus.

With surprising ease, Leon dragged Madeleine's would-be rescuer to his feet and propelled him along to the head of the companionway.

'Call your friend out,' he whispered urgently, gesturing for Guy to wait beside the door.

'He won't come,' the soldier protested. 'He won't leave his post.'

'Think of something,' Leon said, pressing his pistol hard under the fellow's chin.

The soldier sighed then called down to his compatriot.

'Michel! That girl is back and she has brought two friends with her. They are interested in spending time with us, but they want to see you.' He forced a laugh. 'They want to see that you are not old and ugly. Show yourself for a moment.'

Madeleine heard footsteps followed by a brief chuckle and a heavy thud. Glancing around, she saw a fourth Republican sprawled on the deck by the hatchway.

'Now,' Leon demanded of his prisoner, 'where are the *chouan* officers being held?'

For a moment the fellow did not reply, not until Leon had threatened to crack his skull. 'They are in the storeroom at the end of the companionway,' he finally grated.

'Show me!' Leon growled, shoving him down the steps, 'and take care. Salving your pride is not worth your life!'

Madeleine and Guy waited tensely in the shadows for what seemed like an eternity. Moths fluttered in the circle of lantern light that lit the deck a little in front of them, weaving and ducking on satin-soft wings. Below her, she could hear the hiss and gurgle of the river as it sped with increasing rapidity towards the sea. Apart from that, all was quiet. The quay was deserted and the prisoners below deck had obviously settled down for the night. She prayed silently that Leon would be able to find Luc and that they had not all risked their lives in vain.

When the first shadowy figure emerged from the companionway, her breath caught in her throat. 'Luc?' she queried.

'No,' the stranger replied, then, before her disappointment could register, added, 'but he's right behind me.'

The unfamiliar *chouan* officer stepped aside and she saw Luc. Joyfully, she threw herself into his arms.

'Ah, Maddie,' he whispered as he hugged her to him. 'You should not have put yourself in such danger.'

Out of the corner of her eye she saw that there was yet another officer with Leon but there was no sign of the moustachioed Republican. She assumed he had been locked up in Luc's place.

'You can hug each other later,' her big cousin grumbled. 'We'd best go before we are discovered.'

For a moment Luc hung back. 'What about the prisoners in the hold? Are you not going to release them?'

'Not on your life!' Leon replied irritably. 'It would draw too much attention. I only agreed to help rescue you.' He glanced at the other officers. 'These two were lucky because they happened to be with you but I don't want to be involved in anything else.'

Still Luc hesitated and Madeleine gave his hand an impatient tug. 'It's likely they'll be pardoned,' she told him. 'Come on, Luc, please!'

He went with her then, albeit reluctantly. By the time they reached the stern the Lemieus had already joined Thierry in the dinghy and one of the other officers was just clambering down. It was going to be a squeeze, seven people in a boat meant for three, but they had little choice.

At that moment, the moon came out from behind the clouds sending a thread of silvery light across the inky water. Madeleine saw that the the current was really racing now, and the dinghy was bouncing and tugging at its line. Luc gestured for her to climb down first and she smiled lovingly at him.

The smile turned almost instantly to an expression of terror picked out into stark relief by the luminous moonlight. Behind Luc, the sergeant was lurching towards them, blood streaming down his face like black ink and his mouth drawn back in a snarl. She saw his rifle level at Luc and knew there was only one way to save her husband. She lunged at him with all her might and together they toppled off the boat and down into the cold, dark river.

She did not hear the shot that echoed out in the night or see the sergeant trip, fall, then bang his head and lie senseless. All she heard was the splash and gurgle of water as it clutched at her, dragging her down, wrapping her in its icy darkness and making it impossible for her to see or breathe. She had reacted instinctively to save Luc and had not considered the fact that she could not swim.

Strong arms grasped her and helped her to claw her way upwards. Gasping and drenched, their bodies and senses numbed by the cold of the water, Luc and Madeleine managed to reach the surface. Somehow her hair had come loose to swirl about her and cling like wet silk to her face. A primeval kind of panic swept over her and she began to struggle.

'I won't let go of you! For once, trust me!' Luc rasped, his lips close to her ear as he caught hold of her shoulders and held her head above the water.

Madeleine could only whimper; shivers racked her body and icy water burned her throat. Desperately, she struggled to control her panic and trust in the man she loved more than life itself. And she could trust him; she knew that now. She could trust him with her life and with her heart.

As Madeleine managed to control her fear, so Luc could feel his own rising. He was managing to keep them both afloat but already his strength was waning. The bank of the river seemed a long way off and the current was carrying them swiftly towards the sea. In one way it was good for it was taking them further and further away from the disturbance that had erupted behind them, but he was very much afraid that they were escaping from it only to drown.

Determinedly, he kicked towards the shore, hampered by his clothing and his heavy boots. They were well past the built-up section of quay but the bank was still too steep to climb up even if he could reach it. Cold water slopped into his face, nearly choking him. His limbs felt like lead and there was a buzzing in his ears. It was not long before he had passed the point of exhaustion and was keeping them both afloat by sheer willpower. He could not, would not, let Madeleine drown, not when he loved her so much, when she had risked so much for him. Surely she must love him to have done that? The thought broke through the clouds that were forming in his brain, warming and revitalising him.

Lifting his head he searched for the dinghy. He thought he caught sight of it being carried along behind them but water slapped into his face, blinding him, and he could not be sure. Renewing his efforts, he struck out again for the bank and to his relief found that they were edging closer. Not too far ahead, he could see a place where the branches of a partly fallen tree dipped down into the water and he knew that if only he could reach it, then he might be able to prevent them being swept on down the river and out to sea.

Kicking again, he brought them in line with the

vegetation and the current swept them into it. Spiky
branches scratched his face and ripped at his clothes.
With his free hand he reached out, grasping the damp
wood and hanging on. Still the current tugged at him
and at Madeleine, tossing them about like twigs in a mill
race.

'Luc!' Above the roaring of the water, he heard
Madeleine scream as she was wrenched away from him.

Frantically he reached out for her, his fingers sliding
down her outstretched arm and finally grasping her
wrist. Gritting his teeth he hung on, feeling as if he was
being torn in two. The partly healed wound in his
shoulder felt like a burning brand, sending rivers of pain
down towards the hand that held her but he would not
let go, not until the dinghy had reached them and she
was safe.

He tried to divorce himself from the pain and the
intense cold, thinking only of Madeleine, of her soft
flesh and sweet lips, of the way the sunlight would light
up her golden hair. He thought of Kercholin and of the
children they would make together; he thought of their
love.

Madeleine's head dipped below the surface and the
salty water burned her lungs. The darkness that filled
her mind was deeper than that of the night or the ink-
black water surrounding her, trying to pull her down.
She was not aware of the dinghy approaching them or
the rough hands that yanked at her hair, lifting her face
from the suffocating current, and neither she nor Luc
heard Leon's glad cry.

They had to prise Luc's hand from the rough branch
in order to drag both him and Madeleine into the dinghy

and still, with his other hand, he grasped Madeleine's wrist with fingers that seemed turned to steel.

'You can let her go now, friend,' one of the *chouans* said, but Luc was beyond hearing the words.

As gently as they could they levered his fingers apart so that they could release Madeleine and one of the *chouans* could wrap her in his coat. She coughed and retched then, as soon as her vision cleared, turned to Luc, putting her arms around him and sobbing against his chest.

'It's all right,' he rasped as he too struggled back to consciousness. 'Don't. . .cry, Maddie.'

Carefully, he pushed himself in to a sitting position against the gunwale, settling Madeleine across his thighs. He was very cold and glad of her warmth against his chest. The small craft had shipped a dangerous amount of water whilst they had both been hauled on board and he could feel it sloshing against his legs.

'Oh, God, Luc, your shoulder!' Madeleine suddenly exclaimed, remembering the way he had held on to her; but when she reached for the buttons on his jacket, he stayed her hand.

'Leave it,' he grated. 'I shall live; never fear.'

In fact, his shoulder was killing him but he had no intention of letting her know that. The fight at the fort had opened the wound and the incident in the river had done nothing to help. His chest hurt from inhaling seawater and his neck stung where the tree branches had scratched him, yet in spite of all this, he smiled. Madeleine loved him; he was sure of it now. She loved him enough to come after him, to risk her life to save his. She was so brave, so beautiful, so much more than he deserved.

Thierry lifted his oars and allowed the current to take the boat further downstream, away from the commotion behind them. The single shot had alerted the soldiers on the other boat and Luc could hear a great deal of shouting and swearing. He realised that he must have dozed, for the next thing he knew Madeleine was shaking his arm. Groggily he realised that the water level in the bottom of the dingy was still rising.

'It's Roland in *Bihan*,' he heard Thierry say, 'and not before time. Another ten minutes and we would have gone down.'

With great care, he eased himself up. A short distance behind them and to the centre of the river he could see the dark shape of a fishing boat heading towards them. Cautiously, Thierry began to steer the overloaded dinghy on a course that would intercept the *Bihan* a short distance downstream.

Luc was in the bows; when Roland threw them a rope, he caught it and, after pulling the dinghy against the *Bihan*'s stern, fastened it next to Roland's own coracle-like craft. The *Bihan* was much larger then Thierry's boat and Luc needed the help of both the old fisherman and his mate in order to scramble aboard. It was a further strain on his shoulder, and for a moment afterwards he could only lean weakly against the gunwhale.

'I thought you'd be downriver somewhere,' the old fishermen told Thierry when he, too, had scrambled aboard. 'I'd have been here sooner but the Republicans insisted on searching the boat before they would let me leave. I was afraid they would cause me to miss the tide. As it is, we will have to hurry or we shall end up aground.'

Whilst the others helped Roland to hoist more sail, Madeleine led Luc into the tiny cabin to dry off. There, amid a tangle of nets and other tackle, she stripped off her outer clothes then turned to help him with his coat and shirt. He was being very careful with his left arm and she knew he was in pain. After persuading him to sit back on the bunk, she moved the lantern a little nearer, then began to unwind the soiled bandages. Her hair still hung in rats' tails and a frown of concern puckered her smooth brow, but Luc didn't think she had ever looked more beautiful.

'It's been bleeding quite a lot,' she commented anxiously. 'Does it hurt very much?'

He shook his head dismissively and, grasping her wrists, kissed her hard.

'I've been wanting to do that for hours,' he said when he finally released her. 'It's a pity we do not have the privacy of a bed!'

'You need a bed, but only for rest,' she gently admonished as she peeled away the last layer of bandage and carefully examined the injury. It was raw and swollen but it appeared to have been cleansed rather than damaged by the salt water and was not nearly as bad as she had feared.

Luc sat with his back against the bulkhead, frowning.

'Am I hurting you?' she asked.

He shook his head and did not even wince as she covered the wound with a small pad of sailcloth that Roland had given her, then fastened it in place with a strip of the old dressing.

'It's not very good,' she told him, 'but it's the best I can do.'

'It's fine,' he replied shortly. Then he swore, '*Dieu*, Madeleine, you might as well say it!'

When she glanced questioningly at him, his frown intensified. 'You might as well tell me that you love me for I know that you do!' More gently he added, 'I need the words too.'

She had intended to tell him the moment she saw him again but events and her concern about his wound had put the matter from her mind. Gently, she smoothed back his hair. She smiled at his irritation and resisted the urge to tease him just a little.

'I love you,' she said earnestly. 'I have done since before you asked me to marry you. It began on our journey from Paris, I think.'

'*Dieu!*' he sighed. 'That long?'

She nodded. 'I wouldn't have married you if I hadn't loved you, although I knew you didn't love me.'

'I didn't know that I loved you,' he corrected, drawing her into his arms and rocking her gently. 'I know now that I loved you from the first moment I saw you.'

'That was lust, Luc!' She was able to tease him now, now that she felt secure.

He shrugged. 'I'm still not sure where the one ends and the other begins. . .but I loved you on our wedding night. Why else was I so angry? Your accusations hurt, Maddie. I could not bear that you should think so poorly of me. Moreover, I was convinced you had only married me for my title. You must admit that you weren't exactly loving on our wedding night.'

Before she could apologise or explain her own inse-curity, Luc continued, his chin resting against her hair. 'I should have explained about the dowry. I should have explained about a lot of things. I never resumed my affair with Edith.'

'I think I knew that,' she said, gently touching his cheek. 'I began to realise it whilst we were on the peninsula. But you were kissing her and most passionately!'

He closed his eyes briefly, as if in pain, and his next words confirmed what she had thought. 'I was so angry with you, Maddie, and my pride was hurt. It wasn't the first time you had believed the worst of me. Then, when you left, I didn't think you cared whether I lived or died. That duel—it was really for you. I couldn't challenge de Brunnière openly on your behalf, not without drawing attention to the very thing we wanted to conceal, but in Edith's name I was not so constrained. I flirted with her to draw his comment and then I challenged him for it. I know I should have explained but I am not very good at justifying myself. I've never had to, I suppose. In the future I will try, but I'm afraid you're going to have to be patient with me.'

De Brunnière! Up until that moment Madeleine had not known the name of the other party in the duel. No wonder Luc had been so angry.

'I should have stayed,' she said. 'I would have, only I was convinced you wanted me gone. For weeks, you had not even shared my bed.'

He gave a wry little laugh. 'That nearly killed me. I wanted you, believe me, but you had begun to look quite ill and I was convinced I had been too demanding with you.'

'I looked ill because you did not come to me,' she explained. 'Oh, Luc, I missed you so. The time after I returned to Kercholin was the most miserable in my life.

Then on the beach at Penthièvre you were so distant, so cold.'

'I found myself hurting, Maddie, more than I would ever have thought possible and my reaction was to try and cut you out of my life. It was foolish I know, because it was like cutting out my heart. Even then, though, I wanted to take care of you. I have felt the need to do so since the moment I first set eyes on you. I have always, always had your interest at heart.'

A lone tear trickled down Madeleine's face and she hugged him close. He had done so much for her. How shabbily she had treated him. It occurred to her that she had never forgotten the way he had propositioned her; in fact, she had continually allowed it to colour her judgement of him. He was not a shallow, pleasure-seeking aristo—he was brave and chivalrous and kind and he always had been.

'I am so sorry I doubted you,' she said.

He sighed. 'You needed reassurance, Maddie, and in my arrogance I refused to give it to you.'

He then proceeded to reassure her in the most effective way, kissing her until her head swam and she forgot entirely where she was.

When Leon Lemieu went in to offer them some of the calvados that Roland had given him, he cleared his throat loudly. Even that did not distract them and chuckling, he went back out, closing the tiny door behind him. Onward, the little boat sped, out into Quiberon Bay before turning towards the beautiful gulf of Morbihan.

Luc sat with a blanket draped across his shoulders, holding his sleeping wife in his arms and he vowed it would take more than another Royalist uprising to prise

him from her and Ketcholin. The Dauphin was dead; he
had heard the sad news from their guards aboard *La
Chartreuse*, and with the boy had died Luc's passionate
commitment to the Royalist cause. It had always been a
personal thing for him, a promise to the sad, bewildered
king who had asked for his help so long ago. He owed
no allegiance to the late king's brothers, d'Artois and
Provence; in fact, he didn't even like them very much.
The monarchy was finished, the aristocracy too. He
would never again be more than simple Luc Valori and
he found that it did not bother him at all.

He looked down at Madeleine's bright head and
prayed that the good Lord would give them one more
thing—a child whose laughter would fill their house and
their hearts. He did not know that his prayer had already
been answered, that a son had been conceived that last
night at the fort, a fair-haired, dark-eyed son who would
grow strong and tall and that there would later be a
lively daughter to play with him.

'*Gwellan-karet*,' he whispered in Breton. 'Dearest
one. I love you with all my heart.'

GET 4 BOOKS
AND A MYSTERY GIFT

Return the coupon below and we'll send you 4 Historical Romance™ novels and a mystery gift absolutely FREE! We'll even pay the postage and packing for you.

We're making you this offer to introduce you to the benefits of Reader Service: FREE home delivery of brand-new Historical Romance novels, at least a month before they are available in the shops, FREE gifts and a monthly Newsletter packed with information.

Accepting these FREE books and gift places you under no obligation to buy, you may cancel at any time, even after receiving just your free shipment. Simply complete the coupon below and send it to:

MILLS & BOON® READER SERVICE, FREEPOST, CROYDON, SURREY, CR9 3WZ.

No stamp needed

Yes, please send me 4 free Historical Romance novels and a mystery gift. I understand that unless you hear from me, I will receive 4 superb new titles every month for just £2.99* each postage and packing free. I am under no obligation to purchase any books and I may cancel or suspend my subscription at any time, but the free books and gifts will be mine to keep in any case.
(I am over 18 years of age)

2EP6M

Ms/Mrs/Miss/Mr _____

Address _____

_____

_____ Postcode _____

Historical Romance™

Coming next month

RAVENSDENE'S BRIDE
Julia Byrne
REGENCY ENGLAND

Nicholas, 5th Earl of Ravensdene, had rarely spent time in
his ancestral home in Sussex, but now there was need.
Somewhere in the area was a traitor, and Nick, as one of
Wellington's spies, was intent on finding him. What Nick
hadn't bargained for were the local matchmaking mamas,
and the only way out of *that* imbroglio was a marriage of
convenience to his neighbour's niece. Miss Sarah Lynley
was a constant surprise to him, and aroused a level of
desire that amazed him—so much so that it was hard to
remember that her family topped his list of suspects...

KING'S PAWN
Joanna Makepeace
ENGLAND 1484/5

Martyn, Earl of Wroxeter, would sacrifice almost
anything for his king, Richard III, but he was deeply
reluctant to undertake a marriage solely to bind a possible
enemy to Richard's cause, when he was still grieving
for his betrothed.

Cressida Gretton was not thrilled either. Having led an
untrammelled life on the Welsh borders, she knew
marriage to a sophisticated stranger would be both
difficult and dangerous, as Henry Tudor began his
campaign to overthrow Richard. She was treading a
minefield, made more perilous by her growing love for
Martyn, who, it appeared, had yet to forget Elinor...